THE EAR IN THE WALL

SHE HAD RISEN AND NOW, HALF CHAGRINED, HALF FRIGHTENED,
STOOD IRRESOLUTE

THE
EAR IN THE WALL

BY
ARTHUR B. REEVE

FRONTISPIECE BY
WILL FOSTER

WILDSIDE PRESS
BERKELEY HEIGHTS • NEW JERSEY

Another great publication from...

Wildside Press
PO Box 45
Gillette, NJ 07933-0045
www.wildsidepress.com

First Wildside Press edition:
September 2000

CONTENTS

v

CONTENTS

THE EAR IN THE WALL

THE EAR IN THE WALL

I

THE VANISHER

"HELLO, Jameson, is Kennedy in?"
I glanced up from the evening papers to
encounter the square-jawed, alert face of District
Attorney Carton in the doorway of our apartment.

"How do you do, Judge?" I exclaimed. "No,
but I expect him any second now. Won't you sit
down?"

The District Attorney dropped, rather wearily I
thought, into a chair and looked at his watch.

I had made Carton's acquaintance some years
before as a cub reporter on the *Star* while he was a
judge of an inferior court. Our acquaintance had
grown through several political campaigns in which
I had had assignments that brought me into contact with him. More recently some special writing
had led me across his trail again in telling the story
of his clean-up of graft in the city. At present his
weariness was easily accounted for. He was in the
midst of the fight of his life for re-election against
the so-called " System," headed by Boss Dorgan, in

which he had gone far in exposing evils that ranged all the way from vice and the drug traffic to bald election frauds.

"I expect a Mrs. Blackwell here in a few minutes," he remarked, glancing again at his watch. His eye caught the headline of the news story I had been reading and he added quickly, "What do the boys on the *Star* think of that Blackwell case, anyhow?"

It was, I may say, a case deeply shrouded in mystery—the disappearance without warning of a beautiful young girl, Betty Blackwell, barely eighteen. Her family, the police, and now the District Attorney had sought to solve it in vain. Some had thought it a kidnaping, others a suicide, and others had even hinted at murder. All sorts of theories had been advanced without in the least changing the original dominant note of mystery.

Photographs of the young woman had been published broadcast, I knew, without eliciting a word in reply. Young men whom she had known and girls with whom she had been intimate had been questioned without so much as a clue being obtained. Reports that she had been seen had come in from all over the country, as they always do in such cases. All had been investigated and had turned out to be based on nothing more than imagination. The mystery remained unsolved.

"Well," I replied, "of course there's a lot of talk now in the papers about aphasia and amnesia and all that stuff. But, you know, we reporters are a sceptical lot. We have to be shown. I can't say we put much faith in *that.*"

"But what is your explanation? You fellows always have an opinion. Sometimes I think the newspapermen are our best detectives."

"I can't say that we have any opinion in this case —yet," I returned frankly. "When a girl just simply disappears on Fifth Avenue and there isn't even the hint of a clue as to any place she went or how, well—oh, there's Kennedy now. Put it up to him."

"We were just talking of that Betty Blackwell disappearance case," resumed Carton, when the greetings were over. "What do you think of it?"

"Think of it?" repeated Kennedy promptly with a keen glance at the District Attorney; "why, Judge, I think of it the same as you evidently do. If you didn't think it was a case that was in some way connected with your vice and graft investigation, you wouldn't be here. And if I didn't feel that it promised surprising results, aside from the interest I always have naturally in solving such mysteries, I wouldn't be ready to take up the offer which you came here to make."

"You're a wizard, Kennedy," laughed Carton, though it was easily seen that he was both pleased and relieved to think that he had enlisted Craig's services so easily.

"Not much of a wizard. In the first place, I know the fight you're making. Also, I know that you wouldn't go to the police in the present state of armed truce between your office and Headquarters. You want someone outside. Well, I'm more than willing to be that person. The whole thing, in its larger aspects, interests me. Betty Blackwell in particular, arouses my sympathies. That's all."

"Exactly, Kennedy. This fight I'm in is going to be the fight of my life. Just now, in addition to everything else, people are looking to me to find Betty Blackwell. Her mother was in to see me to-day; there isn't much that she could add to what has already been said. Betty was a most attractive girl. The family is an excellent one, but in reduced circumstances. She had been used to a great deal as a child, but now, since the death of her father, she has had to go to work—and you know what that means to a girl like that."

Carton laid down a new photograph which the newspapers had not printed yet. Betty Blackwell was slender, petite, chic. Her dark hair was carefully groomed, and there was an air with which she wore her clothes and carried herself, even in a portrait, which showed that she was no ordinary girl.

Her soft brown eyes had that magnetic look which is dangerous to their owner if she does not know how to control it, eyes that arrested one's gaze, invited notice. Even the lens must have felt the spell. It had caught, also, the soft richness of the skin of her oval face and full throat and neck. Indeed one could not help remarking that she was really the girl to grace a fortune. Only a turn of the hand of that fickle goddess had prevented her from doing so.

I had picked up one of the evening papers and was looking at the newspaper half-tone which more than failed to do justice to her. Just then my eye happened on an item which I had been about to discuss with Carton when Kennedy entered.

"As a scientist, does the amnesia theory appeal to you, Craig?" I asked. "Now, here is an explanation by one of the special writers, headed, 'Personalities Lost Through Amnesia.' Listen."

The article was brief:

Mysterious disappearances, such as that of Betty Blackwell, have alarmed the public and baffled the police before this—disappearances that have in their suddenness, apparent lack of purpose, and inexplicability much in common with her case.

Leaving out of account the class of disappearances for their own convenience—embezzlers, blackmailers, and so forth—there is still a large number of recorded cases where the subjects have dropped out of sight without apparent cause or reason and have left behind them untarnished reputations and solvent back accounts. Of these, a small percentage are found to have met with violence; others have been victims of suicidal mania, and sooner or later a clue has come to light which has established the fact. The dead are often easier to find than the living.

Of the remaining small proportion, there are on record, however, a number of carefully authenticated cases where the subject has been the victim of a sudden and complete loss of memory.

This dislocation of memory is a variety of aphasia known as amnesia, and when the memory is recur-

rently lost and restored, we have alternating personality. The Society for Psychical Research and
many eminent psychologists, among them the late
William James, Dr. Weir Mitchell, Dr. Hodgson
of Boston, and Dr. A. E. Osborn of San Francisco,
have reported many cases of alternating personality.

Studious efforts are being made to understand
and to explain the strange type of mental phenomena
exhibited in these cases, but as yet no one has given a
clear and comprehensive explanation of them. Such
cases are by no means always connected with disappearances, and exhaustive studies have been made of
types of alternating personality that have from first
to last been carefully watched by scientists of the first
rank.

The variety known as the ambulatory type, where
the patient suddenly loses all knowledge of his own
identity and of the past and takes himself off, leaving no trace or clue, is the variety which the present
case of Miss Blackwell seems to suggest.

There followed a number of most interesting
cases and an elaborate argument by the writer to
show that Betty Blackwell was a victim of this psychological aberration, that she was, in other words,
"a vanisher."

I laid down the paper with a questioning look at
Kennedy.

"As a scientist," he replied deliberately, "the
theory, of course, does appeal to me, especially in
the ingenious way in which that writer applied it.
However, as a detective"—he shook his head
slowly—"I must deal with facts—not speculations.
It leaves much to be explained, to say the least."

Just then the door buzzer sounded and Carton himself sprang to answer it.

"That's Mrs. Blackwell now—her mother. I told her that I was going to take the case to you, Kennedy, and took the liberty of asking her to come up here to meet you. Good-afternoon, Mrs. Blackwell. Let me introduce Professor Kennedy and Mr. Jameson, of whom I spoke to you."

She bowed and murmured a tremulous greeting. Kennedy placed a chair for her and she thanked him.

Mrs. Blackwell was a slender little woman in black, well past middle age. Her face and dress spoke of years of economy, even of privation, but her manner was plainly that of a woman of gentle breeding and former luxury. She was precisely of the type of decayed gentlewoman that one meets often in the city, especially at some of the middle-class boarding-houses.

Deeply as the disappearance of her daughter had affected her, Mrs. Blackwell was facing it bravely. That was her nature. One could imagine that only when Betty was actually found would this plucky little woman collapse. Instinctively, one felt that she claimed his assistance in the unequal fight she was waging against the complexities of modern life for which she had been so ill prepared.

"I do hope you will be able to find my daughter," she began, controlling her voice with an effort. "Mr. Carton has been so kind, more than kind, I am sure, in getting your aid. The police seem to be able to do nothing. They make out reports, put me off, tell me they are making progress—but they don't find Betty."

There was a tragic pathos in the way she said it.

" Betty was such a good girl, too," she went on, her emotions rising. " Oh, I was so proud of her when she got her position down in Wall Street, with the broker, Mr. Langhorne."

" Tell Mr. Kennedy just what you told me of her disappearance," put in Carton.

Again Mrs. Blackwell controlled her feelings. " I don't know much about it," she faltered, " but last Saturday, when she left the office early, she said she was going to do some shopping on Fifth Avenue. I know she went there, did shop a bit, then walked on the Avenue several blocks. But after that there is no trace of her."

" You have heard nothing, have no idea where she might have gone—even for a time? " queried Kennedy.

He asked it with a keen look at the face of Mrs. Blackwell. I recalled one case where a girl had disappeared in which Kennedy had always asserted that if the family had been perfectly frank at the start much more might have been accomplished in unravelling the mystery.

There was evident sincerity in Mrs. Blackwell as she replied quickly, " Absolutely none. Another girl from the office was with her part of the time, then left her to take the subway. We don't live far uptown. It wouldn't have taken Betty long to get home, even if she had walked, after that, through a crowded street, too."

"Of course, she may have met a friend, may have gone somewhere with the friend," put in Kennedy, as if trying out the remark to see what effect it might have.

"Where could she go?" asked Mrs. Blackwell in naïve surprise, looking at him with a counterpart of the eyes we had seen in the picture. "I hope you don't think that Betty——"

The little widow was on the verge of tears again at the mere hint that her daughter might have had friends that were not all, perhaps, that they should be.

Carton came to the rescue. "Miss Blackwell," he interposed, "was a very attractive girl, very. She had hosts of admirers, as every attractive girl must have. Most of them, all of them, as far as Mrs. Blackwell knows and I have been able to find out, were young men at the office where she worked, or friends of that sort—not the ordinary clerk, but of the rising, younger, self-made generation. Still, they don't seem to have interested her particularly as far as I have been able to discover. She merely liked them. There is absolutely nothing known to point to the fact that she was any different from thousands of girls in that respect. She was vivacious, full of fun and life, a girl any fellow would have been more than proud to take to a dance. She was ambitious, I suppose, but nothing more."

"Betty was not a bad girl," asserted Mrs. Black-

well vehemently. "She was a good girl. I don't
believe there was much, in fact anything important,
on which she did not make me her confidanté. Yes,
she was ambitious. So am I. I have always hoped
that Betty would bring our family—her younger
sister—back to the station where we were before
the panic wiped out our fortune and killed my husband. That is all."

"Yes," added Carton, "nothing at all is known
that would make one think that she was what young
men call a ' good fellow ' with them."

Kennedy looked up, but said nothing. I thought
I could read the unspoken word on his lips, as he
glanced from Carton to Mrs. Blackwell, " known."

She had risen and was facing us.

"Is there no one in all this great city," appealed
the distracted little woman with outstretched arms,
"who can find my daughter? Is it possible that a
girl can disappear in broad daylight in the streets
and never be heard of again? Oh, won't you find
her? Tell me she is safe—that she is still the little
girl I——"

Her voice failed and she was crying softly in her
lace handkerchief. It was touching and I saw that
Kennedy was deeply moved, although at once to his
practical mind the thought must have occurred that
nothing was to be gained by further questions of
Mrs. Blackwell.

"Believe me, Mrs. Blackwell," he said in a low
tone, taking her hand, "I will do all that is in my
power to find her."

" Thank you," murmured the mother, overcome.

A moment later, however, she had recovered her composure to some degree and rose to go. There was a flattering look of relief on her face which in itself must have been ample reward to Craig, a retainer worth more to him in a case like this than money.

" I'm going back to my office," remarked Carton. " If I learn anything, I shall let you know."

The District Attorney went out with Mrs. Blackwell. Busy as he was, he had time to turn aside to help this bereaved woman, and I admired him for it.

" Do you think it is one of those cases like some that Carton has uncovered on the East Side and among girls newly arrived in the city? " I asked Craig when the door was shut.

" Can't say," he returned, in an abstracted study.

" It's awful if it is," I pursued. " And if it is, I suppose all that will result from it will be a momentary thrill of the newspaper-readers, and then they will fall back on the old saying that after all it is only a result of human nature that such things happen—they always have happened and always will— that old line of talk."

" That sort of thing is *not* a result of human nature," returned Kennedy earnestly. " It's a System. I mean to say that if it should turn out to be connected with the vice investigations of Carton, and not a case of aphasia, such a disappearance you would find to be due to the persistent, cunning, and unprincipled exploitation of young girls.

" No, Walter, it is not that women are weak or that men are inherently vicious. That doesn't account for a case like this. Then, too, some mawkish people to-day are fond of putting the whole evil on low wages as a cause. It isn't that—alone. It isn't even lack of education or of moral training. Human nature is not so bad in the mass as some good people think. No, don't you, as a reporter, see it? It is big business, in its way, that Carton is fighting—big business in the commercialized ruin of girls, such, perhaps, as Betty Blackwell—a vicious system that enmeshes even those who are its tools. I'm glad if I can have a chance to help smash it.

" Now, I'll tell you what I want you to do, just so that we can start this thing with a clear understanding of what it amounts to. I want you to look up just what the situation is. I know there is an army of ' vanishers ' in New York. I want to know something about them in the mass. Can't you dig up something from your *Star* connections? "

Kennedy had some matters concerning other cases to clear up before he felt free to devote his whole time to this. As there was nothing we could do immediately, I spent some time getting at the facts he wanted. Indeed, it did not take me long to discover that the disappearance of Betty Blackwell, in spite of the prominence it had been given, was by no means an isolated case. I found that the *Star* alone had chronicled scores of such disappearances during the past few months, cases of girls who had simply been swallowed up in the big city. They were the daughters of neither the rich nor of the poor, most of them, but girls rather in ordinary circumstances.

Even the police records showed upward of a thousand missing young girls, ranging in age from fourteen to twenty-one years and I knew that the police lists scarcely approximated the total number of missing persons in the great city, especially in those cases where a hesitancy on the part of parents and relatives often concealed the loss from public records.

I came away with the impression that there were literally hundreds of cases every bit as baffling as that of Betty Blackwell, of young girls who had left absolutely no trace behind, who had made no preparations for departure and of whom few had been heard from since they disappeared. Many from homes of refinement and even high financial standing had disappeared, leaving no clues behind. It was not alone the daughters of the poor that were affected—it was all society.

Many reasons, I found, had been assigned for the disappearances. I knew that there must be many causes at work, that no one cause could be responsible for all or perhaps a majority of the cases. There were suicides and murders and elopements, family troubles, poverty, desire for freedom and adventure; innumerable complex causes, even down to kidnapping.

The question was, however, which of these causes had been in operation in the case of Betty Blackwell? Where had she gone? Where had this whole army of vanishers disappeared? Were these disappearances merely accidents—or was there an epidemic of amnesia? I could bring myself to no such conclusions, but was forced to answer my own queries in lieu of an answer from Kennedy, by propounding another. Was there an organized band?

And, after I had tried to reason it all out, I still found myself back at the original question, as I rejoined Kennedy at the laboratory, "Where had they all—where had Betty Blackwell gone?"

II

THE BLACK BOOK

I HAD scarcely finished pouring out my suspicions to Kennedy when the telephone rang.

It was Carton on the wire, in a state of unsuppressed excitement. Kennedy answered the call himself, but the conversation was brief and, to me, unenlightening, until he hung up the receiver.

"Dorgan—the Boss," he exclaimed, "has just found a detectaphone in his private dining-room at Gastron's."

At once I saw the importance of the news and for the moment it obscured even the case of Betty Blackwell.

Dorgan was the political boss of the city at that time, apparently entrenched, with an organization that seemed impregnable. I knew him as a big, bull-necked fellow, taciturn to the point of surliness, owing his influence to his ability to " deliver the goods " in the shape of graft of all sorts, the arch-enemy of Carton, a type of politician who now is rapidly passing.

"Carton wants to see us immediately at his office," added Craig, jamming his hat on his head. "Come on."

Without waiting for further comment or answer

from me, Kennedy, caught by the infectious excitement of Carton's message, dashed from our apartment and a few minutes later we were whirling downtown on the subway.

"You know, I suppose," he whispered rather hoarsely above the rumble and roar of the train, but so as not to be overheard, "that Dorgan always has kept a suite of rooms at Gastron's, on Fifth Avenue, for dinners and conferences."

I nodded. Some of the things that must have gone on in the secret suite in the fashionable restaurant I knew would make interesting reading, if the walls had ears.

"Apparently he must have found out about the eavesdropping in time and nipped it," pursued Kennedy.

"What do you mean?" I asked, for I had not been able to gather much from the one-sided conversation over the telephone, and the lightning change from the case of Betty Blackwell to this had left me somewhat bewildered. "What has he done?"

"Smashed the transmitter of the machine," replied Kennedy tersely. "Cut the wires."

"Where did it lead?" I asked. "How do you know?"

Kennedy shook his head. Either he did not know, yet, or he felt that the subway was no place in which to continue the conversation beyond the mere skeleton that he had given me.

We finished the ride in comparative silence and

hurried into Carton's office down in the Criminal Courts Building.

Carton greeted us cordially, with an air of intense relief, as if he were glad to have been able to turn to Kennedy in the growing perplexities that beset him.

What surprised me most, however, was that, seated beside his desk, in an easy chair, was a striking looking woman, not exactly young, but of an age that is perhaps more interesting than youth, certainly more sophisticated. She, too, I noticed, had a tense, excited expression on her face. As Kennedy and I entered she had looked us over searchingly.

"Let me present Mr. Kennedy and Mr. Jameson, Mrs. Ogleby," said Carton quickly. "Both of them know as much about how experts use those little mechanical eavesdroppers as anyone—except the inventor."

We bowed and waited for an explanation.

"You understand," continued Carton slowly to us in a tone that enjoined secrecy, "Mrs. Ogleby, who is a friend of Mr. Murtha, Dorgan's right-hand man, naturally is alarmed and doesn't want her name to appear in this thing."

"Oh—it is terrible—terrible," Mrs. Ogleby chimed in in great agitation. "I don't care about anything else. But, my reputation—it will be ruined if they connect my name with the case. As soon as I heard of it—I thought of you, Mr. Carton. I came here immediately. There must be some way

in which you can protect me—some way that you
can get along without using——"

"But, my dear Mrs. Ogleby," interrupted the
District Attorney, "I have told you half a dozen
times, I think, that I didn't put the detectaphone
in——"

"Yes, but you will get the record," she persisted excitedly. "Can't you do something?" she
pleaded.

I fancied that she said it with the air of one who
almost had some right in the matter.

"Mrs. Ogleby," reiterated Carton earnestly, "I
will do all I can—on my word of honour—to protect
your name, but——"

He paused and looked at us helplessly.

"What was it that was overheard?" asked Craig
point-blank, watching Mrs. Ogleby's face carefully.

"Why," she replied nervously, "there was a big
dinner last night which Mr. Dorgan gave at Gastron's. Mr. Murtha took me and—oh—there were
lots of others——" She stopped suddenly.

"Yes," prompted Kennedy. "Who else was
there?"

She was on her guard, however. Evidently she
had come to Carton for one purpose and that was
solely to protect herself against the scandal which
she thought might attach to having been present at
one of the rather notorious little affairs of the Boss.

"Really," she answered, colouring slightly, "I
can't tell you. I mustn't say a word about who was
there—or anything about it. Good heavens—it is

bad enough as it is—to think that my name may be dragged into politics and all sorts of false stories set in motion about me. You must protect me, Mr. Carton, you must."

"How did you find out about the detectaphone being there?" asked Kennedy.

"Why," she replied evasively, "I thought it was just an ordinary little social dinner. That's what Mr. Murtha told me it was. I didn't think anyone outside was interested in it or in who was there or what went on. But, this morning, a—a friend—called me up and told me—something that made me think others besides those invited knew of it, knew too much."

She paused, then resumed hastily to forestall questioning, "I began to think it over myself, and the more I thought of it, the stranger it seemed that anyone else, outside, should know. I began to wonder how it leaked out, for I understood that it was a strictly private affair. I asked Mr. Murtha and he told Mr. Dorgan. Mr. Dorgan at once guessed that there had been something queer. He looked about his rooms there, and, sure enough, they found the detectaphone concealed in the wall. I can't tell any more," she added, facing Carton and using her bewitching eyes to their best advantage. "I can't ask you to shield Mr. Dorgan and Mr. Murtha. They are your opponents. But I have done nothing to you, Mr. Carton. You must suppress—that part of it—about me. Why, it would ruin——"

She cut her words short. But I knew what she

meant, and to a certain extent I could understand, if not sympathize with her. Her husband, Martin Ogleby, club-man and man about town, had a reputation none too savoury. But, man-like, I knew, he would condone not even the appearance of anything that caused gossip in his wife's actions. I could understand how desperate she felt.

"But, my dear lady," repeated Carton, in a manner that showed that he felt keenly, for some reason or other, the appeal she was making to him, "must I say again that I had nothing whatever to do with it? I have sent for Mr. Kennedy and——"

"Nothing—on your honour?" she asked, facing him squarely.

"Nothing—on my honour," he asserted frankly.

She appeared to be dazed. Apparently all along she had assumed that Carton must be the person to see, that he alone could do anything for her, would do something.

Her face paled as she met his earnest look. She had risen and now, half chagrined, half frightened, she stood irresolute. Her lips quivered and tears stood in her eyes as she realized that, instead of protecting herself by her confidence, she had, perhaps, made matters worse by telling an outsider.

Carton, too, had risen and in a low voice which we could not overhear was trying to reassure her.

In her confusion she was moving toward the door, utterly oblivious, now, to us. Carton tactfully took her arm and led her to a private entrance that opened from his office down the corridor and out of sight of the watchful eyes of the reporters and attendants in the outer hall.

I did not understand just what it was all about, but I could see Kennedy's eye following Carton keenly.

"What was that—a plant?" he asked, still trying to read Carton's face, as he returned to us alone a moment later. "Did she come to see whether you got the record?"

"No—I don't think so," replied Carton quickly. "No, I think that was all on the level—her part of it."

"But who did put in the instrument, really—did you?" asked Kennedy, still quizzing.

"No," exclaimed Carton hastily, this time meeting Craig's eye frankly. "No. I wish I had. Why —the fact is, I don't know who did—no one seems to know, yet, evidently. But," he added, leaning forward and speaking rapidly, "I think I could give a shrewd guess."

Kennedy said nothing, but nodded encouragingly.

"I think," continued Carton impressively, "that it must have been Langhorne and the Wall Street crowd he represents."

"Langhorne," repeated Kennedy, his mind working rapidly. "Why, it was his stenographer that Miss Blackwell was. Why do you suspect Langhorne?"

"Because, exclaimed Carton, more excited than ever at Kennedy's quick deduction, bringing his fist down on the desk to emphasize his own suspicion,

" because they aren't getting their share of the graft that Dorgan is passing out—probably are sore, and think that if they can get something on the Boss or some of those who are close to him, they may force him to take them into partnership in the deals."

Carton looked from Kennedy to me, to see what impression his theory made. On me at least it did make an impression. Hartley Langhorne, I knew, was a Wall Street broker and speculator who dealt in real estate, securities, in fact in anything that would appeal to a plunger as promising a quick and easy return.

Kennedy made no direct comment on the theory. " In what shape is the record, do you suppose? " he asked merely.

" I gathered from Mrs. Ogleby," returned Carton watchfully, " that it had been taken down by a stenographer at the receiving end of the detectaphone, transcribed in typewriting, and loosely bound in a book of limp black leather. Oh," he concluded, " Dorgan would give almost anything to find out what is in that little record, you may be sure. Perhaps even, rather than have such a thing out, he would come to terms with Langhorne."

Kennedy said nothing. He was merely absorbing the case as Carton presented it.

" Don't you see? " continued the District Attorney, pacing his office and gazing now and then out of the window, " here's this record hidden away somewhere in the city. If I could only get it—I'd win my fight against Dorgan—and Mrs. Ogleby need not suffer for her mistake in coming to me, at all."

He was apparently thinking aloud. Kennedy did not attempt to quiz him. He was considering the importance of the situation. For, as I have said, it was at the height of the political campaign in which Carton had been renominated independently by the Reform League—of which, more later.

" You don't think that Langhorne is really in the inner ring, then?" questioned Craig.

" No, not yet."

" Well, then," I put in hastily, " can't you approach him or someone close to him, and get——"

" Say," interrupted Carton, " anything that took place in that private dining-room at Gastron's would be just as likely to incriminate Langhorne and some of his crowd as not. It is a difference in degree of graft—that is all. They don't want an open fight. It was just a piece of finesse on Langhorne's part. You may be sure of that. No, neither of them wants a fight. That's the last thing. They're both afraid. What Langhorne wanted was a line on Dorgan. And we should never have known anything about this Black Book, if some of the women, I suppose, hadn't talked too much. Mrs. Ogleby added two and two and got five. She thought it must be I who put the instrument in."

Carton was growing more and more excited again. " It's exasperating," he continued. " There's the record—somewhere—if I could only get it. Think of it, Kennedy—an election going on

3

and never so much talk about graft and vice before!"

"What was in the book—mostly, do you imagine?" asked Craig, still imperturbable.

Carton shrugged his shoulders. "Oh, almost anything. For instance, you know, Dorgan has just put through a new scheme of city planning—with the able assistance of some theoretical reformers. That will be a big piece of real estate graft, unless I am mistaken. Langhorne and his crowd know it. They don't want to be frozen out."

As they talked, I had been revolving the thing over in my head. Dorgan's little parties, as reported privately among the men on the *Star* whom I knew, were notorious. The more I considered, the more possible phases of the problem I thought of. It was not even impossible that in some way it might bear on the Betty Blackwell case.

"Do you think Dorgan and Murtha are hunting the book as anxiously as—some others?" I ventured.

"You have heard of the character of some of those dinners?" answered Carton by asking another question, then went on: "Why, Dorgan has had some of our leading lawyers, financiers, and legislators there. He usually surrounds them with brilliant, clever women, as unscrupulous as himself, and—well—you can imagine the result. Poor little Mrs. Ogleby," he added sympathetically. "They could twist her any way they chose for their purposes."

My own impression had been that Mrs. Ogleby was better able to take care of herself than his words gave her credit for, but I said nothing.

Carton paused before the window and gazed out at the Bridge of Sighs that led from his building across to the city prison.

" What a record that Black Book must hold! " he exclaimed meditatively. " Why, if it was only that I could ' get ' Murtha—I'd be happy," he added, turning to us.

Murtha, as I have said, was Boss Dorgan's right bower, a clever and unscrupulous politician and leader in a district where he succeeded somehow or other in absolutely crushing opposition. I had run across him now and then in the course of my newspaper career and, aside from his well-known character in delivering the " goods " to the organization whenever it was necessary, I had found him a most interesting character.

It was due to such men as Murtha that the organization kept its grip, though one wave of reform after another lashed its fury on it. For Murtha understood his people. He worked at politics every hour—whether it was patting the babies of the district on the head, or bailing their fathers out of jail, handing out shoes to the shiftless or judiciously distributing coal and ice to the deserving.

Yet I had seen enough to know the inherent viciousness of the circle—of how the organization took dollars from the people with one concealed hand and distributed pennies from the other hand, held aloft and in the spotlight. Again and again, Kennedy and I in our excursions into scientific warfare on crime in the underworld had run squarely up against the refined as well as the debased creatures of the " System." Pyramided on what looked like open-handed charity and good-fellowship we had seen vice and crime of all degrees.

And yet, somehow or other, I must confess to a sort of admiration for Murtha and his stamp—if for nothing else than because of the frankness with which he did what he sought to do. Neither Kennedy nor I could be accused of undue sympathy with the System, yet, like many who had been brought in close contact with it, it had earned our respect in many ways.

And so, I contemplated the situation with more than ordinary interest. Carton wanted the Black Book to use in order to win his political fight for a clean city and to prosecute the grafters. Dorgan wanted it in order to suppress and thus protect himself and Murtha. Mrs. Ogleby wanted it to save her good name and prevent even the appearance of scandal. Langhorne wanted it in order to coerce Dorgan to share in the graft, yet was afraid of Carton also.

Was ever a situation of such peculiar, mixed motives?

" I would move heaven and earth for that Black Book!" exclaimed Carton finally, turning from the window and facing us.

Kennedy, too, had risen.

"You can count on me, then, Carton," he said simply, as the recollection of the many fights in which we had stood shoulder to shoulder with the young District Attorney came over him.

A moment later Carton had us each by the hand.

"Thank you," he cried. "I knew you fellows would be with me."

III

THE SAFE ROBBERY

IT was late that night that Kennedy and I left Carton after laying out a campaign and setting in motion various forces, official and unofficial, which might serve to keep us in touch with what Dorgan and the organization were doing.

Not until the following morning, however, did anything new develop in such a way that we could work on it.

Kennedy had picked up the morning papers which had been left at the door of our apartment and was hastily running his eye over the headlines on the first page, as was his custom.

"By Jove, Walter," I heard him exclaim. "What do you think of that—a robbery below the deadline—and in Langhorne's office, too."

I hurried out of my room and glanced at the papers, also. Sure enough, there it was:

SAFE ROBBED IN WALL ST. OFFICE

Door Into Office of Langhorne & Westlake, Brokers, Forced and Safe Robbed.

One of the strangest robberies ever perpetrated was pulled off last night in the office of Langhorne

& Westlake, the brokers, at —— Wall Street, some time during the regular closing time of the office and eight o'clock.

Mr. Langhorne had returned to his office after dining with some friends in order to work on some papers. When he arrived, about eight o'clock, he found that the door had been forced. The office was in darkness, but when he switched on the lights it was discovered that the office safe had been entered.

Nothing was said about the manner in which the safe robbery was perpetrated, but it is understood to have been very peculiar. So far no details have been announced and the robbery was not reported to the police until a late hour.

Mr. Langhorne, when seen by the reporters, stated positively that nothing of great value had been taken and that the firm would not suffer in any way as a result of the robbery.

One of the stenographers in the office, Miss Betty Blackwell, who acted as private secretary to Mr. Langhorne, is missing and the case has already attracted wide attention. Whether or not her disappearance had anything to do with the robbery is not known.

" Naturally he would not report it to the police," commented Kennedy; " that is, if it had anything to do with that Black Book, as I am sure that it must have had."

" It was certainly a most peculiar affair if it did not," I remarked. " There must be some way of finding that out. It's strange about Betty Blackwell."

Kennedy was turning something over in his mind.

"Of course," he remarked, "we don't want to come out into the open just yet, but it would be interesting to know what happened down there at Langhorne's. Have you any objection to going down with me and posing as a reporter from the *Star?*"

"None whatever," I returned.

We stopped at the laboratory on the campus of the University where Craig still retained his professorship. Kennedy secured a rather bulky piece of apparatus, which, as nearly as I can describe, consisted of a steel frame, which could be attached by screws to any wooden table. It contained a lower plate which could move forward and back, two lateral uprights stiffened by curved braces, and a cross piece of steel attached by strong bolts to the tops of the posts. In the face of the machine was a dial with a pointer.

Kennedy quickly took the apparatus apart and made it up into two packages so that between us we could carry it easily, and at about the time that Wall Street offices were opening we were on our way downtown.

Langhorne proved to be a tall, rather slim, man of what might be called youngish middle age. One did not have to be introduced to him to read his character or his occupation. Every line of his faultlessly fitting clothes and every expression of his keen and carefully cared-for face betokened the plunger, the man who lived by his wits and found the process both fascinating and congenial.

"Mr. Langhorne," began Kennedy, after I had taken upon myself the duty of introducing ourselves as reporters, "we are preparing an article for our paper about a new apparatus which the *Star* has imported especially from Paris. It is a machine invented by Monsieur Bertillon just before he died, for the purpose of furnishing exact measurements of the muscular efforts exerted in the violent entry of a door or desk by making it possible to reproduce the traces of the work that a burglar has left on doors and articles of furniture. We've been waiting for a case that the instrument would fit into and it seemed to us that perhaps it might be of some use to you in getting at the real robber of your office. Would you mind if we made an attempt to apply it?"

Langhorne could not very well refuse to allow us to try the thing, though it was plainly evident that he did not want to talk and did not relish the publicity that the news of the morning had brought him.

Kennedy had laid the apparatus down on a table as he spoke and was assembling the parts which he had separated in order to carry it.

"These are the marks on the door, I presume?" he continued, examining some indentations of the woodwork near the lock.

Langhorne assented.

"The door was open when you returned?" asked Kennedy.

"Closed," replied Langhorne briefly. "Before I

put the key into the lock, I turned the knob, as I have a habit of doing. Instead of catching, it yielded and the door swung open without any trouble."

He repeated the story substantially as we had already read it in the papers.

Kennedy had taken a step or two into the office, and was now facing the safe. It was not a large safe, but was one of the most modern construction and was supposed to be burglar proof.

"And you say you lost practically nothing?" persisted Craig.

"Nothing of importance," reiterated Langhorne.

Kennedy had been watching him closely. The man was at least baffling. There was nothing excited or perturbed about his manner. Indeed, one might easily have thought that it was not his safe at all that had been robbed. I wondered whether, after all, he had had the Black Book. Certainly, I felt, if he had lost it he was very cool about the loss.

Craig had by this time reached the safe itself. In spite of Langhorne's reluctance, his assurance had taken Kennedy even up to the point which he wished. He was examining the safe.

On the front it showed no evidence of having been "souped" or drilled. There was not a mark on it. Nor, as we learned later from the police, was there any evidence of a finger-print having been left by the burglar.

Langhorne now but ill concealed his interest. It was natural, too, for here he had one of the most modern of small strong-boxes, built up of the latest chrome steel and designed to withstand any reasonable assault of cracksman or fire.

I was on the point of inquiring how on earth it had been possible to rob the safe, when Kennedy, standing on a chair, as Langhorne directed, uttered a low exclamation.

I craned my neck to look also.

There, in the very top of the safe, yawned a huge hole large enough to thrust one's arm through, with something to spare.

As I looked at the yawning dark hole in the top of what had been only a short time ago a safe worthy of the latest state of the art, it seemed incomprehensible.

Try as I could to reason it out, I could find no explanation. How it had been possible for a burglar to make such an opening in the little more than two hours between closing and the arrival of Langhorne after dinner, I could not even guess. As far as I knew it would have taken many long hours of patient labour with the finest bits to have made anything at all comparable to the destruction which we saw before us.

A score of questions were on my lips, but I said nothing, although I could not help noticing the strange look on Langhorne's face. It plainly showed that he would like to have known what had taken place during the two or more hours when his office had been unguarded, yet was averse to betraying any such interest.

Mystified as I was by what I saw, I was even more amazed at the cool manner in which Kennedy passed it all by.

He seemed merely to be giving the hole in the top of the safe a passing glance, as though it was of no importance that someone should have in such an incredibly short time made a hole through which one might easily reach his arm and secure anything he wanted out of the interior of the powerful little safe.

Langhorne, too, seemed surprised at Kennedy's matter of fact passing by of what was almost beyond the range of possibility.

"After all," remarked Kennedy, "it is not the safe that we care to study so much as the door. For one thing, I want to make sure whether the marks show a genuine breaking and entering or whether they were placed there afterwards merely to cover the trail, supposing someone had used a key to get into the office."

The remark suggested many things to me. Was it that he meant to imply that, after all, the missing Betty Blackwell had had something to do with it? In fact, could the thing have been done by a woman?

"Most persons," remarked Craig, as he studied the marks on the door, "don't know enough about jimmies. Against them an ordinary door-lock or window-catch is no protection. With a jimmy eighteen inches long, even an anemic burglar can exert a pressure sufficient to lift two tons. Not one door-lock in ten thousand can stand this strain. It's like using a hammer to kill a fly. Really, the only use of locks is to keep out sneak thieves and to compel the modern, scientific educated burglar to make a noise. This fellow, however, was no sneak thief."

He continued to adjust the machine which he had brought. Langhorne watched minutely, but did not say anything.

" Bertillon used to call this his mechanical burglar detector," continued Kennedy. " As you see, this frame carries two dynamometers of unequal power. The stronger, which has a high maximum capacity of several tons, is designed for the measurement of vertical efforts. The other measures horizontal efforts. The test is made by inserting the end of a jimmy or other burglar's tool and endeavouring to produce impressions similar to those which have been found on doors or windows. The index of the dynamometer moves in such a way as to make a permanent record of the pressure exerted. The horizontal or traction dynamometer registers the other component of pressure."

He pressed down on the machine. " There was a pressure here of considerably over two tons," he remarked at length, " with a very high horizontal traction of over four hundred pounds. What I wanted to get at was whether this could have been done by a man, woman, or child, or perhaps by several persons. In this case, it was clearly no mere fake to cover up the opening of the door by a key. It was a genuine attempt. Nor could it have been done by a woman. No, that is the work of a man, a powerful man, too, accustomed to the use of the jimmy."

I fancied that a shade of satisfaction crossed the otherwise impassive face of Langhorne. Was it because the Bertillon dynamometer appeared at first sight to exonerate Betty Blackwell, at least so far, from any connection with the crime? It was difficult to say.

Important though it was, however, to clear up at the start just what sort of person was connected with the breaking of the door I could not but feel that Kennedy had some purpose in deferring and minimizing for the present what, to me at least, was the greater mystery, the entering of the safe itself.

He was still studying and comparing the marks on the door and the record made on the dynamometer, when the office telephone rang and Langhorne was summoned to answer it. Instead of taking the call in his own office, he chose to answer it at the switchboard, perhaps because that would allow him to keep an eye also on us.

Whatever his purpose, it likewise enabled us to keep an ear on him, and it was with surprise which both Kennedy and I had great difficulty in concealing, that we heard him reply, " Hello—yes—oh, Mrs. Ogleby, good-morning. How are you? That's good. So you, too, read the papers. No, I haven't lost anything of importance, thank you. Nothing serious, you know. The papers like to get hold of such things and play them up. I have a couple of reporters here now. Heaven knows what they are doing, but I can foresee some more unpaid advertising for the firm in it. Thank you again for your interest. You haven't forgotten the studio dance I'm giving on the twelfth? No—that's fine. I hope you'll come, even if Martin has another engagement. Fine. Well—good-bye."

He hung up the receiver with a mingled air of gratification and exasperation, I fancied.

" Haven't you fellows finished yet? " he asked finally, coming over to us, a little brusquely.

" Just about," returned Kennedy, who had by this time begun slowly to dismember and pack up the dynamometer, determined to take advantage of every minute both to observe Langhorne and to fix in his mind the general lay-out of the office.

" Everybody seems to be interested in me this morning," he observed, for the moment forgetting the embargo he had imposed on his own words.

As for myself, I saw at once that others besides ourselves were keenly interested in this robbery.

" There," remarked Kennedy when at last he had finished packing up the dynamometer into two packages. " At least, Mr. Langhorne, you have the satisfaction of knowing that it was in all probability a man, a strong man, and one experienced in forcing doors who succeeded in entering your office during your brief absence last night."

Langhorne shrugged his shoulders non-committally, but it was evident that he was greatly relieved and he could not conceal his interest in what Kennedy was doing, even though he had succeeded in conveying the impression that it was a matter of indifference to him.

"I suppose you keep a great many of your valuable papers in safety deposit vaults," ventured Kennedy, finishing up the wrapping of the two packages, "as well as your personal papers perhaps at home."

He made the remark in a casual manner, but Langhorne was too keen to fall into the trap.

"Really," he said with an air of finality, "I must decline to be interviewed at present. Good-day, gentlemen."

"A slippery customer," was Craig's comment when we reached the street outside the office. "By the way, evidently Mrs. Ogleby is leaving no stone unturned in her effort to locate that Black Book and protect herself."

I said nothing. Langhorne's manner, self-confident to the point of bravado, had baffled me. I began to feel that even if he had lost the detectaphone record, his was the nature to carry out the bluff of still having it, in much the same manner that he would have played the market on a shoestring or made the most of an unfilled four-card flush in a game of poker.

Kennedy was far from being discouraged, however. Indeed, it seemed as if he really enjoyed

matching his wit against the subtlety of a man like
Langhorne, even more than against one the type of
Dorgan and Murtha.

"I want to see Carton and I don't want to carry
these bundles all over the city," he remarked,
changing the subject for the moment, as he turned
into a public pay station. "I'll ring him up and
have him meet us at the laboratory, if I can."

A moment later he emerged, excited, perspiring
from the closeness of the telephone booth.

"Carton has some news—a letter—that's all he
would say," he exclaimed. "He'll meet us at the
laboratory."

We hastily resumed our uptown journey.

"What do you think it is?" I asked. "About
Betty Blackwell?"

Kennedy shook his head non-committally. "I
don't know. But he has some of his county detectives watching Dorgan and Murtha in that Black
Book case, I know. They are worried. It doesn't
look as though they, at least, had the record—that
is, if Langhorne has really lost it."

I wondered whether Langhorne might not, after
all, as Kennedy had hinted, have concealed it elsewhere. The activity of Dorgan and Murtha might
indicate that they knew more about the robbery than
appeared yet on the surface. Had they failed in
it? Had they been double-crossed by the man they
had chosen for the work, assuming that they knew
of and had planned the "job"?

The safe-breaking and the way Langhorne took
4

it had served to complicate the case even further. While we had before been reasonably sure that Langhorne had the book, now we were sure of nothing.

IV

THE ANONYMOUS LETTER

"WHAT do you make of that?" inquired Carton half an hour later as he met us breathlessly at the laboratory.

He unfolded a letter over which he had evidently been puzzling considerably. It was written, or rather typewritten, on plain paper. The envelope was plain and bore no marks of identification, except possibly that it had been mailed uptown.

The letter ran:

DEAR SIR:

Although this is an anonymous letter, I beg that you will not consider it such, since it will be plain to you that there is good reason for my wishing to remain nameless.

I want to tell you of some things that have taken place recently at a little hotel in the West Fifties. No doubt you know of the place already—the Little Montmartre.

There are several young and wealthy men who frequent this resort. I do not dare tell you their names, but one is a well-known club-man and man about town, another is a banker and broker, also well known, and a third is a lawyer. I might also mention an intimate friend of theirs, though not of their position in society—a doctor who has somewhat of a reputation among the class of people who frequent the Little Montmartre, ready to furnish them with anything from a medical certificate to drugs and treatment.

I have read a great deal in the newspapers lately of the disappearance of Betty Blackwell, and her case interests me. I think you will find that it will repay you to look into the hint I have given. I don't think it is necessary to say any more. Indeed it may be dangerous to me, and I beg that you will not even show this letter to anyone except those associated with you, and then, please, only with the understanding that it is to go no farther.

Betty Blackwell is not at this hotel, but I am sure that some of those whose wild orgies have scandalized even the Little Montmartre know something about her.

Yours truly,

AN OUTCAST.

Kennedy looked up quickly at Carton as he finished reading the letter.

"Typical," he remarked. "Anonymous letters occasionally are of a friendly nature, but usually they reflect with more or less severity upon the conduct or character of someone. They usually receive little attention, but sometimes they are of the most serious character. In many instances they are most important links in chains of evidence pointing to grave crimes.

"It is possible to draw certain conclusions from such letters at once. For instance, it is a surprising fact that in a large number of cases the anonymous letter writer is a woman, who may write what it

does not seem possible she could write. Such letters
often by their writing, materials used, composition
and general form indicate at once the sex of the
writer and frequently show nationality, age, education, and occupation. These facts may often point
to the probable author.

"Now in this case the writer evidently was well
educated. Assumed illiteracy is a frequent disguise,
but it is impossible for an author to assume a lit-
eracy he or she does not possess. Then, too, women
are more apt to assume the characteristics of men
than men of women. There are many things to be
considered. Too bad it wasn't in ordinary hand-
writing. That would have shown much more.
However, we shall try our best with what we have
here. What impressed you about it?"

"Well," remarked Carton, "the thing that impressed me was that as usual and as I fully expected, the trail leads right back to protected vice
and commercialized graft. This Little Montmartre is one of the swellest of such resorts in the city,
the legitimate successor to the scores and hundreds
of places which the authorities and the vice investigators have closed recently. In fact, Kennedy, I
consider it more dangerous, because it is run, on
the surface at least, just like any of the first-class
hotels. There's no violation of law there, at least
not openly."

Craig had continued to examine the letter closely.
"So, you have already investigated the Little Montmartre?" he queried, drawing from his pocket a

little strip of glass and laying it down carefully over the letter.

"Indeed I have," returned the District Attorney, watching Kennedy curiously. "It is a place with a very unsavoury reputation. And yet I have been able to get nothing on it. They are so confounded clever. There is never any outward violation of law; they adhere strictly to the letter of the rule of outward decency."

Over the typewritten characters Kennedy had placed the strip of glass and I could see that it was ruled into little oblongs, into each of which one of the type of the typewritten sheet seemed to fall. Apparently he had forgotten the contents of the letter in his interest in the text itself. He held the paper up to the light and seemed to study its texture and thickness. Then he examined the typed characters more closely with a little pocket magnifying glass, his lips moving as if he were counting something. Next he seized a mass of correspondence on his desk and began comparing the letter with others, apparently to determine just the shade of writing of the ribbon. Finally he gave it up and leaned back in his chair regarding us.

"It is written in the regular pica type," he remarked thoughtfully, "and on a machine that has seen considerable rough usage, although it is not an old machine. It will take me a little time to identify the make, but after I have done that, I think I could identify the particular machine itself the moment I saw it. You see, it is only a clue that would serve to fix it once you found that machine. The point is, after all, to find it. But once found, I am sure we shall be close to the source of the letter. I may keep this and study it at my leisure? "

" Certainly."

For a moment Carton was silent. Then it seemed as though the matter of Betty Blackwell brought to mind what he had read in the morning papers.

" That robbery of Langhorne's safe was a most peculiar thing, wasn't it? " he meditated. " I suppose you know what Miss Blackwell was? "

" Langhorne's stenographer and secretary, of course," I replied quickly.

" Yes, I know. But I mean what she had actually done? I don't believe you do. My county detectives found out only last night."

Kennedy paused in his rummaging among some bottles to which he had turned at the mention of the safe robbery. " No—what was it? " he asked.

Carton bent forward as if our own walls might have ears and said in a low voice: " She was the operator who took down the detectaphone conversations at the other end of the wire in a furnished room in the house next to Gastron's."

He drew back to see what effect the intelligence had on us, then resumed slowly: " Yes, I've had my men out on the case. That is what they think. I believe she often executed little confidential commissions for Langhorne, sometimes things that took her on short trips out of town. There is a possibility that she may be on a mission of that sort. But I think—it's this Black Book case that involves her now."

"Langhorne wouldn't talk much about any-thing," I put in, hastily remembering his manner. "He may not be responsible—but from his actions I'd wager he knows more about her than appears."

"Just so," agreed Carton. "If my men can find out that she was the operator who 'listened in' and got the notes and the transcript of the Black Book, then she becomes a person of importance in the case and the fact must be known to others who are interested. Why," he pursued, "don't you see what it means? If she is out of the way, there is no one to swear to the accuracy of the notes in the record, no one to identify the voices—even if we do man-age finally to locate the thing."

"Dorgan and the rest are certainly leaving noth-ing undone to shake the validity of the record," ru-minated Kennedy, accepting for the moment at least Carton's explanation of the disappearance of Miss Blackwell. "Have you any idea what might have happened to her?"

Carton shook his head negatively. "There are several explanations," he replied slowly. "As far as we have been able to find out she led a model life, at home with her mother and sister. Except for the few commissions for Langhorne and lately when she was out rather late taking the detectaphone notes, she was very quiet,—in fact devoted to her mother and the education of her younger sister."

"What sort of place was it in which the receivers

of the detectaphone were located—do you know?"
asked Kennedy quickly.

"Yes, it seems to be a very respectable boarding-
house," answered Carton. "She came there with a
grip about a week ago and hired a room, saying she
was out of town a great deal. Just about the same
time a young man, who posed as a student in electrical engineering at some school uptown, left. It
must have been he who installed the detectaphone—
perhaps with the aid of a waiter in Gastron's. At
any rate, she seems to have been alone in the board-
ing-house—that is, I mean, not acquainted with any
of the other guests—during the time when she was
taking down the record. Dorgan traced the wires,
outside the two buildings, to her rooms, but she was
not there. In fact there was nothing there but a
grip with a few articles that give no clue to anything. Somehow she must have heard of it, for
no one knows anything about her, since then."

"Perhaps Langhorne is keeping her out of the
way so that no one can tamper with her testimony,"
I suggested.

"It's possible," said Carton in a tone that showed
that he did not believe in that explanation. "How
about that safe robbery, Kennedy? Some of the
papers hinted that she might have known something
of that. I had a man down there watching, afterwards, but I had cautioned him to be careful and
keep under cover. One of the elevator boys told
him that the robbers had made a hole in the safe.
What did he mean? Did you see it?"

Rapidly Kennedy sketched what we had done, telling the story of how the dynamometer had at least partly exonerated Betty Blackwell.

When he reached the description of the hole in the safe, Carton was absolutely incredulous. As for myself, it presented a mystery which I found absolutely inexplicable. How it was possible in such a short time to make a hole in a safe by any known means, I could not understand. In fact, if I had not seen it myself, I should have been even more sceptical than Carton.

Kennedy, however, made no reply immediately to our expressions of doubt. He had found and set apart from the rest a couple of little glass bottles with ground glass stoppers. Then he took a thick piece of steel and laid it across a couple of blocks of wood, under which was a second steel plate.

Without a word of explanation, he took the glass stopper out of the larger bottle and poured some of the contents on the upper plate of steel. There it lay, a little mound of reddish powder. Then he took a little powder of another kind from the other bottle.

He lighted a match and ignited the second pile of powder.

"Stand back—close to the wall—shield your eyes," he called to us.

He had dropped the burning mass on the red powder and in two or three leaps he joined us at the far end of the room.

Almost instantly a dazzling, intense flame broke

out. It seemed to sizzle and crackle. With bated breath we waited and, as best we could, shielding our eyes from the glare, watched.

It was almost incredible, but that glowing mass of powder seemed literally to be sinking, sinking right down into the cold steel. In tense silence we waited. On the ceiling we could see the reflection of the molten mass in the cup which it had burned for itself in the cold steel plate.

At last it fell through to the lower piece of steel, on which it burnt itself out—fell through as the burning roof of a frame building might have fallen into the building.

Neither Carton nor I spoke a word, but as we now cautiously advanced with Kennedy and peered over the steel plate we instinctively turned to Craig for an explanation. Carton seemed to regard him as if he were some uncanny mortal. For, there in the steel plate, was a hole. As I looked at the clean-cut edges, I saw that it was smaller but identical in nature with that which we had seen in the safe in Langhorne's office.

"Wonderful!" ejaculated Carton. "What is it?"

"Thermit," was all Kennedy said, as just a trace of a smile of satisfaction flitted over his face.

"Thermit?" echoed Carton, still as mystified as before.

"Yes, an invention of a chemist named Gold-schmidt, of Essen, Germany. It is composed of iron oxide, such as comes off a blacksmith's anvil or the rolls of a rolling-mill, and powdered metallic aluminum. You could thrust a red-hot bar into it without setting it off, but when you light a little magnesium powder and drop it on thermit, a combustion is started that quickly reaches fifty-four hundred degrees Fahrenheit. It has the peculiar property of concentrating its heat to the immediate spot on which it is placed. It is one of the most powerful oxidizing agents known, and it doesn't even melt the rest of the steel surface. You see how it ate its way directly through this plate. Steel, hard or soft, tempered, annealed, chrome, or Harveyized—it all burns just as fast and just as easily. And it's comparatively inexpensive, also. This is an experiment Goldschmidt it fond of showing his students—burning holes in one- and two-inch steel plates. It is the same with a safe—only you need more of the stuff. Either black or red thermit will do the trick equally well, however."

Neither of us said anything. There was nothing to say except to feel and express amazement.

"Someone uncommonly clever or instructed by someone uncommonly clever, must have done that job at Langhorne's," added Craig. "Have you any idea who might pull off such a thing for Dorgan or Murtha?" he asked of Carton.

"There's a possible suspect," answered Carton slowly, "but since I've seen this wonderful exhibition of what thermit can do, I'm almost ashamed to mention his name. He's not in the class that would be likely to use such things."

"Oh," laughed Kennedy, "never think it. Don't you suppose the crooks read the scientific and technical papers? Believe me, they have known about thermit as long as I have. Safes are constructed now that are proof against even that, and other methods of attack. No indeed, your modern scientific cracksman keeps abreast of the times in his field better than you imagine. Our only protection is that fortunately science always keeps several laps ahead of him in the race—and besides, we have organized society to meet all such perils. It may be that the very cleverness of the fellow will be his own undoing. The unusual criminal is often that much the easier to run down. It narrows the number of suspects."

"Well," rejoined Carton, not as confident now as when he had first met us in the laboratory, "then there is a possible suspect—a fellow known in the underworld as 'Dopey' Jack—Jack Rubano. He's a clever fellow—no doubt. But I hardly think he's capable of that, although I should call him a rather advanced yeggman."

"What makes you suspect him?" asked Kennedy eagerly.

"Well," temporized Carton, "I haven't anything 'on' him in this connection, it's true. But we've been trying to find him and can't seem to locate him in connection with primary frauds in Murtha's own district. Dopey Jack is the leader of a gang of gunmen over there and is Murtha's first lieutenant whenever there is a tough political battle of the organization either at the primaries or on Election Day."

"Has a record, I suppose?" prompted Kennedy.

"Would have—if it wasn't for the influence of Murtha," rejoined Carton.

I had heard, in knocking about the city, of Dopey Jack Rubano. That was the picturesque title by which he was known to the police and his enemies as well as to his devoted followers. A few years before, he had begun his career fighting in "preliminaries" at the prize fight clubs on the lower East Side.

He had begun life with a better chance than most slum boys, for he had rugged health and an unusually sturdy body. His very strength had been his ruin. Working decently for wages, he had been told by other petty gang leaders that he was a "sucker," when he could get many times as much for boxing a few rounds at some "athletic" club. He tried out the game with many willing instructors and found that it was easy money.

Jack began to wear better clothes and study the methods of other young men who never worked but always seemed to have plenty of money. They were his pals and showed him how it was done. It wasn't long before he learned that he could often get more by hitting a man with a blackjack than by using his fists in the roped ring. Then, too, there were various ways of blackmail and extortion that were simple, safe, and lucrative. He might be arrested, but he early found that by making himself useful to some politicians, they could fix that minor difficulty in the life.

Thus because he was not only strong and brutal, but had a sort of ability and some education, Dopey Jack quickly rose to a position of minor leadership— had his own incipient " gang," his own " lobby-gows." His following increased as he rose in gangland, and finally he came to be closely associated with Murtha himself on one hand and the " guns " and other criminals of the underworld who frequented the stuss games, where they gambled away the products of their crimes, on the other.

Everyone knew Dopey Jack. He had been charged with many crimes, but always through the aid of " the big fellows " he avoided the penitentiary and every fresh and futile attempt to end his career increased the numbers and reverence of his followers. His had been the history and he was the pattern now of practically every gang leader of consequence in the city. The fight club had been his testing ground. There he had learned the code, which can be summarized in two words, " Don't squeal." For gangland hates nothing so much as a " snitch." As a beginner he could be trusted to commit any crime assigned to him and go to prison, perhaps the chair, rather than betray a leader. As a leader he had those under him trained in the same code. That still was his code to those above him in the System.

" We want him for frauds at the primaries," repeated Carton, " at least, if we can find him, we can hold him on that for a time. I thought perhaps he might know something of the robbery—and about the disappearance of the girl, too.

"Oh," he continued, "there are lots of things against him. Why, only last week there was a dance of a rival association of gang leaders. Against them Dopey Jack led a band of his own followers and in the ensuing pistol battle a passer-by was killed. Of course we can't connect Dopey Jack with his death, but—then we know as well as we know anything in gangland that he was responsible."

"I suppose it isn't impossible that he may know something about the disappearance of Miss Blackwell," remarked Kennedy.

"No," replied Carton, "not at all, although, so far, there is absolutely no clue as far as I can figure out. She may have been bought off or she may have been kidnapped."

"In either case the missing girl must be found," said Craig. "We must get someone interested in her case who knows something about what may happen to a girl in New York."

Carton had been revolving the matter in his mind. "By George," he exclaimed suddenly, "I think I know just the person to take up that case for us—it's quite in her line. Can you spare the time to run down to the Reform League headquarters with me?"

"Nothing could be more important, just at the minute," replied Craig.

The telephone buzzed and he answered it, a moment later handing the receiver to Carton.

"It's your office," he said. "One of the assistant district attorneys wants you on the wire."

As Carton hung up the receiver he turned to us with a look of great satisfaction.

"Dopey Jack has just been arrested," he announced. "He has shut up like an oyster, but we think we can at least hold him for a few days this time until we sift down some of these clues."

V

THE SUFFRAGETTE SECRETARY

CARTON took us directly to the campaign headquarters of the Reform League, where his fight for political life was being conducted.

We found the offices in the tower of a skyscraper, whence was pouring forth a torrent of appeal to the people, in printed and oral form of every kind, urging them to stand shoulder to shoulder for good government and vote the "ring" out of power.

There seemed to me to be a different tone to the place from that which I had ordinarily associated with political headquarters in previous campaigns. There was a notable absence of the old-fashioned politicians and of the air of intrigue laden with tobacco.

Rather, there was an air of earnestness and efficiency, which was decidedly encouraging and hopeful. It seemed to speak of a new era in politics when things were to be done in the open instead of at secret meetings and scandalous dinners, as Dorgan did them at Gastron's.

Maps of the city were hanging on the walls, some stuck full of various coloured pins, denoting the condition of the canvass. Other maps of the city in colours, divided into all sorts of districts, told how fared the battle in the various strongholds of Boss Dorgan and Sub-boss Murtha.

Huge systems of card indexes, loose leaf devices, labour-saving appliances for getting out a vast amount of campaign " literature " in a hurry; in short, a perfect system, such as a great, well-managed business might have been proud of, were in evidence everywhere one looked.

Work was going ahead in every department under high pressure, for the campaign, which had been more than usually heated, was now drawing to a close. Indeed, it would have taken no great astuteness, even without one's being told, to deduce merely from the surroundings that the people here were engaged in the annual struggle of seeking the votes of their fellow-citizens for reform and were nearly worn out by the arduous endeavour.

It had been, as I have said, the bitterest campaign in years. Formerly the reformers had been of the " silk-stocking " type, but now a new and younger generation was coming upon the stage, a generation which had been trained to achieve results, ambitious to attain what in former years had been considered impossible. The Reform League was making a stiff campaign and the System was, by the same token, more frightened than ever before.

Carton was fortunate in having shaken off the thralldom of the old bosses even before the popular uprising against them had assumed such proportions as to warrant anyone in taking his political life in his hands by defying the powers that ruled behind the scenes. In fact, the Reform League itself owed its existence to a fortunate conjunction of both moral and economic conditions which demanded progress.

Of course, the League did not have such a big "barrel" as their opponents under Dorgan. But, at least they did have many willing workers, men and women, who were ready to sacrifice something for the advancement of the principles for which they stood.

In one part of the suite of offices which had been leased by the League, Carton had had assigned to him an office of his own, and it was to this office that he led us, after a word with the boy who guarded the approach to the door, and an exchange of greetings with various workers and visitors in the outside office.

We seated ourselves while Carton ran his eye through some letters that had been left on his desk for his attention.

A moment later the door of his office opened and a young lady in a very stunning street dress, with a pretty little rakish hat and a tantalizing veil, stood a moment, hesitated, and then was about to turn back with an apology for intruding on what looked like a conference.

"Good-morning, Miss Ashton," greeted Carton, laying down the letters instantly. "You're just the person I want to see."

The girl, with a portfolio of papers in her hand, smiled and he quickly crossed the room and held the door open, as he whispered a word or two to her.

She was a handsome girl, something more than even pretty. The lithe gracefulness of her figure spoke of familiarity with both tennis and tango, and her face with its well-chiselled profile denoted intellectuality from which no touch of really feminine charm had been removed by the fearsome process of the creation of the modern woman. Sincerity as well as humour looked out from the liquid depths of her blue eyes beneath the wavy masses of blonde hair. She was good to look at and we looked, irresistibly.

"Let me introduce Professor Kennedy and Mr. Jameson, Miss Ashton," began Carton, adding: "Of course you have heard of Miss Margaret Ashton, the suffragist leader? She is the head of our press bureau, you know. She's making a great fight for us here—a winning fight."

It seemed from the heightened look of determination which set Carton's face in deeper lines that Miss Ashton had that indispensable political quality of inspiring both confidence and enthusiasm in those who worked with her.

"It is indeed a great pleasure to meet you," remarked Kennedy. "Both Mr. Jameson and myself have heard and read a great deal about your work, though we seem never before to have had the pleasure of meeting you."

Miss Ashton, I recalled, was a very clever girl, a graduate of a famous woman's college, and had had several years of newspaper experience before she became a leader in the cause of equal suffrage.

The Ashtons were well known in society and it was a sore trial to some of her conservative friends that she should reject what they considered the proper " sphere " for women and choose to go out into life and devote herself to doing something that was worth while, rather than to fritter her time and energy away on the gaiety and inconsequentiality of social life.

Among those friends, I had understood, was Hartley Langhorne himself. He was older than Miss Ashton, but had belonged to the same social circle and had always held her in high regard. In fact the attentions he paid her had long been noticeable, the more so as she seemed politely unaffected by them.

Carton had scarcely more than introduced us, yet already I felt sure that I scented a romance behind the ordinarily prosaic conduct of a campaign press bureau.

It is far from my intention even to hint that the ability or success of the head of the press bureau were not all her own or were in any degree over-rated. But it struck me, both then and often later, that the candidate for District Attorney had an extraordinary interest in the newspaper campaign, much more, for instance, than in the speakers' bureau. I am sure that it was not wholly accounted for by the fact that publicity is playing a more and more important part in political campaign-ing.

Nevertheless, as we came to know afterwards

such innovations as her card index system by election districts all over the city, showing the attitude
of the various newspaper editors, local leaders, and
other influential citizens, recording changes of senti-
ment and possible openings for future work, all
were very full and valuable. Kennedy, who had a
regular pigeon-hole mind for facts himself, was visibly impressed by the huge mechanical memory
built up by Miss Ashton.

Though he said nothing to me, I knew that Craig
also had observed the state of affairs between the
reform candidate and the suffrage leader.

"You see, Miss Ashton," explained Carton,
"someone has placed a detectaphone in the private
dining-room of Dorgan at Gastron's. I heard of it
first through Mrs. Ogleby, who attended one of the
dinners and was terribly afraid her name would be
connected with them if the record should ever be
published."

"Mrs. Ogleby?" cried Miss Ashton quickly.
"She—at a dinner—with Mr. Murtha? I—I can't
believe it."

Carton said nothing. Whether he knew more
about Mrs. Ogleby than he cared to tell, I could
not even guess.

As he went on briefly summarizing the story, Miss
Ashton shot a quick glance or two at him.

Carton noticed it, but appeared not to do so. "I
suppose," he concluded, "that she thought I was
the only person capable of eavesdropping. As a
matter of fact, I think the instrument was put in

by Hartley Langhorne as part of the fight that is going on fiercely under the surface in the organization."

It was Carton's turn now, I fancied, to observe Miss Ashton more closely. As far as I could see, the information was a matter of perfect indifference to her.

Carton did not say it in so many words, but one could not help gathering that rather than seem to be pursuing a possible rival and using his official position in order to do it, he was not considering Langhorne in any other light than as a mere actor in the drama between himself and Dorgan and Murtha.

"Now," he concluded, "the point of the whole thing is this, Miss Ashton. We have learned that Betty Blackwell—you know the case—who took the notes over the detectaphone for the Black Book, has suddenly and mysteriously disappeared. If she is gone, it may be difficult to prove anything, even if we get the book. Miss Blackwell happens to be a stenographer in the office of Langhorne & Westlake."

For the first time, Miss Ashton seemed to show a sign of embarrassment. Evidently she would just as well have had Miss Blackwell in some other connection.

"Perhaps you would rather have nothing to do with it," suggested Carton, "but I know that you were always interested in things of the sort that happen to girls in the city and thought perhaps you could advise us, even if you don't feel like personally taking up the case."

"Oh, it doesn't—matter," she murmured. "Of course, the first thing for us to do is, as you say, to find what has become of Betty Blackwell."

Carton turned suddenly at the word "us," but Miss Ashton was still studying the pattern of the rug.

"Do you know any more about her?" she asked at length.

As fully as possible the District Attorney repeated what he had already told us. Miss Ashton seemed to be more than interested in the story of the disappearance of Langhorne's stenographer.

As Carton unfolded the meagre details of what we knew so far, Miss Ashton appeared to be torn by conflicting opinions. The more she thought of what might possibly have happened to the unfortunate girl, the more aroused about the case she seemed to become.

Carton had evidently calculated on enlisting her sympathies, knowing how she felt toward many of the social and economic injustices toward women, and particularly girls.

"If Mr. Murtha or Mr. Dorgan is responsible in any way for any harm to her," she said finally, her earnest eyes now ablaze with indignation, "I shall not rest until someone is punished."

Kennedy had been watching her emotions keenly, I suspect, to see whether she connected Langhorne in any way with the disappearance. I could see it interested him that she did not seem even to consider that Langhorne might be responsible. Whether her intuition was correct or not, it was at least better at present than any guess that we three might have made.

" They control so many forces for evil," she went on, " that there is no telling what they might command against a defenceless girl like her when it is a question of their political power."

" Then," pursued Kennedy, pacing the floor thoughtfully, " the next question is, How are we to proceed? The first step naturally will be the investigation of this Little Montmartre. How is it to be done? I presume you don't want to go up there and look the place over yourself, do you, Carton? "

" Most certainly not," said Carton emphatically. Not if you want this case to go any further. Why, I can't walk around a corner now without a general scurry for the cyclone cellars. They all know me, and those who don't are watching for me. On the contrary, if you are going to start there I had better execute a flank movement in Queens or Jersey to divert attention. Really, I mean it. I had better keep in the background. But I'll tell you what I would like to do."

Carton hesitated and came to a full stop.

" What's the matter? " asked Kennedy quickly, noticing the hesitation.

" Why—I—er—didn't know just how you'd take a suggestion—that's all."

" Thankfully. What is it? "

" You know young Haxworth? "

" You mean the son of the millionaire who is investigating vice and whom the newspapers are poking fun at? "

" Yes. Those papers make me tired. He has been working, you know, with me in this matter. He is really serious about it, too. He has a corps of investigators of his own already. Well, there is one of them, a woman detective named Clare Kendall, who is the brains of the whole Haxworth outfit. If you would be willing to have them—er—to have her co-operate with you, I think I could persuade Haxworth——"

" Oh," broke in Kennedy with a laugh. " I see. You think perhaps there might be some professional jealousy? On the contrary, it solves a problem I was already considering. Of course we shall need a woman in this case, one with a rare amount of discretion and ability. Yes, by all means let us call in Miss Kendall, and let us take every advantage we can of what she has already accomplished."

Carton seized the telephone.

" Tell her to meet us at my laboratory in half an hour," interposed Kennedy. " You will come along? "

" I can't. Court opens in twenty minutes and there is a motion I must argue myself."

Miss Ashton appeared to be greatly gratified at Craig's reception of the suggestion, and Carton noticed it.

" Oh, yes," recollected Carton, " by the way, as
I was on my way down here, my office called up and
told me that they had succeeded in locating and ar-
resting Dopey Jack. That ought to please you,—it
will mean cutting down the number of those East
Side ' rackets ' considerably if we succeed with
him."

" Good! " she exclaimed. " Yes, I don't think
there were any worse affairs than the dances of that
Jack Rubano Association. They have got hold of
more young girls and caused more tragedies than
any other gang.. If you need any help in getting
together evidence, Mr. Carton, I shall be only too
glad to help you. I have several old scores myself
to settle with that young tough."

" Thank you," said Carton. " I shall need your
help, if we are to do anything. Of course, we can
hold him only for primary frauds just now, but I
may be able to do something about that dance that
he broke up as a shooting affray."

Miss Ashton nodded encouragingly.

" And," he went on, " it's barely possible that he
may know something, or some of his followers may,
about the robbery of Mr. Langhorne's safe,—if not
about the complete and mysterious disappearance of
Betty Blackwell."

" They'd stop at nothing to save their precious
skins," commented Miss Ashton. " Perhaps that is
a good lead. At any rate I can suggest that to the
various societies and other agencies which I intend
to set in motion trying to trace what has happened

to her. You can have him held until they have time
to report?"

"I shall make it a point to do so at any cost," he
returned, "and I can say only this, that we are all
deeply indebted to you for the interest you have
shown in the case."

"Not at all," she replied enthusiastically, evidently having overcome the first hesitation which
had existed because Miss Blackwell had been Langhorne's stenographer.

Miss Ashton had quickly jotted down in her notebook the best description we could give of the missing girl, her address, and other facts about her, and
a list of those whom she meant to start at work on
the case.

For a moment she hesitated over one name, then
with a sudden resolution wrote it down.

"I intend to see Hartley Langhorne about it,
too," she added frankly. "Perhaps he may tell
something of importance, after all."

I am sure that this final resolution cost her more
than all the rest. Carton would never have asked
it of her, yet was gratified that she saw it to be her
duty to leave nothing undone in tracing the girl, not
even considering the possibility of offending Langhorne.

"Decent people don't seem to realize," she remarked as she shut her little notebook and slipped
it back into her chatelaine, "how the System and
the underworld really do affect them. They think
it is all something apart from the rest of us, and

never consider how closely we are all bound together and how easy it is for the lowest and most
vicious stratum in the social order to pass over and
affect the highest."

"That's exactly the point," agreed Carton.
"Take this very case. It goes from Wall Street to
gangland, from Gastron's down to the underworld
gambling joints of Dopey Jack and the rest."

"Society—gambling," mused Miss Ashton, taking
out her notebook again. "That reminds me of
Martin Ogleby. I must see Mary and try to warn
her against some of those sporty friends of her husband's."

"Please, Miss Ashton," put in Carton quickly,
"don't mention that I have told you of the detectaphone record. It might do more harm than good,
just at present. For a time at least, I think we
should try to keep under cover."

Whether or not that was his real reason, he
turned now to Kennedy for support. We had been,
for the most part, silent spectators of what had
been happening.

"I think so—for the present—at least as far as
our knowledge of the Black Book goes," acquiesced
Craig. He had turned to Miss Ashton and made
no effort to conceal the admiration which he felt for
her, after even so brief an acquaintance. "I think
Miss Ashton can be depended upon to play her part
in the game perfectly. I, for one, want to thank
her most heartily for the way in which she has
joined us."

" Thank you," she smiled, as she rose to go to her own office. " Oh, you can always depend on me," she assured us as she gathered up her portfolio of papers, " where there are the interests of a girl like Betty Blackwell involved !"

VI.

THE WOMAN DETECTIVE

HALF an hour later, a tall, striking, self-reliant young woman with an engaging smile opened the laboratory door and asked for Professor Kennedy.

"Miss Kendall?" Craig inquired, coming forward to meet her.

She was dark-haired, with regular features and an expression which showed a high degree of intelligence. Her clear grey eyes seemed to penetrate and tear the mask off you. It was not only her features and eyes that showed intelligence, but her gown showed that without sacrificing neatness she had deliberately toned down the existing fashions which so admirably fitted in with her figure in order that she might not appear noticeable. It was clever, for if there is anything a good detective must do it is to prevent people from looking twice.

I knew something of her history already. She had begun on a rather difficult case for one of the large agencies and after a few years of experience had decided that there was a field for an independent woman detective who would appeal particularly to women themselves. Unaided she had fought her way to a position of keen rivalry now with the best men in the profession.

Narrowly I watched Kennedy. Here, I felt instinctively, were the " new " woman and the " new " man, if there are such things. I wondered just how they would hit it off together. For the moment, at least, Clare Kendall was an absorbing study, as she greeted us with a frank, jerky straight-arm handshake.

" Mr. Carton," she said directly, " has told me that he received an anonymous letter this morning. May I see it? "

There are times when the so-called " new " woman's assumed masculine brusqueness is a trifle jarring, as well as often missing the point. But with Clare Kendall one did not feel that she was eternally trying to assert that she was the equal or the superior of someone else, although she was, as far as the majority of detectives I have met are concerned. It was rather that she was different; in fact, almost from the start I felt that she was indispensable. She seemed to have that ability to go straight to the point at issue, a sort of faculty of intuition which is often more valuable than anything else, the ability to feel or sense things for which at first there was no actual proof. No good detective ever lacks that sort of instinct, and Clare Kendall, being a woman, had it in large degree. But she had more. She had the ability to go further and get the facts and actual proof; for, as she often said during the course of a case, " Woman's intuition may not be good evi-

6

dence in a court of law, but it is one of the best means to get good evidence that will convince a court of law."

"My investigators have been watching that place for some time," she remarked as she finished the letter. "Of course, having been closely in touch with this sort of thing for several months in my work, I have had all the opportunity in the world to observe and collect information. The letter does not surprise me."

"Then you think it is a good tip?" asked Kennedy.

"Decidedly, although without the letter I should not have started there, I think. Still, as nearly as I can gather, there is a rather nondescript crowd connected in one way or another with the Montmartre. For instance, there is a pretty tough character who seems to be connected with the people there, my investigators tell me. It is a fellow named 'Ike the Dropper,' one of those strong-arm men who have migrated up from the East Side to the White Light District. At least my investigators have told me they have seen him there, for I have never bothered with the place myself. There has been plenty of work elsewhere which promised immediate results. I'm glad to have a chance to tackle this place, though, with your help."

"What do you think of the rest of the letter?" asked Craig.

"I think I could make a pretty shrewd guess from what I have heard, as to the identity of some of those hinted at. I'm not sure, but I think the lawyer may be a Mr. Kahn, a clever enough attorney who has a large theatrical clientele and none too savoury a reputation as a local politician. The banker may be Mr. Langhorne, although he is not exactly a young man. Still, I know he has been associated with the place. As for the club-man I should guess that that was Martin Ogleby."

Kennedy and I exchanged glances of surprise.

"As a first step," said Kennedy, at length, "I am going to write a letter to Betty Blackwell, care of the Little Montmartre—or perhaps you had better do the actual writing of it, Miss Kendall. A woman's hand will look less suspicious."

"What shall I write?" she asked.

"Just a few lines. Tell her that you are one of the girls in the office, that you have heard she was at the Montmartre—anything. The actual writing doesn't make any difference. I merely want to see what happens."

Miss Kendall quickly wrote a little note and handed it to him.

"Then direct this envelope," he said, reaching into a drawer of his desk and bringing out a plain white one. "And let me seal it."

Carefully he sealed and stamped the letter and handed it to me to post.

"You will dine with us, Miss Kendall?" he asked. "Then we will plan the next step in our campaign."

"I shall be glad to do so," she replied.

Fifteen minutes later I had dropped the letter in the drop of a branch of the general post-office to ensure its more prompt delivery, and it was on its way through the mails to accomplish the purpose Kennedy may have contemplated.

"Just now it is more important for us to become acquainted with this Little Montmartre," he remarked. "I suppose, Miss Kendall, we may depend on you to join us?"

"Indeed you may," she replied energetically. "There is nothing that we would welcome more than evidence that would lead to the closing of that place."

Kennedy seemed to be impressed by the frankness and energy of the young woman.

"Perhaps if we three should go there, hire a private dining-room, and look about without making any move against the place that would excite suspicion, we might at least find out what it is that we are fighting. Of course we must dine somewhere, and up there at the same time we can plan our campaign."

"I think that would be ripping," she laughed, as the humour of the situation dawned on her. "Why, we shall be laying our plans right in the heart of the enemy's country and they will never realize it. Perhaps, too, we may get a glimpse of some of those people mentioned in the anonymous letter."

To Clare Kendall it was simply another phase of the game which she had been playing against the forces of evil in the city.

The Little Montmartre was, as I already knew, one of the smaller hotels in a side street just off Broadway, eight or ten stories in height, of modern construction, and for all the world exactly like a score of other of the smaller hostelries of the famous city of hotels.

Clare, Craig, and myself pulled up before the entrance in a taxicab, that seeming to be the accepted method of entering with éclat. A boy opened the door. I jumped out and settled with the driver without a demur at the usual overcharge, while Craig assisted Clare.

Laughing and chatting, we entered the bronze plate-glass doors and walked slowly down a richly carpeted corridor. It was elegantly furnished and decorated with large palms set at intervals, quite the equal in luxuriousness, though on a smaller scale, of any of the larger and well-known hotels. Beautifully marked marbles and expensive hangings greeted the eye at every turn. Faultlessly liveried servants solicitously waited about for tips.

Craig and Clare, who were slightly ahead of me, turned quickly into a little alcove, or reception room and Craig placed a chair for her. Farther down the corridor I could see the office, and beyond a large main dining-room from which strains of music came and now and then the buzz of conversation and laughter from gay parties at the immaculately white tables.

" Boy," called Kennedy quietly, catching the eye of a passing bell hop and unostentatiously slipping a quarter into his hand, which closed over the coin almost automatically, " the head waiter, please. Oh —er—by the way—what is his name? "

" Julius," returned the boy, to whom the proceeding seemed to present nothing novel, although the whole atmosphere of the place was beyond his years. " I'll get him in a minute, sir. He's in the main dining-room. He's having some trouble with the cabaret singers. One of them is late—as usual."

We sat in the easy chairs watching the people passing and repassing in the corridor. There was no effort at concealment here.

A few minutes later Julius appeared, a young man, tall and rather good-looking, suave and easy. A word or two with Kennedy followed, during which a greenback changed hands—in fact that seemed to be the open sesame to everything here—and we were in the elevator decorously escorted by the polished Julius.

The door of the elevator shut noiselessly and it shot up to the next floor. Julius preceded us down the thickly carpeted corridor leading the way to a large apartment, or rather a suite of rooms, as handsomely furnished as any in other hotels. He switched on the lights and left us, with the remark, " When you want the waiter or anything, just press the button."

In the largest of the rooms was a dining-table and several chairs of Jacobean oak. A heavy sideboard and serving-table stood against opposite walls. Another, smaller room was furnished very attractively as a sitting-room. Deep, easy chairs stood in the corners and a wide, capacious davenport stretched across one wall. In another nook was a little divan or cosy corner.

Electric bulbs burned pinkly in the chandeliers and on silver candelabra on the table, giving a half light that was very romantic and fascinating. From a curtained window that opened upon an interior court we could catch strains from the cabaret singers below in the main dining-room. Everything was new and bright.

Kennedy pressed the button and a waiter brought a menu, imposing in length and breath-taking in rates.

"The cost of vice seems to have gone up with the cost of living," remarked Miss Kendall, as the waiter disappeared as silently as he had responded to the bell. It was a phrase that stuck in my head, so apt was it in describing the anomalous state of things we found as the case unrolled.

Craig ordered, now and then consulting Clare about some detail. The care and attention devoted to us could not have been more punctilious if it had been an elaborate dinner party.

"Well," he remarked, as the waiter at last closed the door of the private dining-room to give the order in downstairs in the kitchen, "the Little Montmartre makes a brave showing. I suppose it will be some time before the dinner arrives, though. There is certainly some piquancy to this," he added, looking about at the furnishings.

"Yes," remarked Miss Kendall, "*risqué* from the moment you enter the door."

She said it with an impersonal tone as if there were complete detachment between herself as an observer and as a guest of the Montmartre.

"Miss Kendall," asked Kennedy, "did you notice anything particularly downstairs? I'd like to check up my own impressions by yours."

"I noticed that Titian beauty in the hotel office as we left the reception room and entered the elevator."

Craig smiled.

"So did I. I thought you would be both woman enough and detective enough to notice her. Well, I suppose if a man likes that sort of girl that's the sort of girl he likes. That's point number one. But did you notice anything else—as we came in, for instance?"

"No—except that everything seems to be a matter of scientific management here to get the most out of the suckers. This is no place for a piker. It all seems to run so smoothly, too. Still, I'm sure that our investigators might get something on the place if they kept right after it, although on the surface it doesn't look as if any law was being openly violated here. What do you mean? What is your point number two?"

"In the front window," resumed Craig, "just as you enter, I noticed one of those little oblong signs printed neatly in black on white—'Dr. Vernon Harris, M. D.' You recall that the letter said something about a doctor who was very friendly with that clique the writer mentioned? It's even money that this Harris is the one the writer meant. I suppose he is the 'house physician' of this gilded palace."

Clare nodded appreciatively. "Quite right," she agreed. "Just how do you think he might be involved?"

"Of course I can't say. But I think, without going any further, that a man like that in a place like this will bear watching anyway, without our needing more than the fact that he is here. Naturally we don't know anything about him as a doctor, but he must have some training; and in an environment like this—well, a little training may be a dangerous thing."

"The letter said something about drugs," mused Clare.

"Yes," added Kennedy. "As you know, alcohol is absolutely necessary to a thing like this. Girls must keep gay and attractive; they must meet men with a bright, unfaltering look, and alcohol just dulls the edge of conscience. Besides, look over that wine list—it fills the till of the Montmartre, judging by the prices. But then, alcohol palls when the pace is as swift as it seems to be here. Even more essential are drugs. You know, after all, it is no wonder so many drug fiends and drunkards are created by this life. Now, a doctor who is not over-scrupulous, and he would have to be not over-scrupulous to be here at all, would find a gold mine in the

dispensing of drugs and the toning up of drug fiends
and others who have been going the pace too rapidly."

"Yes," she said. "We have found that some of
these doctors are a great factor in the life of various
sections of the city where they hang out. I know
one who is deeply in the local politics and boasts
that any resort that patronizes him is immune. Yes,
that's a good point about Dr. Harris."

"I suppose your investigators have had more or
less to do with watching the progress of drug habits?" ventured Craig.

"Very much," she replied, catching the drift of
his remarks. "We have found, for instance, that
there are a great many cases where it seems that
drugs have been used in luring young and innocent
girls. Not the old knockout drops—chloral, you
know—but modern drugs, not so powerful, perhaps,
but more insidious, and in that respect, I suppose,
more dangerous. There are cocaine fiends, opium
smokers; oh, lots of them. But those we find in the
slums mostly. Still, I suppose there are all kinds of
drugs up here in the White Light District—bella-
donna to keep the eyes bright, arsenic to whiten the
complexion, and so on."

"Yes," asserted Craig. "This section of the city
may not be so brutal in its drug taking as others, but
it is here—yes, and it is over on Fifth Avenue, too,
right in society. Before we get through I'm sure
we'll both learn much more than we even dream of
now."

The door opened after a discreet tap from the waiter and the lavish dinner which Craig had ordered appeared. The door stayed open for a moment as the bus boy carried in the dishes. A rustle of skirts and low musical laughter was wafted in to us and we caught a glimpse of another gay party passing down the hall.

"How many private dining-rooms are there?" asked Craig of the waiter.

"Just this one, sir, and the next one, which is smaller," replied the model waiter, with the air of one who could be blind and deaf and dumb if he chose.

"Oh, then we were lucky to get this."

"Yes, sir. It is really best to telephone first to Julius to make sure and have one of the rooms reserved, sir."

Craig made a mental note of the information. The party in the next room were hilariously ordering, mostly from the wine list. None of us had recognized any of them, nor had they paid much attention to us.

Craig had eaten little, although the food was very good.

"It's a shame to come here and not see the whole place," he remarked. "I wonder if you would excuse me while I drop downstairs to look over things there—perhaps ingratiate myself with that Titian? Tell Miss Kendall about our visit to Langhorne's office while I am gone, Walter."

There was not much that I could tell except the

bare facts, but I thought that Miss Kendall seemed especially interested in the broker's reticence about his stenographer.

I had scarcely finished when Craig returned. A glance at his face told me that even in this brief time something had happened.

" Did you meet the Titian? " I asked.

" Yes. She is the stenographer and sometimes works the switchboard of the telephone. I happened to strike the office while the clerk was at dinner and she was alone. While I was talking to her I was looking about and my eye happened to fall on one of the letter boxes back of the desk, marked ' Dr. Harris.' Well, at once I had an overwhelming desire to get a note which I saw sticking in it. So I called up a telephone number, just as a blind, and while she was at the switchboard I slipped the note into my pocket. Here it is."

He had laid an envelope down before us. It was in a woman's hand, written hastily.

" I'd like to know what was in it without Dr. Harris knowing it," he remarked. " Now, the secret service agents abroad have raised letter-opening to a fine art. Some kinds of paper can be steamed open without leaving a trace, and then they follow that simple operation by reburnishing the flap with a bone instrument. But that won't do. It might make this ink run."

Among the ornaments were several with flat wooden bases. Kennedy took one and placed it on the edge of the table, which was perfectly square.

Then he placed the envelope between the table and the base.

" When other methods fail," he went on, " they place the envelope between two pieces of wood with the edges projecting about a thirty-second of an inch."

He had first flattened the edge of the envelope, then roughened it, and finally slit it open.

" Scientific letter-opening," he remarked, as he pulled out a little note written on the hotel paper. It read:

DEAR HARRY:
Called you up twice and then dropped into the hotel, but you seem to be out all the time. Have something *very important* to tell you. Shall be busy to-night and in the morning, but will be at the *thé dansant* at the Futurist Tea Room to-morrow after-noon about four. Be sure to be there.
MARIE.

" I shall," commented Kennedy. " Now the question is, how to seal up this letter so that he won't know it has been opened. I saw some of this very strong mucilage in the office. Ring the bell, Walter. I'll get that impervious waiter to borrow it for a moment."

Five minutes later he had applied a hair line of the strong, colourless gum to the inside of the en-velope and had united the edges under pressure be-tween the two pieces of wood. As soon as it was dry he excused himself again and went back to the office, where he managed to secure an opportunity to stick the letter back in the box and chat for a few minutes longer with the Titian.

"There's a wild cabaret down in the main dining-room," he reported on his return. "I think we might just as well have a glimpse of it before we go."

Kennedy paid the cheque, which by this time had mounted like a taximeter running wild, and we drifted into the dining-room, a rather attractive hall, panelled in Flemish oak with artificial flowers and leaves about, and here and there a little bird con-cealed in a cage in the paper foliage.

As cabarets go, it was not bad, although I could imagine how wild it might become in the evening or on special occasion.

"That Dr. Harris interests me," remarked Ken-nedy across the table at us. "We must get some-thing in writing from him in some way. And then there's that girl in the office, too. She seems to be right in with all these people here."

Evidently the cabaret had little of interest to Miss Kendall, who, after a glance that took in the whole dining-room and disclosed none there in the gay crowd who, as far as we could see, had any relation to the case, seemed bored.

Craig noticed it and at once rose to go.

As we passed out and into the corridor, Miss Kendall turned and whispered, "Look over at the desk—Dr. Harris."

Sure enough, chatting with the stenographer was a man with one of those black bags which doctors carry. He was a young man in appearance, one of those whom one sees in the White Light District, with unnaturally bright eyes which speak of late hours and a fast pace. He wore a flower in his buttonhole—a very fetching touch with some women. Debonair, dapper, dashing, his face was not one readily forgotten. As we passed hurriedly I observed that he had torn open the note and had thrown the envelope, unsuspectingly, into the basket.

VII

THE GANG LEADER

WITH the arrest of Dopey Jack, it seemed as if all the forces of the gang world were solidified for the final battle.

Carton had been engaged in a struggle with the System so long that he knew just how to get action, the magistrates he could depend on, the various pitfalls that surrounded the snaring of one high in gangland, the judges who would fix bail that was prohibitively high.

As he had anticipated and prepared for, every wire was pulled to secure the release of Rubano. But Carton was fortunate in having under him a group of young and alert assistants. It took the combined energies of his office, however, to carry the thing through and Kennedy and I did not see Carton again for some time.

Meanwhile we were busy gathering as much information as we could about those who were likely to figure in the case. It was remarkable, but we found that the influence of Dorgan and Murtha was felt in the most unexpected quarters. People who would have talked to us on almost any other subject, absolutely refused to become mixed up in this

affair. It was as though the System practised ter-
rorism on a large scale.

Late in the afternoon we met in Carton's office,
to compare notes on the progress made during the
day.

The District Attorney greeted us enthusiastically.

" Well," he exclaimed as he dropped into his big
office chair, " this has been a hard day for me—but
I've succeeded."

" How? " queried Kennedy.

" Of course the newspapers haven't got it yet,"
pursued Carton, " but it happened that there was a
Grand Jury sitting and considering election cases.
It went hard, but I made them consider this case of
Dopey Jack. I don't know how it happened, but I
seem to have succeeded in forcing action in record
time. They have found an indictment on the election charges, and if that falls through, we shall have
time to set up other charges against him. In fact
we are ' going to the mat,' so to speak, with this
case."

The office telephone rang and after a few sentences of congratulation, Carton turned to us, his
spirits even higher than before. " That was one of
my assistants," he explained, " one of the cleverest.
The trial will be before Judge Pomeroy in General
Sessions and it will be an early trial. Pomeroy is
one of the best of them, too—about to retire, and
wants to leave a good record on the bench behind
him. Things are shaping up as well as we could
wish for."

7

The door opened and one of Carton's clerks started to announce the name of a visitor.

" Mr. Carton, Mr.——"

" Murtha," drawled a deep voice, as the owner of the name strode in, impatiently brushing aside the clerk. " Hello, Carton," greeted the Sub-boss aggressively.

" Hello, Murtha," returned Carton, retaining his good temper and seeing the humour of the situation, where the practice of years was reversed and the mountain was coming to Mahomet. " This is a little—er—informal—but I'm glad to see you, nevertheless," he added quietly. " Won't you sit down? By the way, meet Mr. Kennedy and Mr. Jameson. Is there anything I can do for you? "

Murtha shook hands with us suspiciously, but did not sit down. He continued to stand, his hat tilted back over his head and his huge hands jammed down into his trousers pockets.

" What's this I hear about Jack Rubano, Carton? " he opened fire. " They tell me you have arrested him and secured an indictment."

" They tell the truth," returned Carton shortly. " The Grand Jury indicted Dopey Jack this afternoon. The trial——"

" Dopey Jack," quoted Murtha in disgusted tones. " That's the way it is nowadays. Give a dog a bad name—why,—I suppose this bad name's going to stick to him all his life, now. It ain't right. You know, Carton, as well as I do that if they charged him with just plain fighting and got him before a

jury, all you would have to say would be, ' Gentlemen, the defendant at the bar is the notorious gangster, Dopey Jack.' And the jurors wouldn't wait to
hear any more, but'd say, ' Guilty ! ' just like that.
And he'd go up the river for the top term. That's
what a boy like that gets once the papers give him
such an awful reputation. It's fierce ! "

Carton shook his head. " Oh, Murtha," he
remonstrated with just a twinkle in his eye, " you
don't think I believe that sort of soft stuff, do you?
I've had my eye on this ' boy '—he's twenty-eight,
by the way—too long. You needn't tell me anything about his respectable old father and his sorrowing mother and weeping sister. Murtha, I've
been in this business too long for that heart throb
stuff. Leave that to the lawyers the System will hire
for him. Let's cut that out, between ourselves, and
get down to brass tacks."

It was a new and awkward rôle for Murtha as
suppliant, and he evidently did not relish it. Aside
from his own interest in Dopey Jack, who was one
of his indispensables, it was apparent that he came
as an emissary from Dorgan himself to spy out the
land and perhaps reach some kind of understanding.

He glanced about at us, with a look that broadly
hinted that he would prefer to see Carton alone.
Carton made no move to ask us to leave and Kennedy met the boss's look calmly. Murtha smoth-
ered his rage, although I knew he would with pleasure have had us stuck up or blackjacked.

" See here, Carton." he blurted out at length, ap-

proaching the desk of the District Attorney and lowering his big voice as much as he was capable, " can't
we reach some kind of agreement between ourselves? You let up on Rubano—and—well, I might
be able to get some of my friends to let up on Carton. See? "

He was conveying as guardedly as he could a
proposal that if the District Attorney would consent
to turn his back while the law stumbled in one of the
numerous pitfalls that beset a criminal prosecution,
the organization would deliver the goods, quietly
pass the word along to knife its own man and allow
Carton to be re-elected.

I studied Carton's face intently. To a man of another stripe, the proposal might have been alluring.
It meant that although the organization ticket won,
he would, in the public eye at least, have the credit
of beating the System, of going into office unham-
pered, of having assured beyond doubt what was at
best only problematical with the Reform League.

Carton did not hesitate a moment. I thought I
saw in his face the same hardening of the lines of his
features in grim determination that I had seen when
he had been talking to Miss Ashton. I knew that,
among other things, he was thinking how impossible
it would be for him ever to face her again in the
old way, if he sold out, even in a negative way, to
the System.

Murtha had shot his huge face forward and was
peering keenly at the man before him.

" You'll—think it over? " he asked.

" I will not—I most certainly will not," returned Carton, for the first time showing exasperation, at the very assumption of Murtha. " Mr. Murtha," he went on, rising and leaning forward over the desk, " we are going to have a fair election, if I can make it. I may be beaten—I may win. But I will be beaten, if at all, by the old methods. If I win—it will be that I win—honestly."

A half sneer crossed Murtha's face. He neither understood nor cared to understand the kind of game Carton played.

" You'll never get anything on that boy," blustered Murtha. " Do you suppose I'm fool enough to come here and make a dishonest proposition—here—right in front of your own friends? " he added, turning to us. "-I ain't asking any favours, or anything dishonest. His lawyers know what they can do and what you can do. It ain't because I care a hang about you, Carton, that I'm here. If you want to know the truth, it's because you can make trouble, Carton,—that's all. You can't convict him, in the end, because—you can't. There's nothing ' on ' him. But you can make trouble. We'll win out in the end, of course."

" In other words, you think the Reform League has you beaten? " suggested Carton quietly.

" No," ejaculated Murtha with an oath. " We don't know—but maybe *you* have us beaten. But not the League. We don't want you for District Attorney, Carton. You know it. But here's a practical proposition. All you have to do is just to let this

Rubano case take its natural course. That's all I ask."

He dwelt on the word " natural " as if it were in itself convincing. " Why," he resumed, " what foolishness it is for you to throw away all your chances just for the sake of hounding one poor fellow from the East Side. It ain't right, Carton,— you, powerful, holding an important office, and he a poor boy that never had a chance and has made the most of what little nature gave him. Why, I've known that boy ever since he hardly came up to my waist. I tell you, there ain't a judge on the bench that wouldn't listen to what we can show about him —hounded by police, hounded by the District Attorney, driven from pillar to post, and——"

" You will have a chance to tell the story in court," cut in Carton. " Pomeroy will try the case."

" Pomeroy? " repeated Murtha in a tone that quite disguised the anger he felt that it should come up before the one judge the System feared and could not control. " Now, look here, Carton. We're all practical men. Your friend—er—Kennedy, here, he's practical."

Murtha had turned toward us. He was now the Murtha I had heard of before, the kind that can use a handshake or a playful slap on the back, as between man and man, to work wonders in getting action or carrying a point. Far from despising such men as Murtha, I think we all rather admired his good qualities. It was his point of view, his method, his aim that were wrong. As for the man himself

he was human—in fact, I often thought far more
human than some of the reformers.

"I'll leave it to Kennedy," he resumed. "Suppose you were running a race. You knew you were
going to win. Would you deliberately stop and
stick your foot out, in order to trip up the man who
was coming in second?"

"I don't know that the cases are parallel," returned Kennedy with an amused smile.

Murtha kept his good nature admirably.

"Then you would stick your foot out—and perhaps lose the race yourself?" persisted Murtha.

"I'll relieve Kennedy of answering that," interrupted Carton, "not because I don't think he can
do it better than I can, perhaps, but because this is
my fight—my race."

"Well," asked Murtha persuasively, "you'll
think it over, first, won't you?"

Carton was looking at his opponent keenly, as if
trying to take his measure. He had some scheme in
mind and Kennedy was watching the faces of both
men intently.

"This race," began Carton slowly, in a manner
that showed he wanted to change the subject, "is
different from any other in the politics of the city
as either of us have ever known it, Murtha."

Murtha made as though he would object to the
proposition, but Carton hurried on, giving him no
chance to inject anything into the conversation.

"It may be possible—it is possible," shot out the
young District Attorney, "to make use of secret

records—conversations—at conferences—dinners
—records that have been taken by a new invention
that seems to be revolutionizing politics all over the
country."

The look that crossed Murtha's face was positively apoplectic. The veins in his forehead stood
out like whipcords.

He started to speak, but choked off the words
before he had uttered them. I could almost read
his mind. Carton had said nothing directly about
the Black Book, and Murtha had caught himself
just in time not to betray anything about it.

"So," he shouted at last, "you are going to try
some of those fine little scientific tricks on us, are
you?"

He was pacing up and down the room, storming
and threatening by turns.

"I want to tell you, Carton," pursued Murtha,
"that you're up against a crowd who were playing
this game before you were born. You reformers
think you are pretty smooth. But we know a thing
or two about you and what you are doing. Be·
sides," he leaned over the desk again, "Carton,
there ain't many men that can afford to throw
stones. I admit my life hasn't been perfect—but,
then I ain't posing as any saint. I don't mind telling you that the organization, as you call it, is looking into some of the things that you reformers have
done. It may be that some of your people—some
of the ladies," he insinuated, "don't look on life in
the broad-minded way that some of the rest do.

Mind you—I ain't making any threats, but when it comes to gossip and scandal and mud-slinging—look out for the little old organization—that's all! "

Carton had set his tenacious jaw. " You can go as far as you like, Murtha," was all he said, with a grim smile.

Murtha looked at him a moment, then his manner changed.

" Carton," he said in a milder tone, at length, " what's the use of all this bluffing? You and I understand each other. These men understand—life. It's a game—that's what it is—a game. Sometimes one move is right, sometimes another. You know what you want to accomplish here in this city. I show you a way to do it. Don't answer me," persisted Murtha, raising a hand, " just—think it over."

Carton had taken a step forward, the tense look on his face unchanged. " No," he exclaimed, and we could almost hear his jaw snap as if it had been a trap. " No—I'll not think it over. I'll not yield an inch. Dopey Jack goes to trial before election."

As Carton bit off the words, Murtha became almost beside himself with rage and chagrin. He was white and red by turns. For a moment I feared that he might do Carton personal violence.

" Carton," he ground out, as he reached the door, " you will regret this."

" I hope not," returned the other summoning with a mighty effort at least the appearance of suavity. " Good-bye."

The only answer was the vicious slam which Murtha gave the door.

As the echo died, the District Attorney turned to us. " Apparently, then, Dorgan did not secure the Black Book," was all he said, " even supposing Dopey Jack planned and executed that robbery of Langhorne."

VIII

THE SHYSTER LAWYER

"THAT'S a declaration of war," remarked Kennedy, as Carton resumed his seat at the desk unconcernedly after the stormy ending of the interview with Murtha.

"I suppose it is," agreed the District Attorney, "and I can't say that I am sorry."

"Nor I," added Craig. "But it settles one thing. We are now out in what I call the 'open' investigation. They have forced us from cover. We shall have to be prepared to take quick action now, whatever move they may make."

Together we were speculating on the various moves that the System might make and how we might prepare in advance for them.

Evidently, however, we were not yet through with these indirect dealings with the Boss. The System was thorough, if nothing else, and prompt.

We had about decided to continue our conference over the dinner table in some uptown restaurant, when the officer stationed in the hall poked his head in the door and announced another visitor for the District Attorney.

This time the entrance was exactly the opposite to the bluster of Murtha. The man who sidled deferentially into the room, a moment after Carton had said he would see him, was a middle-sized fellow, with a high, slightly bald forehead, a shifty expression in his sharp ferret eyes, and a nervous, self-confident manner that must have been very impressive before the ignorant.

"My name is Kahn," he introduced himself. "I'm a lawyer."

Carton nodded recognition.

Although I had never seen the man before, I recollected the name which Miss Kendall had mentioned. He was one of the best known lawyers of the System. He had begun his career as an "ambulance chaser," had risen later to the dignity of a police court lawyer, and now was of the type that might be called, for want of a better name, a high class "shyster"—unscrupulous, sharp, cunning.

Shyster, I believe, has been defined as a legal knave, a lawyer who practises in an unprofessional or tricky manner. Kahn was all that—and still more. If he had been less successful, he would have been the black sheep of the overcrowded legal flock. Ideals he had none. His claws reached out to grab the pittance of the poverty-stricken client as well as the fee of the wealthy. He had risen from hospitals to police courts, coroner's court, and criminal courts, at last attaining the dignity of offices opposite an entrance to the criminal courts building, from which vantage point his underlings surveyed the scene of operations like vultures hovering over bewildered cattle.

Carton knew him. Kahn was the leader among some score of men more or less well dressed, of more or less evil appearance, who are constantly prowling from one end to the other of the broad first floor of the criminal courts building during the hours of the day that justice is being administered there.

These are the shyster lawyers and their runners and agents who prey upon the men and women whom misfortune or crime have delivered into the hands of the law. Others of the same species are wandering about the galleries on other floors of the building, each with a furtive eye for those who may be in trouble themselves or those who seem to be in need of legal assistance for a relative or friend in trouble.

Perhaps the majority of lawyers practising in the courts are reputable to the highest degree, and many of the rest merely to a safe degree. Many devote themselves to philanthropic work whenever a prisoner is penniless. But the percentage of shysters is high. Kahn belonged in the latter class, although his days of doing dirty work himself were passed. He had a large force of incipient shysters for that purpose. As for himself, he handled only the big cases in which he veneered the dirty work by a sort of finesse.

Kahn bowed and smiled ingratiatingly. " Mr. Carton," he began in a conciliatory tone, " I have intruded on your valuable time in the interest of my client, Mr. Jack Rubano."

" Huh ! " grunted Carton. " So they've retained you, have they, Ike ? " he mused familiarly, closely regarding the visitor.

Kahn, far from resenting the familiarity, seemed rather to enjoy it and take it as his due measure of fame.

" Yes, Mr. Carton, they have retained me. I have just had a talk with the prisoner in the Tombs and have gone over his case very carefully, sir."

Carton nodded, but said nothing, willing to let Kahn do the talking for the present until he exposed his hand.

" He has told me all about his case," pursued Kahn evenly. " It is not such a bad case. I can tell you that, Mr. Carton, because I didn't have to resort to the ' friend of the judge ' gag in order to show him that he had a good chance."

Kahn looked knowingly at Carton. At least he was frank about his own game before us; in fact, utterly shameless, it seemed to me. Probably it was because he knew it was no use, that Carton had no illusions about him. Still, there was an uncanny bravado about it all. Kahn was indeed very successful in making the worst appear the better reason. He knew it and knew that Carton knew it. That was his stock in trade.

He had seated himself in a chair by the District Attorney's desk and as he talked was hitching it closer and closer, for men of Kahn's stamp seem unable to talk without getting into almost personal contact with those with whom they are talking.

Carton drew back and folded his hands back of his head as he listened, still silent.

"You know, Mr. Carton," he insinuated, "it is a very different thing to be sure in your own mind that a man is guilty from being able to prove it in court. There are all sorts of delays that may be granted, witnesses are hard to hold together, in fact there are many difficulties that arise in the best of cases."

"You don't need to tell me that, Kahn," replied Carton quietly.

"I know it, Mr. Carton," rejoined the other apologetically. "I was just using that as a preface to what I have to say."

He took another hitch of the chair nearer Carton and lowered his voice impressively. "The point, sir, at which I am driving is simply this. There must be some way in which we can reach an agreement, compromise this case, satisfactorily to the people with a minimum of time and expense—some way in which the indictment or the pleadings can be amended so that it can be wound up and—you understand—both of us win—instead of dragging it out and perhaps you losing the case in the end."

Carton shook his head. "No, Kahn," he said in a low tone, but firmly, "no compromise."

Kahn bent his ferret eyes on Carton's face as if to bore through into his very mind.

"No," added the District Attorney, "Murtha was just here, and I may as well repeat what I said to him—although I might fairly assume that he went from this room directly across the street to your office and that you know it already. This case has gone too far, it has too many other ramifications for me to consent to relax on it one iota."

Kahn was baffled, but he was cleverer than Murtha and did not show it.

"Surely," he urged, "you must realize that it is not worth your while at such a critical time for yourself to waste energies on a case when there are so many more profitable things that you could do. The fact is that I would be the last one to propose anything that was not open and above board and to our mutual advantage. There must be some way in which we can reach an agreement which will be satisfactory to all parties in interest, sir."

"Kahn," repeated Carton a little testily, "how often must I repeat to you and your people that I am *not* going to compromise this case in any shape, form, or manner? I am going to fight it out on the lines I have indicated if I have to disrupt this entire office to get men to do it. I have plenty to do seeking re-election, but my first duty is to act as public prosecutor in the office to which I have been already elected. Otherwise, it would be a poor recommendation to the people to return me to the same position. No, you are merely wasting your time and ours talking compromise."

Kahn had been surveying Carton keenly, now and then taking a shifty glance at Kennedy and myself.

As Carton rapped out the last words, as if in the nature of an ultimatum, Kahn gazed at him in amazement. Here was a man whom he knew he could neither bribe, bully, or bulldoze.

"You must consider this, too," he added pointedly. "There has been a good deal of mud-slinging in this campaign. We may find it necessary to go back into the antecedents and motives of those who represent the people in this case."

It was a subtle threat. Just what it implied I could not even guess, nor did Carton betray anything by look or word. Carton had voluntarily placed himself in the open and in a position from which he could not retreat. Evidently, now, he was willing to force the fight, if the other side would accept the issue. It meant much to him but he did not balk at it.

"No, Kahn," he repeated firmly, "no compromise."

Kahn drew back a bit and hastily scanned the face of the prosecutor. Evidently he saw nothing in it to encourage him. Yet he was too smooth to let his temper rise, as Murtha had. By the same token I fancied him a more dangerous opponent. There was something positively uncanny about his assurance.

Kahn rose slowly. "Then it is war—without quarter?" asked Kahn shrewdly.

"War—without quarter," repeated Carton positively.

He withdrew quietly, with an almost feline tread, quite in contrast with the bluster of Murtha. I felt for the first time a sort of sinking sensation, as I

8

began to realize the varied character of the assault that was preparing.

Not so, Carton and Kennedy. It seemed that every event that more clearly defined our position and that of our opponents added zest to the fight for them. And I had sufficient confidence in the combination to know that their feelings were justified.

Carton silently pulled down and locked the top of his desk, then for a moment we debated where we should dine. We decided on a quiet hotel uptown and, leaving word where we could be found, hurried along for the first real relaxation and refreshment after a crowded day's work.

If, however, we thought we could escape even for a few minutes we were mightily mistaken. We had not fairly done justice to the roast when a boy in buttons came down the line of tables.

" Mr. Carton—please."

The District Attorney crooked his finger at the page.

" You're wanted at the telephone, sir."

Carton rose and excused himself.

The message must have given him food of another kind, for when he returned after a long absence, he pushed aside the now cold roast and joined us in the coffee and cigars.

" One of my men," he announced, " has been doing some shadowing for me. Evidently, both Murtha and Kahn having failed, they are resorting to other tactics. It looks as if they had in some way, probably from some corrupt official of the court or employee in charge of the jury list, obtained a copy of the panel which Justice Pomeroy has summoned for the case."

" It ought to be a simple thing to empanel another set of talesmen and let these fellows serve in some other part of the court," I suggested, considering the matter hastily.

" Much better to let it rest as it is," cut in Craig quickly, " and try to catch Kahn with the goods. It would be great to catch one of these clever fellows trying to ' fix ' the jury, as well as intimidate witnesses, as he already hinted himself."

" Just the thing," exclaimed Carton, whose keen sense of proportion showed what a valuable political asset such a coup would make in addition to its effect on the case.

" We'll get Kahn right, if we have a chance," planned Craig. " You are acquainted more or less with his habits, I suppose. Where does Kahn hang out? Most fellows like him have a sort of Amen Corner where they meet their henchmen, issue orders, receive reports and carry on business that wouldn't do for an office downtown."

" Why, I believe he goes to Farrell's—has an interest in the place, I think."

Farrell's, we recognized, as a rather well-known all-night café which managed to survive the excise vicissitudes by dint of having no cabaret or entertainment.

We finished the dinner in silence, Kennedy turning various schemes over in his mind, and rejecting them one after another.

"There's nothing we can do immediately, I suppose," he remarked at length. "But if you and Carton care to come up to the laboratory with me, I might in time of peace prepare for war. I have a little apparatus up there which I think may fit in somehow and if it does, Mr. Kahn's days of jury fixing are numbered."

A few minutes later, we found ourselves in Kennedy's laboratory, where he had gathered together an amazing collection of paraphernalia in the warfare of science against crime which he had been waging during the years that I had known him.

Carton looked about in silent admiration. As for myself, although one might have thought it was an old story with me, I had found that no sooner had I become familiar with one piece of apparatus to perform one duty, than another situation, entirely different and unprecedented in our cases arose which called for another, entirely new. I had learned to have implicit confidence in Kennedy's ability to meet each new emergency with something fully capable of solving the problem.

From a cabinet, Kennedy took out what looked like the little black leather box of a camera, with, however, a most peculiar looking lens.

IX

THE JURY FIXER

"LET'S visit Farrell's," remarked Craig, after looking over the apparatus and slinging it over his shoulder.

It was early yet, and the theatres were not out, so that there were comparatively few people in the famous all-night café. We entered the bar cautiously and looked about. Kahn at least was not there.

In the back of this part of the café were several booths, open to conform to the law, yet sufficiently screened so that there was at least a little privacy.

Above the booths was a line of transoms.

" What's back there? " asked Kennedy, under his breath.

" A back room," returned Carton.

" Perhaps Kahn is there," Craig suggested. "Walter, you're the one whom he would least likely recognize. Suppose you just stick your head in the door and look about as quietly as you can."

I lounged back, glanced at the records of sporting events posted on the wall at the end of the bar, then, casually, as if looking for someone, swung the double-hinged door that led from the bar into the back room.

The room was empty except for one man, turned sidewise to the door, reading a paper, but in a position so that he could see anyone who entered. I had not opened the door widely enough to be noticed, but I now let it swing back hastily. It was Kahn, pompously sipping something he had ordered.

" He's back there," I whispered to Kennedy, as I returned, excitedly motioning toward one of the transoms over the booths back of which Kahn was seated.

" Right there? " he queried.

" Just about," I answered.

A moment later Kennedy led the way over to the booth under the transom and we sat down. A waiter hovered near us. Craig silenced him quickly with a substantial order and a good-sized tip.

From our position, if we sat well within the booth, we were effectually hidden unless someone purposely came down and looked in on us. We watched Kennedy curiously. He had unslung the little black camera-like box and to it attached a pair of fine wires and a small pocket storage battery which he carried.

Then he looked up at the transom. It was far too high for us to hear through, even if those in the back room talked fairly loud. Standing on the leather wall seats of the booth to listen or even to look over was out of the question, for it would be sure to excite suspicion among the waiters, or the customers who were continually passing in and out of the place.

Kennedy was watching his chance, and when the café emptied itself after being deluged between the acts from a neighbouring theatre, he jumped up quickly in the seat, stood on his toes and craned his neck through the diagonally opened transom. Before any of the waiters, who were busy clearing up the results of the last theatre raid, had a chance to notice him, Craig had slipped the little black box into the shadow of the corner.

From it dangled down the fine wires, not noticeable.

"He's sitting just back of us yet," reported Kennedy. "I don't know about that flaming arc light in the middle of the room, but I think it will be all right. Anyhow, we shall have to take a chance. It looks to me as if he were waiting for someone— didn't it to you, Walter?"

I nodded acquiescence.

"He has wasted no time in getting down to work," put in Carton, who had been a silent spectator of the preparations of Kennedy. "What's that thing you put on the ledge up there—a detectaphone?"

Kennedy smiled. "No—they're too clever to do any talking, at least in a place like this, I'm afraid," he said, carefully hiding the wires and the battery beside him in the shadow of the corner of the booth. "It may be that nothing will happen, anyhow, but if it does we can at least have the satisfaction of having tried to get something. Carton, you had better sit as far back in the booth as I am. The longer we can stay here unnoticed the better. Let Walter sit on the outside."

We changed places.

"Lawyers have been complaining to me lately," remarked Carton in a well modulated voice, "about jury fixing. Some of them say it has been going on on a large scale and I have had several of my county detectives working on it. But they haven't landed anything yet,—except rumours, like this one about the Dopey Jack jury. I've had them out posing as jurymen who could be 'approached' and would arrange terms for other bribable jurymen."

"And you mean to say that that's going on right here in this city?" I asked, scenting a possible newspaper story.

"This campaign I have started," he replied, "is only the beginning of our work in breaking up the organized business of jury bribing. I mean to put an end to the work of what I have reason to believe is a secret ring of jury fixers. Why, I understand that the prices for 'hanging' a jury range all the way from five to five hundred dollars, or even higher in an important case. The size of the jury fixer's 'cut' depends upon the amount the client is willing to pay for having his case made either a disagreement or a dismissal. Usually a bonus is demanded for a dismissal in criminal cases. But such things are very difficult to——"

"Sh!" I cautioned, for from my vantage point I saw two men approaching.

They saw me in the booth, but not the rest of us,

and turned to enter the next one. Though they were talking in low tones, we could catch words and phrases now and then, which told us that we ourselves would have to be very careful about being overheard.

" We've got to be careful," one of them remarked in a scarcely audible undertone. " Carton has detectives mingling with the talesmen in every court of importance in the city."

The reply of the other was not audible, but Carton leaned over to us and whispered, " One of Kahn's runners, I think."

Apparently Kahn was taking extreme precautions and wanted everything in readiness so that whatever was to be done would go off smoothly. Kennedy glanced up at the little black leather box perched high above on the sill of the partition.

" The chief says that a thousand dollars is the highest price that he can afford for ' hanging' this jury—providing you get on it, or any of your friends."

The other man, whose voice was not of the vibrating, penetrating quality of the runner, seemed to hesitate and be inclined to argue.

" We've had 'em as low as five dollars," went on the runner, at which Carton exchanged a knowing glance with us. " But in a special case, like this, we realize that they come high."

The other man grumbled a bit and we could catch the word, " risky."

Back and forth the argument went. The runner,

however, was a worthy representative of his chief, for at last he succeeded in carrying both his point and his price.

"All right," we heard him say at last, "the chief is in the back room. Wait until I see whether he is alone."

The runner rose and went around to the swinging door. From the other side of the transom we could, as we had expected, hear nothing. A moment later the runner returned.

"Go in and see him," he whispered.

The man rose and made his way through the swinging door into the back room.

None of us said a word, but Kennedy was literally on his toes with excitement. He was holding the little battery in his hand and after waiting a few moments pressed what looked like a push button.

He could not restrain his impatience longer, but had jumped up on the leather seat and for a moment looked at the black leather box, then through the half open transom, as best he could.

"Press it—press it!" he whispered to Carton, pointing at the push button, as he turned a little handle on the box, then quickly dropped down and resumed his seat.

"Craig—one of the waiters," I cried hurriedly.

The outside bar had been filling up as the evening advanced and the sight of a man standing on one of the seats had attracted the attention of a patron. A waiter had followed his curious gaze and saw Kennedy.

With a quick pull on the wire, Kennedy jerked the black leather box from its high perch and deftly caught it as it fell.

"Say—what are youse guys doin', huh?" demanded the waiter pugnaciously.

Carton and I had risen and stood between the man and Craig.

The sound of voices in high pitch was enough to attract a crowd ever ready to watch a scrap. Mindful of the famous " flying wedge " of waiters at Farrell's for the purpose of hustling objectionable and obstreperous customers with despatch to the sidewalk, I was prepared for anything.

The runner who was sitting alone in the next booth, leaned out and gazed around the corner into ours.

"Carton!" he shouted in a tone that could have been heard on the street.

The effect of the name of the District Attorney was magical. For the moment, the crowd fell back. Before the tough waiters or anyone else could make up their minds just what to do, Kennedy, who had tucked the box into his capacious side pocket, took each of us by the arm and we shoved our way through the crowd.

The head waiter followed us to the door, but offered no resistance. In fact no one seemed to know just what to do and it was all over so quickly that even Kahn himself had not time to get a glimpse of us through the swinging door.

A moment later we had piled into a taxicab at

the curb and were speeding through the now deserted streets uptown to the laboratory.

Kennedy was jubilant. "I may have almost precipitated a riot," he chortled, "but I'm glad I stood up. I think it must have been at the psychological moment."

At the laboratory he threw off his coat and prepared to plunge into work with various mysterious pans of chemicals, baths, jars, and beakers.

"What is it?" asked Carton, as Kennedy carefully took out the dark leather box, shielding it from the glare of a mercury vapour light.

"A camera with a newly-invented electrically operated between-lens shutter of great illumination and efficiency," he explained. "It has always been practically impossible to get such pictures as I wanted, but this new shutter has so much greater speed than anything else ever invented before, that it is possible to use it in this sort of detective work. I've proved its speed up to one two-thousandth of a second. It may or may not have worked, but if it has we've caught someone, right in the act."

Kennedy had a "studio" of his own which was quite equal to the emergency of developing the two pictures which he had taken with the new camera.

Late as it was, we waited for him to finish, just as we would have waited down in the *Star* office if one of our staff photographers had come in with something important.

At last Kennedy emerged from his workshop. As he did so, he slapped down two untoned prints.

Both were necessarily indistinct owing to the conditions under which they had had to be taken. But they were quite sufficient for the purpose.

As Carton bent over the second one, which showed Kahn in the very act of handing over a roll of bills to the rather anemic man whom his runner had brought to him, Carton addressed the photograph as if it had been Kahn himself.

"I have you at last," he cried. "This is the end of your secret ring of jury fixers. I think that will about settle the case of Kahn, if not of Dopey Jack, when we get ready to spring it. Kennedy, make another set of prints and let me lock them in a safe deposit vault. That's as precious to me as if it were the Black Book itself!"

Craig laughed. "Not such a bad evening's work, after all," he remarked, clearing things up. "Do you realize what time it is?"

Carton glanced perfunctorily at his watch. "I had forgotten time," he returned.

"Yes," agreed Craig, "but to-morrow is another day, you know. I don't object to staying up all night, or even several nights, but there doesn't seem to be anything more that we can do now, and it may be that we shall need our strength later. This is, after all, only a beginning in getting at the man higher up."

"The man highest up," corrected Carton, with elation as we parted on the campus, Kennedy and I to go to our apartment.

"See you in the morning, Carton," bade Kennedy. " By that time, no doubt, there will be some news of the Black Book."

We arrived at our apartment a few minutes later. On the floor was some mail which Kennedy quickly ran over. It did not appear to be of any importance —that is, it had no bearing on the case which was now absorbing our attention.

" Well, what do you think of that? " he exclaimed as he tore open one diminutive letter. " That was thoughtful, anyhow. She must have sent us that a few minutes after we left headquarters."

He handed me an engraved card. It was from Miss Ashton, inviting us to a non-partisan suffrage evening at her studio in her home, to be followed by a dance.

Underneath she had written a few words of special invitation, ending, " I shall try to have some people there who may be able to help us in the Betty Blackwell matter."

X

THE AFTERNOON DANCE

IT was early the following morning that I missed Kennedy from our apartment. Naturally I guessed from my previous experiences with that gentleman that he would most likely be found at his laboratory, and I did not worry, but put the finishing touches on a special article for the *Star* which I had promised for that day and had already nearly completed.

Consequently it was not until the forenoon that I sauntered around to the Chemistry Building. Precisely as I had expected, I found Kennedy there at work.

I had been there scarcely a quarter of an hour when the door opened and Clare Kendall entered with a cheery greeting. It was evident that she had something to report.

"The letter to Betty Blackwell which you sent to the Montmartre has come back, unopened," she announced, taking from her handbag a letter stamped with the post-office form indicating that the addressee could not be found and that the letter was returned to the sender. The stamped hand of the post-office pointed to the upper left-hand corner where Clare had written in a fictitious name and used an address to which she frequently had mail sent when she wanted it secret.

"Only on the back," she pursued, turning the letter over, "there are some queer smudges. What are they? They don't look like dirt."

Kennedy glanced at it only casually, as if he had fully expected the incident to turn out as it did.

"Not unopened, Miss Kendall," he commented. "We have already had a little scientific letter-opening. This was a case of scientific letter-sealing. That was a specially prepared envelope."

He reached down into his desk and pulled out another, sealed it carefully, dried it, then held it over a steaming pan of water until the gum was softened and it could be opened again. On the back were smudges just like those on the letter that had been returned.

"On the thin line of gum on the flap of the envelope," he explained, "I have placed first a coating of tannin, over which is the gum. Then on the part of the envelope to which the flap adheres when it is sealed I placed some iron sulphate. When I sealed the envelope so carefully I brought the two together separated only by the thin film of gum. Now when steam is applied to soften the gum, the usual method of the letter-opener, the tannin and the sulphate are brought together. They run and leave these blots or dark smudges. So, you see, someone has been found at the Montmartre, even if it is not Betty Blackwell herself, who has interest enough in the case to open a letter to her before handing it back to the postman.   That shows us that we are on the right trail at least, even if it does not tell us who is at the end of the trail.   Here's another thing: This 'Marie' is a new one.   We must find out about her."

"At the Futurist Tea Room at four this after-noon, when she meets our good friend, young Dr. Harris," reminded Clare.   "Between cabarets and tea rooms I don't know whether this is work or play."

"It's work, all right," smiled Kennedy, adding, "at least it would be if it weren't lightened by your help."

It was the middle of the afternoon when Craig and I left the laboratory to keep our appointment with Miss Kendall at the Futurist Tea Room, where we hoped to find Dr. Harris's friend "Marie," who seemed to want to see him so badly.

A long line of touring and town cars as well as taxicabs bore eloquent testimony not only to the popularity of this tea room and cabaret, but to the growth of afternoon dancing.   One never realizes how large a leisure class there is in the city until after a visit to anything from a baseball game to a matinée—and a dance.   People seemed literally to be flocking to the Futurist.   They seemed to like its congeniality, its tone, its "atmosphere."

As we left our hats to the tender mercies of the "boys" who had the checking concession we could see that the place was rapidly filling up.

"If we are to get a table that we want here, we'd
9

better get it now," remarked Kennedy, slipping the inevitable piece of change to the head waiter. " If we sit over there in that sort of little bower we can see when Miss Kendall arrives and we shall not be so conspicuous ourselves, either "

The Futurist was not an especially ornate place, although a great deal of money had evidently been expended in fitting it up to attract a *recherché* clientele.

Our table, which Kennedy had indicated, was, as he had said, in a sort of little recess, where we could see without being much observed ourselves, although that seemed almost an impossibility in such a place. In fact, I noticed before we had had time to seat ourselves that we had already attracted the attention of two show girls who sat down the aisle and were amusing themselves at watching us by means of a mirror. It would not have been very difficult to persuade them to dispense with the mirror.

A moment later Clare Kendall entered and paused at the door an instant, absorbing the gay scene as only a woman and a detective could. Craig rose and advanced to meet her, and as she caught sight of us her face brightened. The show girls eyed her narrowly and with but slight approval.

" We feel more at ease with a lady in the party," remarked Craig, as they reached the table and I rose to greet her. " Two men alone here are quite as noticeable as two ladies. Walter, I know, was quite uncomfortable."

" To say nothing of the fact which you omitted,"

I retaliated, " that it is a pleasure to be with Miss Kendall—even if we must talk shop all the time."

Clare smiled, for her quick intuition had already taken in and dismissed as of no importance the two show girls. We ordered as a matter of course, then settled back for a long interval until the waiter out of the goodness of his heart might retrieve whatever was possible from the mob of servitors where refreshments were dispensed.

" Opposite us," whispered Clare, resting her chin on her interlocked fingers and her elbows on the tip-edge of the table, " do you see that athletic-looking young lady, who seems to be ready for anything from tea to tango? Well, the man with her is Martin Ogleby."

Ogleby was of the tall, sloping-shouldered variety, whom one can see on the Avenue and in the clubs and hotels in such numbers that it almost seems that there must be an establishment for turning them out, even down to a trademark concealed somewhere about them, " Made in England." Only Ogleby seemed a little different in the respect that one felt that if all the others were stamped by the same die, he was the die, at least. Compared to him many of the others took on the appearance of spurious counterfeits.

" Dr. Harris," Craig whispered, indicating to us the direction with his eyes.

Outside on a settee, we could see in the corridor a man waiting, restless and ill at ease. Now and then he looked covertly at his watch as if he expected someone who was late and he wondered if anything could be amiss.

Just then a superbly gowned woman alighted from a cab. The starter bowed as if she were familiar. It was evident that this was the woman for whom Harris waited, the " Marie " of the letter.

She was a carefully groomed woman, as artificial as French heels. Yet indeed it was that studied artificiality which constituted her chief attraction. As Harris greeted her I noted that Clare was amazed at the daring cut of her gown, which excited comment even at the Futurist.

Her smooth, full, well-rounded face with its dark olive skin and just a faint trace of colour on either cheek, her snappy hazel eyes whose fire was heightened by the penciling of the eyebrows, all were a marvel of the dexterity of her artificial beautifier. And yet in spite of all there was an air of unextinguishable coarseness about her which it was difficult to describe, but easy to feel.

" Her lips are too thick and her mouth too large," remarked Clare, " and yet in some incomprehensible way she gives you the impression of daintiness. What is it? "

" The woman is frankly deceptive from the tip of her aigrette to the toes of her shoes," observed Craig.

" And yet," smiled Clare, watching with interest the little stir her arrival had made among the revellers, " you can see that she is the envy of every woman here who has slaved and toiled for that same

effect without approaching within miles of it or attracting one quarter the notice for her pains that
this woman receives."

Dr. Harris was evidently in his element at the
attention which his companion attracted. They
seemed to be on very good terms indeed, and one
felt that Bohemianism could go no further.

They paused, fortunately, at a just vacated table
around an " L " from us and sat down. For once
waiters seemed to vie in serving rather than in
neglecting.

By this time I had gained the impression that the
Futurist was all that its name implied—not up to
the minute, but decidedly ahead of it. There was
an exotic flavour to the place, a peculiar fascination,
that was foreign rather than American, at seeing
demi-monde and decency rubbing elbows. I felt sure
that a large percentage of the women there were
really young married women, whose first step down-
ward was truly nothing worse than saying they had
been at their whist clubs when in reality it was tango
and tea. What the end might be to one who let the
fascination blind her perspective I could imagine.

Dr. Harris and " Marie " were nearer the dancing floor than we were, but seemed oblivious to it.
Now and then as the music changed we could catch
a word or two.

He was evidently making an effort to be gay, to
counteract the feeling which she had concealed as
she came in, but which had the upper hand now that
they were seated.

" Won't you dance? " I heard him say.

" No, Harry. I came here to tell you about how things are going."

There was a harshness about her voice which I recognized as belonging exclusively to one class of women in the city. She lowered it as she went on talking earnestly.

" It looks as though someone has squealed, but who——" I caught in the fragmentary lulls of the revelry.

" I didn't know it was as bad as that," Dr. Harris remarked.

They talked almost in whispers for several moments while I strained my ears to catch a syllable, but without success. What were they talking about? Was it about Dopey Jack? Or did they know something about Betty Blackwell? Perhaps it was about the Black Book. Even when the music stopped they talked without dropping a word.

The music started again. There was no mistaking the appeal that the rocking whirl of the rhythmic dance made. From the side of the table where Kennedy was seated he could catch an occasional glimpse of the face of Marie. I noticed that he had torn a blank page off the back of the menu and with a stub of a pencil was half idly writing.

At the top he had placed the word, " Nose," followed by " straight, with nostrils a trifle flaring," and some other words I could not quite catch. Beneath that he had written " Ears," which in turn was followed by some words which he was setting

down carefully. Eyes, chin, and mouth followed,
until I began to realize that he was making a sort
of scientific analysis of the woman's features.

"I shall need some more——" I caught as the
music softened unexpectedly.

A singer on the little platform was varying the
programme now by a solo and I shifted my chair so
as to get a better view and at the same time also a
look at the table around the corner from us.

As I did so I saw Dr. Harris reach into his
breast pocket and take out a little package which he
quickly handed to Marie. As their hands met, their
eyes met also. I fancied that the doctor struggled
to demagnetize, so to speak, the look which she gave
him.

"You'll come to see me—afterwards?" she
asked, dropping the little package into her handbag
of gold mesh and rattling the various accoutrements
of beautification which tinkled next to it.

Harris nodded.

"You're a life saver to some——" floated over
to me from Marie.

The solo had been completed and the applause
was dying away.

" . . . tells me he needs . . . badly off
. . . don't forget to see . . . "

The words came in intervals. What they meant
I did not know, but I strove to remember them.
Evidently Marie and a host of others were depend-
ing on Harris for something. At any rate, it
seemed, now that she had talked she felt easier in

mind, as one does after carrying a weight a long time in secret.

"*Tanguez-vous?*" he asked as the orchestra struck up again.

"Yes—thank you, Harry—just one."

We watched the couple attentively as they were alternately lost and found in the dizzy swaying mass. The music became wilder and they threw themselves into the abandon of the dance.

They had been absorbed so much in each other and the unburdening of whatever it was she had wanted to tell him, that neither had noticed the other couple on the other side of the floor whose presence had divided our own attention.

Martin Ogleby and his partner were not dancing. It was warm and they were among the lucky ones who had succeeded in getting something besides a cheque from the waiters. Two tall glasses of ginger ale with a long curl of lemon peel sepentining through the cracked ice stood before them.

The dance had brought Dr. Harris and Marie squarely around to within a few feet of where Ogleby was sitting. As Harris swung around she faced Ogleby in such a way that he could not avoid her, nor could she have possibly missed seeing him.

For a moment their eyes met. Not a muscle in either face moved. It was as if they were perfect strangers. She turned and murmured something to her partner. Ogleby leaned over, without the least confusion, and made a witty remark to his partner.

It was over in a minute. The acting of both could not have been better if they had deliberately practised their parts. What did it mean?

As the dance concluded I saw Ogleby glance hastily over in the direction of Marie. He gave a quick smile of recognition, as much as to say " Thank you."

It was evident now that both Dr. Harris and Marie, whoever she was, were getting ready to leave. As they rose to move to the door, Kennedy quickly paid our own cheque, leaving the change to the waiter, and without seeming to do so we followed them.

Harris was standing near the starter with his hat off, apparently making his adieux. Deftly Kennedy managed to slip in behind so as to be next in line for a cab.

" Walter and I will follow Harris if they separate," he whispered to Clare Kendall. " You follow the woman."

The afternoon was verging toward dinner and people were literally bribing the taxicab starter. Our own cab stood next in line behind that which Harris had called.

" I have certainly enjoyed this little glimpse of Bohemia," commented Kennedy to Miss Kendall as we waited. " I shouldn't mind if detective work took me more often to afternoon dances. There, they are going down the steps. Here's the cab I called. Let me know how things turn out. Goodbye. Here—chauffeur, around that way—where that other cab is going—the lady will tell you where to drive."

Harris hesitated a moment as if considering whether to take a cab himself, then slowly turned and strolled down the street.

We followed, slowly also. There was something unreal about the bright afternoon sunshine after the atmosphere of the Futurist Tea Room, where everything had been done to promote the illusion of night.

Harris walked along meditatively, crossing one street after another, not as if debating where he was going, but rather in no great hurry to get there.

Instead of going down Broadway he swerved into Seventh Avenue, then after a few blocks turned into a side street, quickened his pace, and at last dived down into a basement under a saloon.

It was a wretched neighbourhood, one of those which reminds one of the life of an animal undergoing a metamorphosis. Once it had evidently been a rather nice residential section. The movement of population uptown had left it stranded to the real estate speculators, less desirable to live in, but more valuable for the future. The moving in of anyone who could be got to live there had led to rapid deterioration and a mixed population of whites and negroes against the day when the upward sweep of business should bring the final transformation into office and loft buildings. But for the present it was decaying, out of repair, a mass of cheap rooming-houses, tenements, and mixed races.

The joint into which Harris had gone was the

only evidence of anything like prosperity on the block, and that evidence was confined to the two entrances on the street, one leading into the ground floor and the other down a flight of steps to the basement.

"Do you want to go in?" asked Kennedy in a tone that indicated that he himself was going.

Just then a negro, dazzling in the whiteness of his collar and the brilliancy of his checked suit, came up the stairs accompanied by a light mulatto.

"It's a black and tan joint," Craig went on, "at least downstairs—negro cabaret, and all that sort of thing."

"I'm game," I replied.

We stumbled down the worn steps, past a swinging door near which stood the proprietor with a careful eye on arrivals and departures. The place was deceiving from the outside. It really extended through two houses, and even at this early hour it was fairly crowded.

There were negroes of all degrees of shading, down to those who were almost white. Scattered about at the various tables were perhaps half a dozen white women, tawdry imitations of the faster set at the Futurist which we had just left, the left-overs of a previous generation in the Tenderloin. There was also a fair sprinkling of white men, equally degraded. White men and coloured women, white women and coloured men, chatted here and there, but for the most part the habitués were ne-groes. At any rate the levelling down seemed to have produced something like an equality of races in viciousness.

As we sat down at a table, Kennedy remarked: "They used to drift down to Chinatown, a good many of these relics. You used to see them in the old 'suicide halls' of the Bowery, too. But that is all passing away now. Reform and agitation have closed up those old dives. Now they try to veneer it over with electric lights and bright varnish, but I suppose it comes to the same thing. After they are cast off Broadway, the next step lower is the black and tan joint. After that it is suicide, unless it is death."

"I don't think this is any improvement over the —the bad old days," I ventured.

Kennedy shook his head in agreement. "There's Harris, down there in the back, talking to someone, a white man, alone."

A waiter came over to us grinning, for we had assumed the rôle of sightseers.

"Who is that, 'way back there, with his chair tipped to the wall, talking to the man with his back to us?" asked Kennedy.

"Ike the Dropper, sah," informed the waiter with obvious pride that such a celebrity should be harboured here.

I looked with a feeling akin to awe at the famous character who, in common with many others of his type, had migrated uptown from the proverbial haunts of the gunmen on the East Side in search of pastures new and untroubled.

Ike the Dropper may have once been a strong-
arm man, but at present I knew that he was chiefly
noted for the fact, and he and his kind were reputed
to be living on the earnings of women to whom they
were supposed to afford " protection." I reflected
on the passing glories of brutality which had sunk
so low.

There were noise and life a plenty here. At a
discordant box of a piano a negro performer was
playing with a keen appreciation of time if of nothing else, and two others with voices that might not
have been unpopular in a decent minstrel show were
rendering a popular air. They wore battered straw
hats and a make-up which was intended to be gro-
tesque.

From time to time, as the pianist was moved, he
played snatches of the same music as that which we
had heard at the Futurist, and between us and Harris and Ike the Dropper several couples were one-
stepping, each in their own sweet way. As the
music became more lively their dancing came more
and more to resemble some of the almost brutal
Apache dances of Paris, in that the man seemed to
exert sheer force and the woman agility in avoiding
him. It was an entirely new phase of afternoon
dancing, an entirely new " leisure class," this strange
combination of Bohemia and Senegambia.

At a table next to us, so near that we could almost
rub elbows with them, sat a white man and a white
woman. They had been talking in low tones, but I
could catch whole sentences now and then, for they

seemed to be making no extraordinary effort at concealment.

"He was framing a sucker to get away with a whole front," I heard the man say, " or with a poke or a souper, but instead he got dropped by a flatty and was canned for a sleep."

"Two dips—pickpockets," whispered Craig. "Someone was trying to take everything a victim had, or at least his pocketbook or watch, but instead he was arrested by a detective and locked up over night."

"Good work," I laughed. "You are 'some' translator."

I looked at our neighbours with a certain amount of respect. Were they framing up something themselves? At any rate I felt that I would rather see them here and know what they were than to be jostled by them in a street car. The sleek proprietor kept a careful eye on them and I knew that a sort of unwritten law would prevent them from trying on anything that would endanger their welcome in a joint none too savoury already.

Nevertheless I was quite interested in the bits of pickpocket argot that floated across to us, expressions like "crossing the mit," "nipping a slang," a "mouthpiece," "making a holler" and innumerable other choice bits as unintelligible to me as "Beowulf."

After a few minutes the woman got up and went out, leaving the man still sitting at the table. Of course it was none of my business what they were doing, I suppose, but I could not help being interested.

That diversion being ended, I joined Kennedy in his scrutiny of Harris and his choice friend. Of course at our distance it was absolutely impossible to gain any idea of what they were talking about, and indeed our chief concern was not to attract any attention. Whatever it was, they were very earnest about it and paid no attention to us.

The dancing had ceased and the two " artists " were entertaining the select audience with some choice bits of ragtime. We could see Ike the Dropper and Dr. Harris still talking.

Suddenly Kennedy nudged me. I looked up in time to see Dr. Harris reach into his inside breast pocket again and quietly slip out a package much like that which we had already seen him hand to Marie at the Futurist. Ike took it, looked at it a moment with some satisfaction, then stuffed it down carefully into the right-hand outside pocket of his coat.

" I wonder what that is that Harris seems to be passing out to them? " mused Craig.

" Drugs, perhaps," I ventured offhand.

" Maybe. I'd like to know for certain."

Just then Harris and Ike rose and walked down on the other side of the place toward the door. Kennedy turned his head so that even if they should look in our direction they would not see his face. I did the same. Fortunately neither seemed interested in the other occupants. Harris having evi-

dently fulfilled his mission, whether of delivering
the package or receiving news which Ike seemed to
be pouring into his ear, had but one thought, to
escape from a place which was evidently distasteful
to him. At the door they paused for a moment and
spoke with the proprietor. He nodded reassuringly
once or twice to Dr. Harris, much to the relief, I
thought, of that gentleman.

Kennedy was chafing under the restraint which
kept him in the background and prevented any of his
wizardry of mechanical eavesdropping. I fancied
that his roving eye was considering various means
of utilizing his seemingly inexhaustible ingenuity if
occasion should arise.

At last Harris managed to shake hands good-bye
and disappeared up the steps to the sidewalk still
followed by Ike.

Kennedy leaned over and looked the " dip " sitting alone back of us squarely in the face.

" Would you like to make twenty-five dollars—
just like that? " he asked with a quick gesture that
accorded very well with the slang.

The man looked at him very suspiciously, as if
considering what kind of new game this was.

" That was your gun moll who just went out,
wasn't it? " pursued Kennedy with assurance.

" Aw, come off. Whatyer givin' us? " responded
the man half angrily.

" Don't stall. I know. I'm not one of the bulls,
either. It's just a plain proposition. Will you or
won't you take twenty-five of easy money? "

Kennedy's manner seemed to mystify him.   For
a moment he looked us over, then seemed to decide
that we were all right.

" How ? " he asked in a harsh but not wholly un-
gracious whisper.   " I'll tip yer off if the boss is
lookin'.   He don't like no frame-ups in here."

" You saw Ike the Dropper go out with that
man ? "

" The guy with the glasses ? "

" Yes."

" Well ? "

" The guy with the glasses gave Ike a little package which Ike put into the right-hand outside pocket
of his coat.   Now it's worth twenty-five beans to me
to get that package—get me ? "

" I gotyer.   Slip me a five now and the other
twenty if I get it."

Kennedy appeared to consider.

" I'm on the level," pursued the dip.   " Me and
the goil is in hard luck with a mouthpiece who wants
fifty bucks to beat the case for one of the best tools
we ever had in our mob that they got right to-day."

" From that I take it that one of your pals needs
fifty dollars for a lawyer to get him out of jail.
Well, I'll take a chance.   Bring the package to me at
—well, the Prince Henry café.   I'll be there at
seven o'clock."   \

The pickpocket nodded, slid from his place and
sidled out of the joint without attracting any attention.

" What's the lay ? " I asked.

10

" Oh, I just want that package; that's all. Come on, Walter. We might as well go before any of these yellow girls speak to us and frame up something on us."

The proprietor bowed as much as to say, " Come again and bring your friends."

XI

THE TYPEWRITER CLUE

IKE was nowhere to be seen when we reached the street, but down the block we caught sight of Dr. Harris on the next corner. Kennedy hastened our pace until we were safely in his wake, then managed to keep just a few paces behind him.

Instead of turning into the street where the Futurist was, Harris kept on up Broadway. It was easy enough to follow him in the crowd now without being perceived.

He turned into the street where the Little Montmartre was preparing for a long evening of entertainment. We turned, and to cover ourselves got into a conversation with a hack driver who seemed suddenly to have sprung from nowhere with the cryptic whisper, "Drive you to the Ladies' Club, gents?"

Out of the tail of his eye Kennedy watched Harris. Instead of turning into the Montmartre and his office, he went past to a high-stooped brownstone house, two doors away, climbed the steps and entered.

We sauntered down the street and looked quickly at the house. A brass sign on the wall beside the door read, " Mme. Margot's Beauty Shop."

"I see," commented Kennedy. "You know women of the type who frequent the Futurist and the Montmartre are always running to the hairdressing and manicure parlours. They make themselves 'beautiful' under the expert care of the various specialists and beauty doctors. Then, too, they keep in touch that way with what is going on in the demi-monde. That is their club, so to speak. It is part of the beauty shop's trade to impart such information—at least of a beauty shop in this neighbourhood."

I regarded the place curiously.

"Come, Walter, don't stare," nudged Kennedy. "Let's take a turn down to the Prince Henry and wait. We can get a bite to eat, too."

I had hardly expected that the pickpocket would play fair, but evidently the lure of the remaining twenty dollars was too strong. We had scarcely finished our dinner when he came in.

"Here it is," he whispered. "The house man here at the Prince Henry knows me. Slip me the twenty."

Kennedy leisurely tore the wrappings from the packet.

"I suppose you have already looked at this first and found that it isn't worth anything to you compared to twenty dollars. Anyhow, you kept your word. Hello—what is it?"

He had disclosed several small packets. Inside each, sealed, was a peculiar glistening whitish powder.

" H'm," mused Kennedy, " another job for the
chemist. Here's the bankroll."

" Thanks," grinned the dip as he disappeared
through the revolving door.

We had returned to the laboratory that night
where Kennedy was preparing to experiment on the
white powder which he had secured in the packet
that came from Dr. Harris. The door opened and
Clare Kendall entered.

" I've been calling you up all over town," she
said, " and couldn't find you. I have something
that will interest you, I think. You said you wanted
something written by Dr. Harris. Well, there
it is."

She laid a sheet of typewriting on the laboratory
table.

" How did you get it? " asked Kennedy in eager
approbation.

" When I left you at the Futurist Tea Room to
follow that woman Marie in the cab, I had a good
deal of trouble. I guess people thought I was
crazy, the way I was ordering that driver about,
but he was so stupid and he would get tangled up
in the traffice on Fifth Avenue. Still, I managed
to hang on, principally because I had a notion already that she was going to the Montmartre. Sure
enough, she turned down that block, but she didn't
go into the hotel after all. She stopped and went
into a place two doors down—Mme. Margot's
Beauty Parlour."

" Just where we finally saw Harris go," ex-

claimed Kennedy. "I beg your pardon for inter-
rupting."

"Of course I couldn't go in right after her, so
I drove around the corner. Then it occurred to
me that it would be a good time to stop in to see
Dr. Harris—when he was out. You know my
experience with the fakers has made me pretty good
at faking up ailments. Then, too, I knew that it
would be easy when he was not there. I said I
was an old patient and had an appointment and
that I'd wait, although I knew those were not his
regular office hours. He has an alleged trained
nurse there all the time. She let me into his waiting-room on the second floor in front—you remember the private dining-rooms are in back. I waited
in momentary fear that he *would* come back. You
see, I had a scheme of my own. Well, I waited
until at last the nurse had to leave the office for
a short time.

"That was my chance. I tiptoed over to his
desk in the next room. On it were a lot of letters.
I looked over them but could find nothing that
seemed to be of interest. They were all letters
from other people. But they showed that he must
have quite an extensive practice, and that he is not
over-scrupulous. I didn't want to take anything
that would excite suspicion unless I had to. Just
then I heard someone coming down the corridor
from the elevator. I had just time to get back to
a chair in the waiting-room when the door opened
and there was that Titian from the office, you re-

member. She saw me without recognizing me, went in and laid some papers on his desk. As soon as she was gone, I went in again and looked them over. Here was one that she had copied for him."

Kennedy had been carefully scrutinizing the sheet of paper as she told how she obtained it.

" It couldn't be better as far as our purposes are concerned," he congratulated. " It seems to consist of some notes he had made and wished to preserve about drugs."

I leaned over and read:

VERONAL.—Diethylmalonyl or diethylbarbituric acid. A hypnotic used extensively. White, crystalline, odourless, slightly bitter. Best in ten to fifteen grain cachets. Does not affect circulatory or respiratory systems or temperature. Toxicity low: 135 gr. taken with no serious result. Unreasonable use for insomnia, however, may lead to death.

HEROIN.—Constant use of heroin has been known to lead to——

I looked inquiringly at Kennedy.

" Just some fragmentary notes which he had evidently been making. Rather interesting in themselves as showing perhaps something of his practice, but not necessarily incriminating."

While we were discussing the contents of the notes, Kennedy had laid over the typewritten sheet the rules and graduated strip of glass which he had used in examining the strange letter signed " An Outcast."

A moment later he pulled the letter itself from a drawer and laid the two pieces of writing side by side, comparing them, going from one to the other successively.

"People generally, who have not investigated the subject," he remarked as he worked, "hold the opinion that the typewriter has no individuality. Fortunately that is not true. The typewriting machine does not always afford an effective protection to the criminal. On the contrary, the typewriting may be a direct means of tracing a document to its source and showing it to be what it really is. This is especially true of typewritten anonymous letters. Without careful investigation it is impossible to say what can be determined from the examination of any particular piece of typewriting, but typewriting can often be positively identified as being the work of a certain particular typewriting machine and even the date of writing can sometimes be found out."

He had been carefully counting something under the lens of a pocket glass. "Even the number of threads to the inch in the ribbon, as shown in the type impression, plainly seen and accurately measured by the microscope or in an enlarged photograph, may show something about the identity of a disputed writing."

He was pointing to a letter "r." Under the glass I noticed that there was a break in the little curl at the top.

"Now if you find such a break in the same letter

in another piece of typewriting, what would you think ? "

" That they were from the same machine," I replied.

" Not so fast," he cautioned. " True, it might raise a presumption that it was from the same machine. But the laws of chance would be against your enthusiasm, Walter."

" Of course," I admitted on second thought.

" It's just like the finger-print theory. There must be a sort of summation of individual characteristics. Now here's a broken ' l ' and there is an ' a ' that is twisted. Now, if the same defects are found in another piece of writing, that makes the presumption all the stronger, and when you have massed together a number of such characteristics it raises the presumption to a mathematical certainty, does it not ? "

I nodded and he went on. " The faces of many letters inevitably become broken, worn, or battered. Not only does that tend to identify a particular machine, but it is sometimes possible, if you have certain admitted standard specimens of writing covering a long period, to tell just when a disputed writing was made. There are two steps in such an inquiry, the first the determination of the fact that a document was written on a certain particular kind of machine and the second that it was written on a certain individual machine of that make. I have here specimens of the writing of all the leading machines. It is easy to pick out the make used, say in the ' Outcast ' letter. Moreover, as I said when I first saw that letter, it is in the regular pica type. So are they all, but as ninety-five per cent. use the pica style that in itself proved nothing."

. " What is that bit of ruled glass ? " asked Clare, bending over the letters in deep interest.

" In ordinary typewriting," replied Craig, " each letter occupies an imaginary square, ten to the inch horizontally and six to the inch vertically. Typewriting letters are in line both ways. This ruled glass plate is an alinement test plate for detecting defects in alinement. I have also here another glass plate in which the lines diverge each at a very slightly different angle—a typewriting protractor for measuring the slant of divergence of various letters that have become twisted, so to speak.

" When it is in perfect alinement the letter occupies the middle of each square and when out of alinement it may be in any of the four corners, or either side of the middle position or at the top or bottom above or below the middle. That, you see, makes nine positions in all—or eight possible divergences from normal in this particular alone."

Clare had been using the protractor herself, quickly familiarizing herself with it.

" Another possible divergence," went on Kennedy, " is the perpendicular position of the letter in relation to the line. That is of great value in individualizing a machine. It is very seldom that machines, even when they are new, are perfect in this particular. It does not seem much until you magnify it. Then anyone can see it, and it is a characteristic that is fixed, continuous, and not much changed by variations in speed or methods of writing.

"Here's another thing. Typewriter faces are not flat like printing type, but are concaved to conform to the curve of the printing surface of the roller. When they are properly adjusted all portions should print uniformly. But when they are slightly out of position in any direction the two curved surfaces of type and roller are not exactly parallel and therefore don't come together with uniform pressure. The result is a difference in intensity in different parts of the impression."

It was fascinating to see Craig at work over such minute points which we had never suspected in so common a thing as ordinary typewriting.

"Then you can identify these letters positively?" asked Clare.

"Positively," answered Craig. "If two machines of the same make were perfect to begin with and in perfect condition—which is never found to be the case when they are critically examined—the work from one would be theoretically indistinguishable from that of another until actual use had affected them differently. The work of any number of machines begins inevitably to diverge as soon as they are used. Since there are thousands of possible particulars in which differences may develop, it very soon becomes possible to identify positively the work of a particular typewriting machine."

"How about the operator?" I asked curiously.

"Different habits of touch, spacing, speed, arrangement, and punctuation all may also tend to show that a particular piece of writing was or was not done by one operator. In other words, typewriting individuality in many cases is of the most positive and convincing character and reaches a degree of certainty which may almost be described as absolute proof. The identification of a typewritten document in many cases is exactly parallel to the identification of an individual who precisely answers a general description as to features, complexion, size, and in addition matches a long detailed list of scars, birthmarks, deformities, and individual peculiarities."

Together we three began an exhaustive examination of the letters, and as Kennedy called off the various characteristics of each type on the standard keyboard we checked them up. It did not take long to convince us, nor would it have failed to convince the most sceptical, that both had come from the same source and the same writer.

"You see," concluded Kennedy triumphantly, "we have advanced a long step nearer the solution of at least one of the problems of this case."

Miss Kendall had evidently been thinking quickly and turning the matter over in her mind.

"But," she spoke up quickly, "even that does not point to the same person as the author—not the writer, but the author—of the three pieces of writing."

"No indeed," agreed Craig. "There is much left to be done. As a matter of fact, there might have been one author, or there might have been two, although all the mechanical work was done by one person. But we are at least sure that we have localized the source of the writing. We know that it is from the Montmartre that the letter came. We know that it is in some way that that place and some of the people who frequent it are connected with the disappearance of Betty Blackwell."

"In other words," supplied Clare, "we are going to get at the truth through that Titian-haired stenographer."

"Exactly."

Clare had risen to go.

"It quite takes my breath away to think that we are really making such progress against the impregnable Montmartre. At various times my investigators have been piecing together little bits of information about that place. I shall have the whole record put together to-night. I shall let you know about it the first thing in the morning."

The door had scarcely closed when Kennedy turned quickly to me and remarked, "That girl has something on her mind. I wonder what it is?"

XII

THE "PORTRAIT PARLÉ"

WHAT it was that Clare Kendall had on her mind, appeared the following day.

"There's something I want to try," she volunteered, evidently unable to repress it any longer. "I have a plan—or half a plan. Don't you think it would be just the thing, under the circumstances, to ring up District Attorney Carton, tell him what we have accomplished and take him into our confidence? Perhaps he can suggest something. At any rate we have all got to work together, for there is going to be a great fight when they find out how far we have gone."

"Bully idea," agreed Craig.

Twenty minutes later we were seated in the District Attorney's office in the Criminal Courts Building, pouring into his sympathetic ear the story of our progress so far.

Carton seemed to be delighted, as Kennedy proceeded to outline the case, at the fact that he and Miss Kendall had found it possible to co-operate. His own experience in trying to get others to work with the District Attorney's office, particularly the police, had been quite the reverse.

"I wish to heaven you could get the right kind

of evidence against the Montmartre gang," he sighed. "It is a gang, too—a high-class gang. In fact—well, it must be done. That place is a blot on the city. The police never have really tried to get anything on it. Miss Kendall never could, could you? I admit I never have. It seems to be understood that it is practically impossible to prove anything against it. They openly defy us. The thing can't go on. It demoralizes all our other work. Just one good blow at the Montmartre and we could drive every one of these vile crooks to cover."

He brought his fist down with a thud on the desk, swung around in his chair, and emphasized his words with his forefinger.

"And yet, I know as well as I know that you are all in this room that graft is being paid to the police and the politicians by that place and in fact by all those places along there. If we are to do anything with them, that must be proved. That is the first step and I'm glad the whole thing hinges on the Blackwell case. People always sit up and take notice when there is something personal involved, some human interest which even the newspapers can see. That Montmartre crowd, whoever they are, must be made to feel the strong arm of the law. That's what I am in this office to do. Now, Kennedy, there must be some way to catch those crooks with the goods."

"They aren't ordinary crooks, you know," ruminated Kennedy.

"I know they are not. But you and Miss Kendall

and Jameson ought to be able to think out a scheme."

"But you see, Mr. Carton," put in Clare, "this is a brand new situation. Your gambling and vice and graft exposures have made all of them so wary that they won't pass a bill from their right to their left pockets for fear it is marked."

Carton laughed.

"Well, you are a brand new combination against them. Let me see; you want suggestions. Why don't you use the detectaphone—get our own little Black Book?"

Kennedy shook his head.

"The detectaphone is all right, as Dorgan knows. It might work again. But I don't think I'll take any chances. No, these grafters wouldn't say 'Thank you' in an open boat in mid-ocean, for fear of wireless, now. They've been educated up to a lot of things lately. No, it must be something new. What do you know about graft up there?"

"The people who are running those places in the fifties are making barrels of money," summarized Carton quickly. "No one ever interferes with them, either. I know from reliable sources, too, that the police are 'getting theirs.' But although I know it I can't prove it; I can't even tell who is getting it. But once a week a collector for the police calls around in that district and shakes them all down. By Jove, to-day is the day. The trouble with it all is that they have made the thing so underground that no one but the principals know anything about it—not even the agents. I guess you are right about the detectaphone."

"To-day's the day, is it? " mused Craig.

"So I understand."

"I think I can get them with a new machine they never dreamed of," exclaimed Kennedy, who had been turning something over in his mind.

He reached for the telephone and called the Montmartre.

" Julius, please," he said when they answered; then, placing his hand over the transmitter, he turned to Clare. " That was your friend the Titian, Miss Kendall."

" No friend of mine if she happens to remember seeing me in Dr. Harris's office the other day. Still, I doubt if she would."

" Hello—Julius? Good morning. How about a private dining-room for three, Julius? "

We could not hear the reply, but Craig added quickly, " I thought there were two? "

Evidently the answer was in the affirmative, for Craig asked next, " Well, can't we have the small one? "

He hung up the receiver with a satisfied smile after closing with " That's the way to talk. Thank you, Julius. Good-bye."

" What was the difficulty? " I asked.

" Why, I thought I'd take a chance—and it took. Now figure it out for yourself. Carton says it's dough day, so to speak, up there. What is more natural than that the money for all those places

11

leased to various people should be passed over in a place that is public and yet is not public? For instance, there is the Montmartre itself. Now think it out. Where would that be done in the Montmartre? Why, in one of the private dining-rooms, of course."

"That seems reasonable," agreed Carton.

"That was the way I doped it," pursued Craig. "I thought I'd confirm it if I could. You remember they told us to call up always if I wanted a private dining-room and it would be reserved for me. So it was the most natural thing in the world for me to call up. If they had said yes, I should have been disappointed. But they said no, and straightway I wanted one of those rooms the worst way. One seems to be engaged—the large one. He said nothing about the other, so I asked him. Since I knew about it, he could hardly say no. Well, I have engaged it for lunch—an early luncheon, too."

"It sounds all right, as though you were on the right trail," remarked Carton. "But, remember, only the best sort of evidence will go against those people. They can afford to hire the best lawyers that money can retain. And be careful not to let them get anything on you, for they are fearful liars, and they'll go the limit to discredit you."

"Trust us," assured Craig. "Now, Miss Kendall, if you will give us the pleasure of lunching with you at the Montmartre again, I think we may be able to get the Judge just the sort of open and shut evidence he is after."

"I shall be glad to do it. I'm ready now."

Kennedy glanced at his watch. "It's a little early yet. If we take a taxicab we shall have plenty of time to stop at the laboratory on our way."

Arriving at the laboratory, he went to a drawer, from which he took a little box which contained a long tube, and carefully placed it in the breast pocket of his coat. Then from a chest of tools he drew several steel sections that apparently fitted together, and began stuffing the parts into various pockets.

"Here, Walter," he said, "these make me bulge like a yeggman with his outfit under his coat. Can't you help me with some of these parts?"

I jammed several into various pockets—heavy pieces of metal—and we were ready.

Our previous visits to the Montmartre seemed to have given us the *entrée* and the precaution of telephoning made it even easier. Indeed, it appeared that about all that was necessary there was to be known and to be thought "right." We carefully avoided the office, where the stenographer might possibly have recognized Clare, and entered the elevator.

"Is Dr. Harris in?" asked Craig, both by way of getting information and showing that he was no stranger.

The black elevator boy gave an ivory grin. "No, sah. He done gone on one o' them things."

Another question developed the fact that whenever Harris was away it was generally assumed that he was tinting the metropolis vermilion from the Battery to the Bronx.

We passed down the hall to the smaller of the two dining-rooms, and as we went by the larger we could see the door open and that no one was there.

We had ordered and the waiter had scarcely shut the door before Kennedy had divested himself of the heavy steel sections which he had hidden in his pockets. I did the same.

With a quick glance he seemed to be observing just how the furniture was placed. The smaller dining-room was quite as elaborately furnished as the larger, though of course the furniture was more crowded.

He moved the settee and was on his knees in a corner. "Let me see," he considered. "There was nothing on this side of the larger room except the divan in the centre."

As nearly as he could judge he was measuring off just where the divan stood on the opposite side of the wall, and its height. Then he began fitting together the pieces of steel. As he added one to another, I saw that they made a sectional brace and bit of his own design, a long, vicious-looking affair such as a burglar might have been glad to own.

Carefully he started to bore through the plaster and lath back of the settee and to one side of where the divan must have been. He was making just as small a hole as possible, now and then stopping to listen.

There was no noise from the next room, but a

tap on the door announced the waiter with luncheon. He shoved the settee back and joined us. The discreet waiter placed the food on the table and departed without a word or look. Kennedy resumed his work and we left the luncheon still untasted.

The bit seemed to have gone through as Kennedy, turning it carefully, withdrew it now and then to make sure. At last he seemed to be satisfied with the opening he had made.

From the package in his breast pocket he drew a long brass tube which looked as if it might be a putty-blower. Slowly he inserted it into the hole he had bored.

"What is it?" I asked, unable to restrain my curiosity longer.

"I felt sure that there would be no talking done in that room, especially as we are in this one and anyone knows that even if you can't put a detectaphone in a room, it will often work if merely placed against a wall or door, on the other side, in the next room. So I thought I'd use this instead. Put your eye down here."

I did so and was amazed to find that through a hole less than a quarter of an inch in diameter the brass tube enabled me to see the entire room next to us.

I looked up at Kennedy in surprise. "What do you think of this, Miss Kendall?" I asked, moving the settee out of her way. "What do you call it?"

"That is a detectascope," he replied, "a little contrivance which makes use of the fish-eye lens.

"Yes. The detectascope enables you to see what is going on in another room. The focus may be altered in range so that the faces of those in the room may be recognized and the act of passing money or signing cheques, for instance, may be detected. The instrument is fashioned somewhat after the cytoscope of the doctors, with which the human interior may be seen."

"Very remarkable," exclaimed Clare. "But I can't understand how it is possible to see so much through such a little tube. Why, I almost fancy I can see more in that room than I could with my own eyes if I were placed so that I could not move my head."

Kennedy laughed.

"That's the secret," he went on. "For instance, take a drop of water. Professor Wood of Johns Hopkins has demonstrated recently the remarkable refracting power of a drop of water, using the camera and the drop of water as a lens. It is especially interesting to scientists because it illustrates the range of vision of some fishes. They have eyes that see over half a circle. Hence the lens gets its name—'the fish-eye lens.' A globe refracts the light that reaches it from all directions, and if it is placed as the lens is in the detectascope so that one half of it catches the light, all this light will be refracted through it. Ordinary lenses, because of their flatness, have a range of only a few degrees, the widest in use, I believe, taking in only ninety-six degrees, or a little over a quarter of a circle. So you see my detectascope has a range almost twice as wide as that of any other lens."

The little tube was fascinating, and although there was no one in the next room yet, I could not resist the desire to keep on looking through it.

" Since you are so interested, Walter," laughed Craig, " we'll appoint you to take the first shift at watching.   Meanwhile we may as well eat since we shall certainly have to pay.   When you are tired or hungry I'll take a turn."

Kennedy and I had been taking turns at watching through the detectascope while Miss Kendall told us more about how she had come to be associated with the organization to clean up New York.

" We have struck some delicate situations before," she was saying, " times when it meant either that we must surrender and compromise the work of the investigation or offend an interest that might turn out to be more powerful than we realized.   Our rule from the start was, ' No Compromise.'   You know the moment you compromise with one, all the others hear it and it weakens your position.   We've made some powerful enemies, but our idea is that as long as we keep perfectly straight and honest they will never be able to beat us.   We shall win in the end, because so far it has never come to a show-down, when we appealed to the public itself, that the public had not risen and backed us strongly."

I had come to have the utmost confidence in Clare Kendall and her frank way of handling a ticklish yet most important subject without fear or prudishness. There was a refreshing newness about her method. It was neither the holier-than-thou attitude of many religionists, nor the smug monopoly of all knowledge of the social worker, nor the brutal wantonness of the man or woman of the world who excuses everything " because it is human nature, always has been and always will be."

" We have no illusions on the subject," she pursued. " We don't expect to change human nature until the individual standard changes. But we are convinced of this—and it is as far as we go and is what we are out to accomplish—and that is that we can, and are going to, smash protected, commercialized vice as one of the big businesses of New York."

" Sh-h," cautioned Kennedy, whose turn it happened to be just then to watch. " Someone has just entered the room."

" Who is it? " I whispered eagerly.

" A man. I can't see his face. His back is toward me, but there is something familiar about him. There—he is turning around. For Heaven's sake —it's Ike the Dropper! "

We had already recounted to Miss Kendall our experiences in following Dr. Harris to the black and tan joint and the meeting with Ike the Dropper.

" Then Ike the Dropper is the collector for the police or the politicians higher up," she exclaimed under her breath. " If we learned nothing more, that would be enough. It would tell us whom to watch."

Hastily we took turns at getting a good look at Ike through the wonderful little detectascope. Then Kennedy resumed his watch, whispering now and then what he saw. Apparently Ike had proceeded to make himself comfortable in the luxurious surroundings of the private dining-room, against the arrival of the graft payers.

" I wonder who the man higher up is," whispered Miss Kendall.

" Someone is coming in," reported Kennedy. " By George, it is that stenographer from the office downstairs. She is handing him an envelope. Good for her! He tried to kiss her and she backed away in disgust. The scoundrel!

" Isn't it clever, though? Not a word is said by anyone. I don't suppose she could swear to knowing anything about what is in the envelope. There she goes out. He is opening the envelope and counting out the money—ten one-hundred-dollar bills. There they go into the fob pocket of his trousers. I imagined he learned something from my pickpocket. That is the safest pocket a man has. That little contribution, I take it, was from the Montmartre itself."

Then followed an interval in which Ike puffed away on his cigar in silent state.

" Here's another now," announced Craig. " Another woman. I never saw her before."

Both Miss Kendall and I looked and neither of us recognized her. She was slim and would have been young-looking if she had not made such obvious efforts to imitate the healthy colour of the cheeks which she probably would have had if she had lived sensibly and left cosmetics alone.

Kennedy was hastily jotting down some notes on the back of an envelope.

" They are going through the same proceedings again. I guess Ike doesn't like her. There she goes. Only two hundred this time."

Another wait followed, during which Ike smoked down his cigar and lighted another from the stub. Then the door opened again.

Kennedy motioned quickly to Clare to look through the detectascope. Meanwhile he pulled from his pocket the piece of paper he had written on and torn from the back of the menu at the Futurist.

" Marie ! " exclaimed Clare under her breath.

" The same," whispered Kennedy. " Miss Kendall, you have the true ' camera eye ' of the born detective. Now—please—let me see if I can get what occurs."

She yielded her place to him.

" Three hundred more," he murmured. " Marie must be in the game, though. He didn't wait for her to leave before he tore open the envelope. Now they are burning the envelopes in the ash tray. And still not a word. This is clever, clever. Think of it—fifteen hundred dollars of easy money like that ! I wonder how much of it sticks to Ike's hands on the way up. He must have a capacious fob pocket for that. Say, he's a regular fellow with the ladies,

Ike is. Only this one doesn't seem to resent it. By George, I wonder if this fellow Ike isn't giving the police or the politicians the double-cross. He couldn't be on such intimate terms with one who was paying graft to him as collector otherwise; do you think so?"

Craig looked up without waiting for an answer. " You will excuse any levity, but that was some kiss she just gave him."

Kennedy resumed his position for looking through the detectascope, occasionally glancing down at the notes he had made the day before and now and then making a slight alteration.

" There. She is going away now. Well, I guess the collection is all over. He has his hat on and a third cigar, ready to go as soon as somebody signals that the coast is clear. That was a good day's work for Ike and the man higher up, whoever he is. Ah—there he goes. It was a signal from the waiter he was after. Now we may as well finish this luncheon. It cost enough."

For several minutes we ate in silence.

" I wish I could have followed Ike," observed Craig. " But of course it would have been of no use. To go out right after him would have given the whole thing away."

" Who is that dark-haired, dark-skinned woman, Marie, do you suppose?" asked Clare. " Sometimes I almost think she is part negro."

" I don't know. I wouldn't be surprised, though, if you were right. If you have any investigators to spare, they might try to find out who she is and something of her history. I will give them a copy of these notes which I intend to turn over to the Department of Justice men who have been making the white slave investigation for the Federal Government."

Kennedy had laid the notes which he had made on the menu before us and was copying them. Both Clare and I leaned over to read them. It was Greek to me:

Nose—straight, base elevated, nostrils thick, slightly flaring.
Ears—lobe descending oval, traversed by a hollow, antitragus concave; lobe separated from cheek.
Lips—large.
Mouth—large.
Chin—receding.

There was much more that he had jotted down and added to the description.

"Oh," exclaimed Clare, as she ran through the writing, "that is this new *portrait parlé,* the spoken picture, isn't it?"

"Yes," replied Kennedy. "You may know that the Government has been using it in its white slave inquiry and has several thousands of such descriptions. Under the circumstances, I understand that the Government agents find it superior to finger-prints. Finger-prints are all right for identification, as we have found right here, for instance, in the Night Court. But Bertillon's new *portrait parlé* is the thing for apprehension."

" What is it? " I asked.

" Well, take the case before us. We have had no chance to finger-print that woman and what good would it do if we had? No one could recognize her that way until she was arrested or some means had been taken to get the prints again.

" But the *portrait parlé* is scientific apprehension, the step that comes before scientific identification by finger-prints. It means giving the detective an actual portrait of the person he is sent after without burdening him with a photograph. As descriptions are now given, together with a photograph, a person is described as of such a weight, height, general appearance, and so on. A clever crook knows that. He knows how to change his appearance so that there are few even of the best detectives who can recognize him. This new system describes the features so that a man can carry them in his mind systematically, features that cannot be changed.

" Take the nose, for example," explained Kennedy. " There are only three kinds, as Bertillon calls them—convex, straight, and concave. A detective, we will say, is sent out after a man with a concave nose or, as in this case a woman with a straight nose. Thus he is freed from the necessity of taking a second glance at two-thirds of the women, roughly, that he meets—that is, theoretically. He passes by all with convex and concave noses.

" There are four classes of ears—triangular, square, oval, and round, as they may be called. Having narrowed his search to women with straight noses, the detective needs to concern himself with only one-fourth of the women with straight noses. Having come down to women with straight noses and, say, oval ears, he will eliminate all those that do not have the mouth, lips, chin, eyes, forehead, and so on that have been given him. Besides that, there are other striking differences in noses and ears that make his work much easier than you would imagine, once he has been trained to observe such things quickly."

" It sounds all right," I agreed haltingly.

" It is all right, too," he argued warmly. " The proof of it is its use in Paris and other cities abroad and the fact that it has been imported here to New York in the Police Department and has been used by the Government. I could tell you many interesting stories about how it has succeeded where photographs would have failed."

I had been reading over the description again and trying to apply it.

" For instance," Craig resumed thoughtfully. " I believe that this woman is a mulatto, but that is a long way from proving it. Still, I hope that by using the *portrait parlé* and other things we may be able to draw the loose threads together into a net that will catch her—providing, of course, that she ought to be caught."

He had finished making copies of the *portrait parlé* and had called for a cheque for the lunch.

" So you see," he concluded, " this is without any doubt the woman we saw at the Futurist, whom

Miss Kendall followed to Madame Margot's Beauty Shop, two doors down."

Kennedy handed a copy to Miss Kendall.

" Using that and whatever other means you may have, Miss Kendall," he said, " I wish that you would try to find this woman and all you can about her. Walter, take this other copy and see Carton. I think he has a county detective who knows the system. I shall spend the rest of the day getting in touch with the Federal authorities in this city and in Washington trying to find out whether they know anything about her."

We left the Montmartre with as much care as we had entered and seemingly without having yet aroused any suspicion. The rest of the day was spent in setting to work those whom we felt we could trust to use the *portrait parlé* to locate the mysterious dark-haired Marie who seemed to cross our trail at every turn, yet who proved so elusive.

XIII

THE CONVICTION

MEANWHILE, the organization was using every effort to get possession of the Black Book, as Kennedy had suspected.

Miss Ashton had been busy on the case of the missing Betty Blackwell, but as yet there was no report from any of the agencies which she had set in motion to locate the girl. She had seen Langhorne, and, although she did not say much about the result of the interview, I felt sure that it had resulted in a further estrangement between them, perhaps a suspicion on the part of Langhorne that Carton had been responsible for it.

In as tactful a way as possible, Miss Ashton had also warned Mrs. Ogleby of the danger she ran, but, as I had already supposed, the warning had been unnecessary. The rumours about the detectaphone record of the dinner had been quite enough. As for the dinner itself, what happened, and who were present, it remained still a mystery, perhaps only to be explained when at last we managed to locate the book.

Since the visit of Kahn, we had had no direct or indirect communications with either Dorgan or Murtha. They were, however, far from inactive, and I felt that their very secrecy, which had always been the strong card of the organization, boded no good. Although both Carton and Kennedy were straining every nerve to make progress in the case, there was indeed very little to report, either the next day or for some time after the episode which had placed Kahn in our power.

Carton was careful not to say anything about the graphic record we had taken of Kahn's attempt to throw the case. It was better so, he felt. The jury fixing evidence would keep and it would prove all the stronger trump to play when the right occasion arose. That time rapidly approached, now, with the day set for the trial of Dopey Jack.

The morning of the trial found both Kennedy and myself in the part of General Sessions to which the case had been assigned to be tried under Justice Pomeroy.

To one who would watch the sieve through which justice vigorously tries to separate the wheat from the chaff, the innocent from the guilty, a visit to General Sessions is the best means. For it is fed through the channels that lead through the police courts, the Grand Jury chambers, and the District Attorney's office. There one can study the largest assortment of criminals outside of a penal institution, from the Artful Dodger and Bill Sykes, Fagin and Jim the Penman, to the most modern of noted crooks of fact or fiction, all done here in real flesh and blood. It is the busiest of criminal courts.

12

More serious offenders against the law are sentenced here than in any other court in New York. The final chapter in nearly every big crime is written there, sooner or later.

As we crowded in, thanks to the courtesy of Carton, we found a roomy chamber, with high ceiling, and grey, impressive walls in the southeast corner of the second floor of the Criminal Courts Building. Heavy carved oaken doors afforded entrance and exit for the hundreds of lawyers, witnesses, friends, and relatives of defendants and complainants who flocked thither.

Rows upon rows of dark-brown stained chairs filled the west half of the courtroom, facing a three-foot railing that enclosed a jury box and space reserved for counsel tables, the clerk and the District Attorney representing the people.

At the extreme east rose in severe dignity the dais or bench above which ascended a draped canopy of rich brown plush. Here Justice Pomeroy presided, in his robes of silk, a striking, white-haired figure of a man, whose face was seamed and whose eyes were keen with thought and observation.

Across the street, reached by the famous Bridge of Sighs, loomed the great grey hulk of stone and steel bars, the city prison, usually referred to as " The Tombs." As if there had been some cunning design in the juxtaposition, the massive jail reared itself outside the windows as an object lesson. It was a perpetual warning to the lawbreaker. Its towers and projections jutted out as so many rocks on a dangerous shore where had been wrecked thousands of promising careers just embarked on the troublesome seas of life.

Skirting the line of southern windows through which The Tombs was visible, ran a steel wire screen, eight feet high, marking off a narrow chute that hugged the walls to a door at the rear of the courtroom leading to the detention pen. Ordinarily prisoners were brought over the Bridge of Sighs in small droves and herded in the detention pens just outside the courtroom until their cases were called.

The line-up of prisoners at such times awaiting their turn at the bar of justice affords ample opportunity for study to the professional or the amateur criminalist.

Almost daily in this court one might look upon murderers, bank looters, clever forgers, taxicab robbers, safe crackers, highwaymen, second-story men, shoplifters, pickpockets, thieves, big and little—all sorts and conditions of crooks come to pay the price.

The court was crowded, for the gang leaders knew that this was a show-down for them. Carton himself, not one of his assistants, was to conduct the case. If Dopey Jack, who had violated almost every law in the revised statutes and had never suffered anything worse than a suspended sentence, could not get off, then no one could. And it was unthinkable that Dopey should not only be arrested and held in jail without bail, but even be convicted on such a trivial matter as slight irregularities that swung the primaries in a large section of the city for his superior, " higher up."

Rubano's father, a decent, sorrowing old man, sat in the rear of the courtroom, probably wondering how it had all happened, for he came evidently of a clean, law-abiding family.

But there was nothing in the appearance of the insolent criminal at the bar to show that he was of the same breed. He was no longer the athlete, whom " prize fighting " had inculcated with principles of manliness and fair play as well as a strong body. All that, as I had seen often before, was a pitiful lie. He was rat-eyed and soft-handed. His skin had the pastiness that comes of more exposure to the glare of vile dance halls than the sunlight of day. His black hair was slicked down; he was faultlessly tailored and his shoes had those high, bulging toes which are the extreme of Fourteenth Street fashion.

Outside, overflowing into the corridor, were gangsters, followers and friends of Dopey Jack. Only an overpowering show of force preserved the orderliness of the court from their boasting, bragging, and threats.

The work of selecting the jury began, and we watched it carefully. Kahn, cool and cunning, had evidently no idea of what Carton was holding out against him. In the panel I could see the anemic-looking fellow whom we had caught with the goods up at Farrell's. Carton's men had shadowed him and had learned of every man with whom he had spoken. As each, for some reason or other, was objected to by Carton, Kahn began to show exasperation.

At last the anemic fellow came up for examination. Kahn accepted him.

For a moment Carton seemed to fumble among his papers, without even looking at the prospective juror. Then he drew out the print which Kennedy had made. Quietly, without letting anyone else see it, he deliberately walked to Kahn's table and showed it to the lawyer, without a word, in fact without anyone else in the court knowing anything about it.

Kahn's face was a study, as he realized for the first time what it was that Carton and Kennedy had been doing that night at Farrell's. He paled. His hand shook. It was with the utmost effort that he could control his voice. He had been cornered and the yellow streak in him showed through.

In a husky voice he withdrew the juror, and Carton, in the same cold, self-possessed manner resumed his former position, not even a trace of a smile on his features.

It was all done so quickly that scarcely a soul in the court besides ourselves realized that anything had happened.

"Isn't he going to say anything about it?" I whispered to Craig.

"That will come later," was all that Kennedy replied, his eyes riveted still on Carton.

Though no one besides ourselves realized it, Carton had thrown a bombshell that had demolished the

defence.   Others noticed it, but as yet did not know
the cause.   Kahn, the great Kahn by whom all the
forces of the underworld had conjured, was completely unnerved.   Carton had fixed it so that he
could not retreat and leave the case to someone else.
He had knocked the props from under his defence
by uncannily turning down every man whom he had
any reason of suspecting of having been approached.
Then he had given Kahn just a glimpse of the evidence that hinted at what was in store for himself
personally.   Kahn was never the same after that.

Judge Pomeroy, who had been following the progress of the case attentively, threw another bombshell when he announced that he would direct that
the names of the jurors be kept secret until it was
absolutely necessary to disclose them, a most unusual proceeding designed to protect them from re-
prisals of gangmen.

At last the real trial began.   Carton had been
careful to see that none of the witnesses for the
people should be " stiffened " as the process was
elegantly expressed by those of Dopey Jack's class—
in other words, intimidated, bribed, or otherwise
rendered innocuous.   One after another, Carton
rammed home the facts of the case, the fraudulent
registration and voting, the use of the names of dead
men to pad the polling lists, the bribery of election
officials at the primaries—the whole sordid, debas-
ing story of how Dopey Jack had intimidated and
swung one entire district.

It was clever, as he presented it, with scarcely

a reference to the name of Murtha, the beneficiary of such tactics—as though, perhaps, Murtha's case was in his mind separate and would be attended to later when his turn came.

Rapidly, concisely, convincingly, Carton presented the facts. Now and then Kahn would rise to object to something as incompetent, irrelevant, and immaterial. But there was lacking something in his method. It was not the old Kahn. In fact, one almost felt that Carton was disappointed in his adversary, that he would have preferred a stiff, straight from the shoulder, stand-up fight.

Now and then we could hear a whisper circulating about among the spectators. What was the matter with Kahn? Was he ill? Gangdom was in a daze itself, little knowing the smooth stone that Carton had slung between the eyes of the great underworld Goliath of the law.

At last Carton's case was all in, and Kahn rose to present his own, a forced smile on his face.

There was an attempt at a demonstration, but Judge Pomeroy rapped sharply for order, and alert court attendants were about to nip effectively any such outburst. Still, it was enough to show the undercurrent of open defiance of the court, of law, of the people.

What it was no one but ourselves knew but Kahn was not himself. Others saw it, but did not understand. They had waited patiently through the sledge-hammer pounding of Carton, waiting expectantly for Kahn to explode a mine that would de-

molish the work of the District Attorney as if it
had been so much paper. Carton had figuratively
dampened the fuse. It sputtered, but the mine did
not explode.

Once or twice there were flashes of the old Kahn,
but for the most part he seemed to have crumpled
up. Often I thought he was not the equal of even
a police court lawyer. The spectators seemed to
know that something was wrong, though they could
not tell just what it was. Kahn's colleagues whispered among themselves. He made his points, but
they lacked the fire and dash and audacity that once
had caused the epigram that Kahn's appearance in
court indicated two things—the guilt of the accused
and a verdict of acquittal.

Even Justice Pomeroy seemed to notice it. Kahn
had tried many a case before him and the old judge
had a wholesome respect for the wiley lawyer. But
to-day the court found nothing so grave as the
strange dilatoriness of the counsel.

Once the judge had to interfere with the remark,
" I may remind the learned counsel for the defence
that the court intends to finish this case before ad-
journment for the day, if possible; if not, then we
shall sit to-night."

Kahn seemed not to grasp the situation, as he
had of old. He actually hurried up the presentation of the case, oblivious to the now black looks
that were directed at him by his own client. If he
had expected to recover his old-time equanimity as
the case proceeded, he failed. For no one better

than he knew what that little photograph of Carton's meant—disgrace, disbarment, perhaps prison itself. What was this Dopey Jack when ruin stared himself so relentlessly in the face in the person of Carton, calm and cool?

At last the summing up was concluded and both sides rested. Judge Pomeroy charged the jury, I thought with eminent fairness and impartiality, even, perhaps, glossing over some points which Kahn's weak presentation might have allowed him to make more of if Kahn had been bolder and stronger in pressing them.

The jury filed out and the anxious waiting began. On all sides was the buzz of conversation. Kahn himself sat silent, gazing for the most part at the papers before him. There must have been some wrangling of the jury, for twice hope of the gangsters revived when they sent in for the record.

But it was not over an hour later when the jury finally filed back again into their box. As Judge Pomeroy faced them and asked the usual question, the spectators hung, breathless, on the words of the foreman as the jurors stood up silently in their places.

There was a tense hush in the courtroom, as every eye was fastened on the face of the foreman.

The hush seemed to embarrass him. But finally he found his voice. Nervously, as if he were taking his own life in his hands he delivered the verdict.

" We find the defendant guilty as charged in the indictment ! "

Instantly, before anyone could move, the dignified judge faced the prisoner deliberately.

"You have heard the verdict," he said colourlessly. "I shall sentence you Friday."

Three court attendants were at Dopey Jack's side in a moment, but none too soon. The pent-up feeling of the man idolized by blackmailers, and man-killers, and batteners on street-women, who held nothing as disgrace but a sign of respect for law or remorse for capture, burst forth.

He cast one baleful look at Kahn as they hurried him to the wire-screened passageway. "It's all a frame-up—a damned frame-up!" he shouted.

As he disappeared a murmer of amazement ran through the room. The unthinkable had happened. An East Side idol had fallen.

XIV

THE BEAUTY PARLOUR

"IT seems strange," remarked Kennedy the following morning when we had met in his laboratory for our daily conference to plan our campaign,
" that although we seem to be on the right trail
we have not a word yet about Betty Blackwell herself. Carton has just telephoned that her mother,
poor woman, is worrying her heart out and is a
mere shadow of her former self."

" We must get some word," asserted Miss Kendall. " This silence is almost like the silence of
death."

" I'm afraid I shall have to impose on you that
task," said Kennedy thoughtfully to her. " There
seems to be no course open to us but to transfer
our watch from Dr. Harris to this Marie. Of
course it is too early to hear from our search by
means of the *portrait parlé*. But we have both
seen Dr. Harris and Marie enter the beauty parlour of Madame Margot. Now, I don't mean to cast
aspersions on your own good looks, Miss Kendall.
They are of the sort with which no beauty parlour
except Nature can compete."

A girl of another type than Clare would probably have read a half dozen meanings into his sin-

cere compliment. But then, I reflected that a man of another type than Craig could not have made the remark without expecting her to do so. There was a frankness between them which, I must confess, considerably relieved me. I was not prepared to lose Kennedy, even to Miss Kendall.

She smiled. "You want me to try a course in artificial beautification, don't you?"

"Yes. Walter doesn't need it, and as for me, nothing could make me a modern Adonis. Seriously, though, a man couldn't get in there, I suppose. At least that is one of the many things I want you to find out. Under the circumstances, you are the only person in whom I have confidence enough to believe that she can get at the facts there. Find out all you can about the character of the place and the people who frequent it. And if you can learn anything about that Madame Margot who runs the place, so much the better."

"I'll try," she said simply.

Kennedy resumed his tests of the powder in the packets which Dr. Harris had been distributing, and I endeavoured to make myself as little in the way as possible.

It was not until the close of the afternoon that a taxicab drove up and deposited Miss Kendall at the door.

"What luck?" greeted Kennedy eagerly, as she entered. "Do you feel thoroughly beautified?"

"Don't make me smile," she replied, as she swept in with an air that would have done credit to the star in a comic opera. " I'd hate to crack or even crease the enamel on my face. I've been steamed and frozen, beaten and painted and——"

" I'm sorry to have been the cause of such cruel and unusual punishment," apologized Craig.

" No, indeed. Why, I enjoyed it. Let me tell you about the place."

She leaned against the laboratory table, certainly an incongruous picture in her new rôle as contrasted with the stained and dirty background of paraphernalia of medico-legal investigation. I could not help feeling that if Clare Kendall ever had decided to go in for such things, Marie herself would have had to look sharp to her laurels.

" As you enter the place," she began, " you feel a delightful warmth and there is an odour of attar of roses in the air. There are thick half-inch carpets that make walking a pleasure and dreamy Sleepy Hollow rockers that make it an impossibility. It is all very fascinating.

" There are dull-green lattices, little gateways with roses, white enamel with cute little diamond panes of glass for windows, inviting bowers of artificial flowers and dim yellow lights. It makes you feel like a sybarite just to see it. It's a cosmetic Arcadia for that fundamental feminine longing for beauty.

" Well, first there are the little dressing-rooms, each with a bed, a dresser and mirror, and everything in such good taste. After you leave them you go to a white, steamy room and there they bake you.

It's a long process of gentle showers, hot and cold, after that, and massage.

"I thought I was through. But it seems that I had only just started. There was a battery of white manicure tables, and then the hairdressers and the artists who lay on these complexions—what do you think of mine? I can't begin to tell all the secrets of the curls and puffs, and reënforcements, hygienic rolls, transformations, fluffy puffers, and all that, or of the complexions. Why, you can choose a complexion, like wall-paper or upholstery. They can make you as pale as a sickly heroine or they can make you as yellow as a bathing girl. There is nothing they can't do. I asked just for fun. I could have come out as dusky as a gipsy.

"They tried electrolysis on my eyebrows, and one attendant suggested a hypodermic injection of perfume. Ever hear of that? She thought ' new mown hay ' was the best to saturate the skin with. Then another suggested, as long as I had chosen this moonbeam make-up, that perhaps I'd like a couple of dimples. They could make them permanent or lasting only a few hours. I declined. But there is nothing so wild that they haven't either thought of themselves or imported from Paris or somewhere else. I heard them discussing someone who wanted odd eyes—made by pouring in certain liquids. They don't seem to care how they affect sight, hearing, skin, or health. It is decoration run mad."

"How about the people there? " asked Kennedy.

"Oh, I must tell you about that. There's so much to tell, I hardly know where to begin—or stop. I saw some flashy people. You know one customer attracts her friends and so on. There is every class there from the demi-monde up to actresses and really truly society. And they have things for all prices from the comparatively cheap to the most extravagant. They're very accommodating and, in a way, democratic."

"Did it seem—straight?" asked Kennedy.

"On the surface, yes, as far as I could judge. But I'll have to go back again for that. For instance, there was one thing that seemed queer to me. I had finished the steaming and freezing and was resting. A maid brought a tray of cigarettes, those dainty little thin ones with gilt tips. There seemed to be several kinds. I managed to try some of them. One at least I know was doped, although I only had a whiff of it. I think after they got to know you they'd serve anything from a cocktail in a teacup to the latest fads. I am sure that I saw one woman taking some veronal in her coffee."

"Veronal?" commented Craig. "Then that may be where Dr. Harris comes in."

"Partly, I think. I've got to find out more about what is hidden there. Once I heard a man's voice and I know it was Dr. Harris's."

"Harris! Why, the elevator boy at the Montmartre said he was painting the town," I observed.

"I don't believe it. I think he has all he can do keeping up with the beauty shop. You see, it is

more than a massage parlour. They do real deco-
rative surgery, as it is called. They'll engage to
give you a new skin as soft and pink as a baby's.
Or they will straighten a nose, or turn an ear. They
have light treatment for complexions—the ruby ray,
the violet ray, the phosphorescent ray.

"You would laugh at the fake science that is
being handed out to those gullible fools. They can
get rid of freckles and superfluous hair, of course.
But they'll even tell you that they can change your
mouth and chin, your eyes, your cheeks. I should
be positively afraid of some of their electrical appliances there. They sweat down your figure or build
it up—just as you please.

"Oh, no one need be plain in these days, not as
long as Madame Margot's exists. That is where
I think Dr. Harris comes in. He can pose as a
full-fledged, blown-in-the-bottle cosmetic surgeon.
I'll bet there is no limit to the agonized beautification that they can put you through if they think
they can play you for a sucker."

"By the way, did you see Madame Margot herself?" asked Craig.

"No. I made all sorts of discreet inquiries after
her, but they seemed to know nothing. The nearest
I could get was a hint from one of the girls that
she was away. But I'll tell you whom I think I
heard, talking to the man whose voice sounded like
Dr. Harris's, and that was Marie. Of course I
couldn't see, but in the part of the shop that looks
like a fake hospital I heard two voices and I would

wager that Marie is going through some of this beautification herself. Of course she is. You remember how artificial she looked? "

" Did you see anyone else? "

" Oh, yes. You know the place is two doors from the Montmartre. Well, I think they have some connection with that place between them and the Montmartre. Anyhow it looks as if they did, for after I had been there a little while a girl came in, apparently from nowhere. She was the girl we saw paying money to Ike the Dropper, you remember—the one none of us recognized? There's something in that next house, and she seems to have charge of it."

" Well, you have done a good day's work," complimented Kennedy.

" I feel that I have made a start, anyhow," she admitted. " There is a lot yet to be learned of Margot's. You remember it was early in the day that I was there. I want to go back sometime in the afternoon or evening."

" Dr. Harris is apparently the oracle on beauty," mused Kennedy.

" Yes. He must make a lot of money there."

" They must have some graft, though, besides the beauty parlour," went on Kennedy. " They wouldn't be giving up money to Ike the Dropper if that was all there was."

" No, and that is where the doped cigarette comes in. That is why I want to go again. I imagine it's like the Montmartre. They have to know you and

13

think you are all right before you get the real inside
of the place."

" I don't doubt it."

" I can't go around looking like a chorus girl,"
remarked Miss Kendall finally, with a glance at a
little mirror she carried in her bag. " I'm afraid
you'll have to excuse me until I get rid of this beautification."

The telephone rang sharply.

As Kennedy answered, we gathered that it was
Carton. A few minutes of conversation, mostly on
Carton's part, followed. Kennedy hung up the re-
ceiver with an exclamation of vexation.

" I'm afraid I did wrong to start anything with
the *portrait parlé* yet," he said. " Why, this thing
we are investigating has so many queer turns that
you hardly know whom to trust."

" What do you mean?"

" I don't know who could have given the thing
away, but Carton says it wasn't an hour after the
inquiries began about Marie that it became known
in the underworld that she was being looked for in
this way. Oh, they are clever, those grafters. They
have all sorts of ways of keeping in touch. I suppose they remember they had one experience with
the *portrait parlé* and it has made them as wary
as a burglar is over finger-prints. Carton tells me
that Marie has disappeared."

" I could swear I heard her or someone at Margot's," said Clare.

" And Harris has disappeared. Of course you

thought you overheard him, too. But you may have been mistaken."

" Why ? "

" As nearly as Carton can find out," said Kennedy quickly, " Marie is Madame Margot herself."

XV

THE PHANTOM CIRCUIT

"I WANT to go to Margot's again to-day," volunteered Miss Kendall the following morning, adding with a smile, "You see, I've got the habit. Really, though, there is a mystery about that place that fascinates me. I want to find out more about this Marie, or Margot, or whoever it was that I thought I heard there. And then those doped cigarettes interest me. You see, I haven't forgotten what you said about dope the first time we talked about Dr. Harris. They will be more free with me, too, now that I am no longer a stranger."

"That is a good idea," agreed Kennedy, who was now chafing under the enforced inaction of the case. "I hope that this time they will let you into some of the secrets. There is one thing, though, I wish you'd look out for especially."

"What do you mean?" she asked.

"I should like to know what ways there are of communicating with the outside. You realize, of course, that it is very easy for them, if they come to suspect you, to frame up something in a place like that. There are strong-arm women as well as men, and I'm not at all sure that there may not be some men besides Dr. Harris who are acquainted

with that place. At any rate Dr. Harris is unscrupulous enough himself."

"I shall make it a point to observe that," she
said as she left us. "I hope I'll have something
to tell you when I come back."

"Walter," remarked Craig as the door closed,
"that is one of the gamest girls I ever knew."

I looked across at him inquiringly.

"Don't worry, my boy," he added, reading my
expression. "She's not of the marrying kind, any
more than I am."

The morning passed and half of the afternoon
without any word from Miss Kendall. Kennedy
was plainly becoming uneasy, when a hurried footstep in the hall was followed by a more hurried
opening of the door.

"Let me sit down, just a minute, to collect myself," panted Miss Kendall, pressing her hands to
her temples where the blue veins stood out and literally throbbed. "I'm all in."

"Why, what is the matter?" asked Kennedy,
placing a chair and switching on an electric fan,
while he quickly found a bottle of restorative salts
which was always handy for emergencies in the
laboratory.

"Oh—such a time as I've had! Wait—let me
see whether I can recollect it in order."

A few minutes later she resumed. "I went in,
as before. There seemed to be quite a change in
the way they treated me. I must have made a good
impression the first time. A second visit seemed

to have opened the way for everything. Evidently they think I am all right.

"Well, I went through much the same thing as I did before, only I tried to make it not quite so elaborate, down to the point where several of us were sitting in loose robes in the lounging-room. That was the part, you know, that interested me before.

"The maid came in with the cigarettes and I smoked one of the doped ones. They watch everything that you do so closely there, and the moment I smoked one they offered me another. I don't know what was in them, but I fancy there must be just a trace of opium. They made me feel exhilarated, then just a bit drowsy. I managed to make away with the second without inhaling much of the smoke, for my head was in a whirl by this time. It wasn't so much that I was afraid I couldn't take care of myself as it was that I was afraid that it would blunt the keenness of my observation and I might miss something."

"Besides the cigarettes, was there anything else?" asked Craig.

"Yes, indeed. I didn't see anyone there I recognized, but I heard some of them talk. One was taking a little veronal; another said something about heroin. It was high-toned hitting the pipe, if you call it that—a Turkish bath, followed by massage, and then a safe complement of anything you wanted, taken leisurely by these aristocratic dope fiends.

"There was one woman there who I am sure was

snuffing cocaine. She had a little gold and enamelled box like a snuff box beside her from which she would take from time to time a pinch of some white crystals and inhale it vigorously, now and then taking a little sip of a liqueur that was brought in to her."

"That's the way," observed Kennedy. "There are always a considerable number of inhuman beings who are willing to make capital out of the weaknesses of others. This illicit sale of cocaine is one example. Such conditions have existed with the opium products a long time. Now it seems to be the ' coke fiend.' "

"I was glad I did just as I did," resumed Clare, "because it wasn't long before I saw that the thing to do was to feign drowsiness. A maid came over to me and in a most plausible and insinuating way hinted that perhaps I might feel like resting and that if the noise in the beauty parlour annoyed me, they had the entire next house—the one next to the Montmartre, you know—which had been fitted up as a dormitory."

"You didn't go?" cut in Craig immediately.

"I did not. I pleaded an engagement. Why, the place is a regular dope joint."

"Exactly. I suspected as much as you went along. Everything seems to have moved uptown lately, to have been veneered over to meet the fastidious second decade of the twentieth century. But underneath it all are the same old vices. I'm glad you didn't attempt to go into the next house. Anyhow, now we are certain about the character of the place. Did you notice anything about the means of communicating with the outside—the telephones, for instance?"

Miss Kendall was evidently feeling much better now.

"Oh, yes," she answered. "I took particular care to observe that. They have a telephone, but there is a girl who attends to it, although they don't really need one. She listens to everything. Then, too, in the other house—— You remember I spoke about the girl whom we saw paying Ike the Dropper? It seems that she has a similar position at the telephone over there."

"So they have two telephones," repeated Craig.

"Yes."

"Good. There are always likely to be some desperate characters in places like that. If we ever have anyone go into that dope joint we must have some way of keeping in touch and protecting the person."

Miss Kendall had gone home for a few hours of rest after her exciting experience. Craig was idly tapping with his fingers on the broad arm of his chair.

Suddenly he jumped up. "I'm going up there to look that joint over from the outside," he announced.

We walked past the front of it without seeing anything in particular, then turned the corner and were on the Avenue. Kennedy paused and looked at a cheap apartment house on which was a sign, "Flats to Let."

"I think I'll get the janitor to show me one of them," he said.

One was on the first floor in the rear. Kennedy did not seem to be very much interested in the rent. A glance out of the window sufficed to show him that he could see the back of the Montmartre and some of the houses. It took only a minute to hire it, at least conditionally, and a bill to the janitor gave us a key.

"What are you going to do?"

"We can't do anything just yet, but it will be dark by the time I get over to the laboratory and back and then we can do something."

That night we started prowling over the back fences down the street. Fortunately it was a very black night and Craig was careful not to use even the electric bull's-eye which he had brought over from the laboratory together with some wire and telephone instruments.

As we crouched in the shadow of one of the fences, he remarked: "Just as I expected; the telephone wires run along the tops of the fences. Here's where they run into 72—that's the beauty parlour. These run into 70—that's the dope joint. Then next comes the Montmartre itself, reaching all the way back as far as the lot extends."

We had come up close to the backs of the houses by this time. The shades were all drawn and the blinds were closed in both of them, so that we had really nothing to fear provided we kept quiet. Besides the back yards looked unkempt, as if no one cared much about them.

Kennedy flashed the electric bull's-eye momentarily on the wires. They branched off from the back fence down the party fence to the houses, both sets on one fence.

"Good!" he exclaimed. "It is better than I hoped. The two sets go on up to the first floor together, then separate. One set goes into the beauty parlour; the other into the dope joint."

Craig had quietly climbed up on a shed over the basements of both the houses. He was working quickly with all the dexterity of a lineman. To two of the four wires he had attached one other. Then to two others he attached another, all the connections being made at exactly corresponding points.

The next step was to lead these two newly connected wires to a window on the first floor of the house next to the Montmartre. He fastened them lightly to the closed shutter, let himself down to the yard again and we beat a slow and careful retreat to our flat.

In one of the yards down near the corner, however, he paused. Here was an iron box fastened to one of the fences, a switch box or something of the sort belonging to the telephone company. To it were led all the wires from the various houses on the block and to each wire was fastened a little ticket on which was scrawled in indelible pencil the number of the house to which the wire ran.

Kennedy found the two pairs that ran to 70 and 72, cut in on them in the same way that he had done before and fastened two other wires, one to each pair. This pair he led along and into the flat.

"I've fixed it," he explained, "so that anyone who can get into that room on the back of the first floor of the dope joint can communicate with the outside very easily over the telephone, without being overheard, either."

"How?" I asked completely mystified by the apparent simplicity of the proceeding.

"I have left two wires sticking on the outside shutter of that room," he replied. "All that anyone who gets into that room has to do is to open the window softly, reach out and secure them. With them fastened to a transmitter which I have, he can talk to me in the flat around the corner and no one will ever know it."

There was nothing more that we could do that night and we waited impatiently until Clare Kendall came to make her daily report in the morning.

"The question is, whom are we going to get whom we can trust to go to that dope joint and explore it?" remarked Kennedy, after we had finished telling Miss Kendall about our experiences of the night before.

"Carton must have someone who can take a course in beauty and dope," I replied. "Or perhaps Miss Kendall has one of her investigators whom she can trust."

"If the thing gets too rough," added Craig,

" whoever is in there can telephone to us, if she will only be careful first to get that back room in the ' dormitory,' as they call it. Then all we'll have to do will be to jump in there and——"

" I'll do it," interrupted Clare.

" No, Miss Kendall," denied Kennedy firmly.

" Let me do it. There is no one whom I can trust more than myself. Besides, I know the places now."

She said it with an air of quiet determination, as if she had been thinking it over ever since she returned from her visit of the day before.

Kennedy and Miss Kendall faced each other for a moment. It was evident that it was against just this that he had been trying to provide. On her part it was equally evident that she had made up her mind.

" Miss Kendall," said Kennedy, meeting her calm eye, " you are the most nervy detective, barring none, that it has ever been my pleasure to meet. I yield under protest."

I must say that it was with a great deal of misgiving that I saw Clare enter Margot's. We had gone as far as the corner with her, had watched her go in, and then hurried into the unfurnished apartment which Craig had rented on the Avenue.

As we sat on the rickety chairs which we had borrowed from the janitor under pretence of wanting to reach something, the minutes that passed seemed like hours.

I wondered what had happened to the plucky girl in her devotion to the cause in which she had enlisted, and several times I could see from the expression of Craig's face that he more and more regretted that he had given in to her and had allowed her to go, instead of adhering to his original plan. From what she had told us about the two places, I tried to imagine what she was doing, but each time I ended by having an increased feeling of apprehension.

Kennedy sat grimly silent with the receiver of the telephone glued to his ear, straining his hearing to catch even the faintest sound.

At last his face brightened.

"She's there all right," he exclaimed to me. "Managed to make them think in the beauty parlour that she was a dope fiend and pretty far gone. Insisted that she must have the back room on the first floor because she was afraid of fire. She kept the door open so that she would not miss anything, but it was a long time before she got a chance to reach out of the window and get the wires and connect them with the instruments I gave her. But it's all right now.

"Yes, Miss Kendall, right here, listening to everything you get a chance to say. Only be careful. There is no use spoiling the game by trying to talk to me until you have all that you think you can obtain in the way of evidence. Don't let them think you have any means of communication with the outside or they'll go to any length to silence you. We'll be here all the time and the moment you think there is any danger, call us."

Kennedy seemed visibly relieved by the message.

"She says that she has found out a great deal already, but didn't dare take the time to tell it just yet," he explained. "By the way, Walter, while we are waiting, I wish you would go out and see whether there is a policeman on fixed post anywhere around here."

Five minutes later when I returned, having located the nearest peg post a long block away on Broadway, Kennedy raised a warning hand. She was telephoning again.

"She says that attendants come and go in her room so often that it's hard to get a chance to say anything, but she is sure that there is someone hidden there, perhaps Marie or Madame Margot, whoever she is, or it may even be Betty Blackwell. They watch very closely."

"But," I asked, almost in a whisper, as if someone over there might hear me, "isn't this a very dangerous proceeding, Craig? It seems to me you are taking long chances. Suppose one of the telephone girls in either house, whom she told us keep such sharp watch over the wires, should happen to be calling up or answering a call. She would hear someone else talking over the wire and it wouldn't be difficult for her to decide who it was. Then there'd be a row."

"Not a chance," smiled Kennedy. "No one except ourselves, not even Central, can hear a word of what is said over these connections I have made. This is what is called a phantom circuit."

" A phantom circuit? " I repeated.   " What kind of a weird thing is that? "

" It is possible to superimpose another circuit over the four telephone wires of two existing circuits, making a so-called phantom line," he explained, as we waited for the next message.   " It seems fantastic at first, but it is really in accordance with the laws of electricity.   You use each pair of wires as if it were one wire and do not interfere in the least with them, but are perfectly independent of both. The current for the third circuit enters the two wires of one of the first circuits, divides, reunites, so to speak, at the other end, then returns through the wires of the second circuit, dividing and reuniting again, thus just balancing the two divisions of the current and not causing any effect on either of the two original circuits.   Rather wonderful, isn't it? "

" I should say that it was," I marvelled.   " I am glad I see it actually working rather than have to believe it second hand."

" It's all due to a special repeating coil of high efficiency absolutely balanced as to resistances, number of turns of wire, and so on which I have used—— Yes—Miss Kendall—we are here.   Now please don't let things go on too far.   At the first sign of danger, call.   We can get in all right.   You have the evidence now that will hold in any court as far as closing up that joint goes, and I'll take a chance of breaking into—well, Hades, to get to you. Good-bye.

"I guess it is Hades there," he resumed to me. "She has just telephoned that one of the dope fiends upstairs—a man, so that you see they admit both men and women there, after all—had become violent and Harris had to be called to quiet him before he ran amuck. She said she was absolutely sure, this time at least, that it was Harris. As I was saying about this phantom circuit, it is used a good deal now. Sometimes they superimpose a telephone conversation over the proper arrangement of telegraph messages and *vice versa.*

"What's that?" cried Craig, suddenly breaking off. "They heard you talking that last time, and you have locked the door against them? They are battering it down? Move something heavy, if you can, up against it—the bureau, anything to brace it. We'll be there directly. Come on, Walter. There isn't time to get around Broadway for that fixed post cop. We must do it ourselves. Hurry."

Craig dashed breathlessly out on the street. I followed closely.

"Hurry," he panted. "Those people haven't any use for anyone that they think will snitch on them."

As we turned the corner, we ran squarely into a sergeant slowly going his rounds with eyes conveniently closed to what he was paid not to see.

Kennedy stopped and grabbed his arm.

"There's a girl up here in 72 who is being mistreated," he cried. "Come. You must help us get her out."

" Aw, g'wan. Whatyer givin' us? 72? That's a residence."

" Say—look here. I've got your number. You'll be up on the most serious charges of your whole career if you don't act on the information I have. All of Ike the Dropper's money 'll go for attorney's fees and someone will land in Sing Sing. Now, come ! "

We had gained the steps of the house. Outside all was dark, blank, and bare. There was every evidence of the most excessive outward order and decency—not a sign of the conflict that was raging within.

Before the policeman could pull the bell, which would have been a first warning of trouble to the inmates, Kennedy had jumped from the high stoop to a narrow balcony running along the front windows of the first story, had smashed the glass into splinters with a heavy object which he had carried concealed under his coat, and was engaged in a herculean effort to wrench apart some iron bars which had been carefully concealed behind the discreetly drawn shades.

As one yielded, he panted, " No use to try the door. The grill work inside guards that too well. There goes another."

Inside now we could hear cries that told us that the whole house was roused, that even the worst of the drug fiends had come at least partly to his senses and begun to realize his peril. From Margot's beauty parlour a couple of girls and a man

14

staggered forth in a vain effort to seem to leave quietly.

"Close that place, too, officer," cried Kennedy to the now astounded policeman. "We'll attend to this house."

The sergeant slowly lumbered across in time to let two more couples escape. It was evident that he hated the job; indeed, would have arrested Kennedy in the old days before Carton had thrown such a scare into the grafters. But Kennedy's assurance had flabbergasted him and he obeyed.

Another bar yielded, and another. Together we squeezed in and found ourselves in a dark front parlour. There was nothing to distinguish it from any ordinary reception room in the blackness.

Hurried footsteps were heard as if several people were retreating into the next house. Down the hall we hastened to the back room.

A second we listened. All was silent. Was Clare safe? It looked ominous. Still the door, partly battered in, was closed.

"Miss Kendall!" called Craig, bending down close to the door.

"Is it you, Professor Kennedy?" came back a faint voice from the other side.

"Yes. Are you all right?"

There was no answer, but she was evidently tugging at something which appeared to be a heavy piece of furniture braced against the door. At last the bolt was slipped back, and there in the doorway she swayed, half exhausted but safe.

" Yes, all right," murmured Clare, bracing herself against the chiffonier which she had moved away from the door, " just a little shaky from the drugs—but all right. Don't bother about me, now. I can take care of myself. I'll feel better in a minute. Upstairs—that is where I think that woman is. Please, please don't—I'm all right—truly. Upstairs."

Kennedy had taken her gently by the arm and she sank down in an easy chair.

" Please hurry," she implored. " You may be too late."

She had risen again in spite of us and was out in the lower hall. We could hear a footstep on the stairs.

" There she goes, the woman who has been hiding up there, Madame——"

Clare cut the words short.

A woman had hastily descended the steps, evidently seeing her opportunity to escape while we were in the back of the house. She had reached the street door, which now was open, and the flaming arc light in front of the house shone brightly on her.

I looked, expecting to see our dark-haired, oliveskinned Marie. I stared in amazement. Instead, this woman was fair, her hair was flaxen, her figure more slim, even her features were different. She was a stranger. I could not recollect ever having seen her.

Again I strained my eyes, thinking it might be

Betty Blackwell at last, but this woman bore no re-
semblance apparently to her. She looked older,
more mature.

In my haste I noted that she had a bandage about
her face, as if she had been injured recently, for
there seemed to be blood on it where it had worked
itself loose in her flight. She gave one glance at
us, and quickened her pace at seeing us so close.
The bandage, already loose, slipped off her face
and fell to the floor. Still she did not seem other
than a stranger to me, though I had a half-formed
notion that I had seen that face somewhere before.
She did not stop to pick the bandage up. She had
gained the door and was down the front step on
the sidewalk before we could stop her.

Taxicabs in droves seemed to have collected, like
buzzards over a dead body. They were doing a
thriving business carrying away those who sought
to escape. Into one by which a man was waiting
in the shadow the woman hurried. The man looked
for all the world like Dr. Harris. An instant later
the chauffeur was gone.

The policeman had the front door of Madame
Margot's covered all right, so efficiently that he was
neglecting everything else. From the basement now
and then a scurrying figure catapulted itself out and
was lost in the curious crowd that always collects
at any time of day or night on a New York street
when there is any excitement.

" It is of no use to expect to capture anyone
now," exclaimed Craig, as we hurried back into the

dope joint. "I hardly expected to do it. All I wanted was to protect Miss Kendall. But we have the evidence against this joint that will close it for good."

He stooped and picked up the bandage.

"I think I'll keep that," he remarked thoughtfully. "I wonder what that blonde woman wore that for?"

"She *must* be up there," reiterated Clare, who had followed us. "I heard them talking, it seemed to me only the moment before I heard you in the hall."

The excitement seemed now to have the effect of quieting her unstrung nerves and carrying her through.

"Let us go upstairs," said Kennedy.

From room to room we hurried in the darkness, lighting the lights. They were all empty, yet each one gave its mute testimony to the character of its use and its former occupants. There were opium layouts with pipes, lamps, *yen haucks,* and other paraphernalia in some. In others had been cocaine snuffers. There seemed to be everything for drug users of every kind.

At last in a small room in front on the top floor we came upon a girl, half insensible from a drug. She was vainly trying to make herself presentable for the street, ramblingly talking to herself in the meantime.

Again my hopes rose that we had found either the mysterious Marie Margot or Betty Blackwell. A second glance caused us all to pause in surprise and disappointment.

It was the Titian-haired girl from the Montmartre office.

Miss Kendall, recovering from the effects of the drugs which she had been compelled to take in her heroic attempt to get at the dope joint, was endeavouring to quiet the girl from the Montmartre, who, now vaguely recollecting us, seemed to realize that something had gone wrong and was trembling and crying pitifully.

" What's the matter with her? " I asked.

" Chloral," replied Miss Kendall in a low voice aside. " I suppose she has had a wild night which she has followed by chloral to quiet her nerves, with little effect. Didn't you ever see them? They will go into a drug store in this part of the city where such things are sold, weak, shaky, nervous wrecks. The clerk will sell them the stuff and they will retire for a moment into the telephone booth. Sometimes they will come out looking as though they had never felt a moment's effect from their wild debauches. But there are other times when they are too weakened to get over it so quickly. That is her case, poor girl."

The soothing hand which she laid on the girl's throbbing head was quite in contrast with the manner in which I recalled her to have spoken of the girl when first we saw her at the Montmartre. She must have seen the look of surprise on my face.

" I can't condemn these girls too strongly when

I see them themselves," she remarked. "It would be so easy for them to stop and lead a decent life, if they only would forget the white lights and the gay life that allures them. It is when they are so down and out that I long to give them a hand to help them up again and show them how foolish it is to make slaves of themselves."

"Call a cab, Walter," said Kennedy, who had been observing the girl closely. "There is nothing more that we can expect to accomplish here. Everybody has escaped by this time. But we must get this poor girl in a private hospital or sanitarium where she can recover."

Clare had disappeared. A moment later she returned from the room she had had downstairs with her hat on.

"I'm going with her," she announced simply.

"What—you, Miss Kendall?"

"Yes. If a girl ever needed a friend, it is this girl now. There is nothing I can do for the moment. I will take care of her in my apartment until she is herself again."

The girl seemed to half understand, and to be grateful to Clare. Kennedy watched her hovering over the drug victim without attempting to express the admiration which he felt.

Just as the cab was announced, he drew Miss Kendall aside. "You're a trump," he said frankly. "Most people would pass by on the other side from such as she is."

They talked for a moment as to the best place to

go, then decided on a quiet little place uptown where convalescents were taken in.

" I think you can still be working on the case, if you care to do so," suggested Craig as Miss Kendall and her charge were leaving.

" How? " she asked.

" When you get her to this sanitarium, try to be with her as much as you can. I think if anyone can get anything out of her, you can. Remember it is more than this girl's rescue that is at stake. If she can be got to talk she may prove an important link toward piecing together the solution of the mystery of Betty Blackwell. She must know many of the inside secrets of the Montmartre," he added significantly.

They had gone, and Craig and I had started to go also when we came across a negro caretaker who seemed to have stuck by the place during all the excitement.

" Do you know that girl who just went out? " asked Craig.

" No, sah," she replied glibly.

" Look here," demanded Craig, facing her. " You know better than that. She has been here before, and you know it. I've a good mind to have you held for being in charge of this place. If I do, all the Marie Margots and Ike the Droppers can't get you out again."

The negress seemed to understand that this was no ordinary raid.

" Who is she? " demanded Craig.

" I dunno, sah. She come from next door."

" I know she did. She's the girl in the office of the Montmartre. Now, you know her. What is her name ? "

The negress seemed to consider a moment, then quickly answered, " Dey always calls her Miss Sybil here, sah, Sybil Seymour, sah."

" Thank you. I knew you had some name for her. Come, Walter. This is over for the present. A raid without arrests, too ! It will be all over town in half an hour. If we are going to do anything it must be done quickly."

We called on Carton and lost no time in having the men he could spare placed in watching the railroads and steamship lines to prevent if we could any of the gang from getting out of the city that way. It was a night of hard work with no results. I began to wonder whether they might not have escaped finally after all. There seemed to be no trace. Harris had disappeared, there was no clue to Marie Margot, no trace of the new blonde woman, not a syllable yet about Betty Blackwell.

XVI

THE SANITARIUM

"IT seems as if the forces of Dorgan are de-moralized," I remarked the afternoon after the raid on Margot's.

" We have them on the run—that's true," agreed Kennedy, " but there's plenty of fight in them, yet. We're not through, by any means."

Still, the lightning swiftness of Carton's attack had taken their breath away, temporarily, at least. Already he had started proceedings to disbar Kahn, as well as to prosecute him in the courts. According to the reports that came to us Murtha himself seemed dazed at the blow that had fallen. Some of our informants asserted that he was drinking heavily; others denied it. Whatever it was, however, Murtha was changed.

As for Dorgan, he was never much in the lime-light anyhow and was less so now than ever. He preferred to work through others, while he himself kept in the background. He had never held any but a minor office, and that in the beginning of his career. Interviews and photographs he eschewed as if forbidden by his political religion. Since the discovery of the detectaphone in his suite at Gas-tron's he had had his rooms thoroughly overhauled,

lest by any chance there might be another of the
magic little instruments concealed in the very walls,
and having satisfied himself that there was not, he
instituted a watch of private detectives to prevent
a repetition of the unfortunate incident.

Whoever it was who had obtained the Black Book
was keeping very quiet about it, and I imagined
that it was being held up as a sort of sword of
Damocles, dangling over his head, until such time
as its possessor chose to strike the final blow. Of
course, we did not and could not know what was
going on behind the scenes with the Silent Boss, what
drama was being enacted between Dorgan and the
Wall Street group, headed by Langhorne. Langhorne himself was inscrutable. I had heard that
Dorgan had once in an unguarded moment expressed
a derogatory opinion of the social leanings of Langhorne. But that was in the days before Dorgan
had acquired a country place on Long Island and
a taste for golf and expensive motors. Now, in his
way, Dorgan was quite as fastidious as any of those
he had once affected to despise. It amused Langhorne. But it had not furthered his ambitions of
being taken into the inner circle of Dorgan's confidence. Hence, I inferred, this bitter internecine
strife within the organization itself.

Whatever was brewing inside the organization, I
felt that we should soon know, for this was the day
on which Justice Pomeroy had announced he would
sentence Dopey Jack.

It was a very different sort of crowd that overflowed the courtroom that morning from that which had so boldly flocked to the trial as if it were to make a Roman holiday of justice.

The very tone was different. There was a tense look on many a face, as if the owner were asking himself the question, " What are we coming to ? If this can happen to Dopey Jack, what might not happen to me ? "

Even the lawyers were changed. Kahn, as a result of the proceedings that Carton had instituted, had yielded the case to another, perhaps no better than himself, but wiser, after the fact. Instead of demanding anything, as a sort of prescriptive right, the new attorney actually adopted the unheard of measure of appealing to the clemency of the court. The shades of all the previous bosses and gangsters must have turned in disgust at the unwonted sight. But certain it was that no one could see the relaxation of a muscle on the face of Justice Pomeroy as the lawyer proceeded with his specious plea. He heard Carton, also, in the same impassive manner, as in a few brief and pointed sentences he ripped apart the sophistries of his opponent.

The spectators fairly held their breath as the prisoner now stood before the tribune of justice.

" Jack Rubano," he began impressively, " you have been convicted by twelve of your peers—so the law looks on them, although the fact is that any honest man is immeasurably your superior. Even before that, Rubano, the District Attorney having looked into all the facts surrounding this charge had come to the conclusion that the evidence was sufficiently strong to convict you. You were convicted in his mind. In my mind, of course, there could be no prejudgment. But now that a jury has found you guilty, I may say that you have a record that is more than enough to disgrace a man twice your age. True, you have never been punished. But this is not the time or place for me to criticise my colleagues on the bench for letting you off. Others of your associates have served terms in prison for things no whit worse than you have done repeatedly. I shall be glad to meet some of them at this bar in the near future."

The justice paused, then extended a long, lean accusatory finger out from the rostrum at the gangster. "Rubano," he concluded, "your crime is particularly heinous—debauching the very foundations of the state—the elections. I sentence you to not less than three nor more than five years in State's prison, at hard labour."

There was an audible gasp in the big courtroom, as the judge snapped shut his square jaw, bull-dog fashion. It was as though he had snapped the backbone of the System.

The prisoner was hurried from the room before there was a chance for a demonstration. It was unnecessary, however. It seemed as if all the jaunty bravado of the underworld was gone out of it. Slowly the crowd filed out, whispering.

Dopey Jack, Murtha's right-hand man, had been sentenced to State's prison!

Outside the courtroom Carton received an ovation. As quickly as he could, he escaped from the newspapermen, and Kennedy was the first to grasp his hand.

But the most pleasing congratulation came from Miss Ashton, who had dropped in with two or three friends from the Reform League.

" I'm so glad, Mr. Carton—for your sake," she added very prettily, with just a trace of heightened colour in her cheeks and eyes that showed her sincere pleasure at the outcome of the case. " And then, too," she went on, " it may have some bearing on the case of that girl who has disappeared. So far, no one seems to have been able to find a trace of her. She just seems to have dropped out as if she had been spirited away."

" We must find her," returned Carton, thanking her for her good wishes in a manner which he had done to none of the rest of us, and in fact forgetful now that any of us were about. " I shall start right in on Dopey Jack to see if I can get anything out of him, although I don't think he is one that will prove a squealer in any way. I hope we can have something to report soon."

Others were pressing around him and Miss Ashton moved away, although I thought his handshakes were perhaps a little less cordial after she had gone.

I turned once to survey the crowd and down the gallery, near a pillar I saw Langhorne, his eyes turned fixedly in our direction, and a deep scowl on his face. Evidently he had no relish for the proceedings, at least that part in which Carton had just figured, whatever his personal feelings may have been toward the culprit. A moment later he saw me looking at him, turned abruptly and walked toward the stone staircase that led down to the main floor. But I could not get that scowl out of my mind as I watched his tall, erect figure stalking away.

Neither Murtha, nor, of course, Dorgan, were there, though I knew that they had many emissaries present who would report to them every detail of what had happened, down perhaps to the congratulations of Miss Ashton. Somehow, I could not get out of my head a feeling that she would afford them, in some way, a point of attack on Carton and that the unscrupulous organization would stop at nothing in order to save its own life and ruin his.

Carton had not only his work at the District Attorney's office to direct, but some things to clear up at the Reform League headquarters, as well as a campaign speech to make.

"I'm afraid I shan't be able to see much of you, to-day," he apologized to Kennedy, "but you're going to Miss Ashton's suffrage evening and dance, aren't you?"

"I should like to go," temporized Kennedy.

Carton glanced about to see whether there was anyone in earshot. "I think you had better go," he added. "She has secured a promise from Langhorne to be there, as well as several of the organization leaders. It is a thoroughly non-partisan affair—and she can get them all together. You know the organization is being educated. When people of the prominence of the Ashtons take up suffrage and make special requests to have certain persons come to a thing like that, they can hardly refuse. In fact, no one commits himself to anything by being present, whereas, absence might mean hostility, and there are lots of the women in the organization that believe in suffrage, now. Yes, we'd better go. It will be a chance to observe some people we want to watch."

"We'll go," agreed Kennedy. "Can't we all go together?"

"Surely," replied Carton, gratified, I could see, by having succeeded in swelling the crowd that would be present and thus adding to the success of Miss Ashton's affair. "Drop into the office here, and I'll be ready. Good-bye—and thanks for your aid, both of you."

We left the Criminal Courts Building with the crowd that was slowly dispersing, still talking over the unexpected and unprecedented end of the trial.

As we paused on the broad flight of steps that led down to the street on this side, Kennedy jogged my elbow, and, following his eyes, I saw a woman, apparently alone, just stepping into a town car at the curb.

There was something familiar about her, but her face was turned from me and I could not quite place her.

"Mrs. Ogleby," Kennedy remarked. "I didn't

see her in the courtroom. She must have been there, though, or perhaps outside in the corridor. Evidently she felt some interest in the outcome of the case."

He had caught just a glimpse of her face and now that he pronounced her name I recognized her, though I should not have otherwise.

The car drove off with the rattle of the changing gears into high speed, before we had a chance to determine whether it was otherwise empty or not.

" Why was she here? " I asked.

Kennedy shook his head, but did not venture a reply to the question that was in his own mind. I felt that it must have something to do with her fears regarding the Black Book. Had she, too, surmised that Murtha had employed his henchman, Dopey Jack, to recover the book from Langhorne? Had she feared that Dopey Jack might in some moment of heat, for revenge, drop some hint of the robbery—whether it had been really successful or not?

It was my turn to call Kennedy's attention to something, now, for standing sidewise as I was, I could see the angles of the building back of him.

" Don't turn—yet," I cautioned, " but just around the corner back of you, Langhorne is standing. Evidently he has been watching Mrs. Ogleby, too."

Kennedy drew a cigarette from his case, tried to light it, let the match go out, and then as if to shield himself from the wind, stepped back and turned.

15

Langhorne, however, had seen us, and an instant later had disappeared.

Without a word further Kennedy led the way around the corner to the subway and we started uptown, I knew this time, for the laboratory.

He made no comment on the case, but I knew he had in mind some plan or other for the next move and that it would probably involve something at the suffrage meeting at Miss Ashton's that evening.

During the rest of the day, Craig was busy testing and re-testing a peculiar piece of apparatus, while now and then he would despatch me on various errands which I knew were more as an outlet for my excitement than of any practical importance.

The apparatus, as far as I could make it out, consisted of a simple little oaken box, oblong in shape, in the face of which were two square little holes with side walls of cedar, converging pyramid-like in the interior of the box and ending in what looked to be little round black discs.

I had just returned with a hundred feet or so of the best silk-covered flexible wire, when he had evidently completed his work. Two of the boxes were already wrapped up. I started to show him the wire, but after a glance he accepted it as exactly what he had wanted and made it into a smaller package, which he handed to me.

"I think we might be journeying down to Carton's office," he added, looking impatiently at his watch.

It was still early and we did not hurry.

Carton, however, was waiting for us anxiously. "I've called you at the laboratory and the apartment—all over," he cried. "Where have you been?"

"Just on the way down," returned Kennedy. "Why, what has happened?"

"Then you haven't heard it?" asked Carton excitedly, without waiting for Craig's answer. "Murtha has been committed to a sanitarium."

Kennedy and I stared at him.

"Pat Murtha," ejaculated Craig, "in a sanitarium?"

"Exactly. Paresis—they say—absolutely irresponsible."

Coming as it did as a climax to the quick and unexpected succession of events of the past few days, it was no wonder that it seemed impossible.

What did it mean? Was it merely a sham? Or was it a result of his excesses? Or had Carton's relentless pursuit, the raid of Margot's, and the conviction of Dopey Jack, driven the Smiling Boss really insane?

XVII

THE SOCIETY SCANDAL

NOTHING else was talked about at the suffrage reception at Miss Ashton's that evening, not even suffrage, as much as the strange fate that seemed to have befallen Murtha.

And, as usual with an event like that, stories of all sorts, even the wildest improbabilities, were current. Some even went so far as to insinuate that Dorgan had purposely quickened the pace of life for Murtha by the dinners at Gastron's in order to get him out of the way, fearing that with his power within the organization Murtha might become a serious rival to himself.

Whether there was any truth in the rumour or not, it was certain that Dorgan was of the stamp that could brook no rivals. In fact, that had been at the bottom of the warfare between himself and Langhorne. Certain also was it that the dinners and conferences at the now famous suite of the Silent Boss were reputed to have been often verging on, if not actually crossing, the line of the scandalous.

Miss Ashton's guests assembled in force, coming from all classes of society, all parties in politics, and all religions. Her object had been to show that, although she personally was working with the Reform League, suffrage itself was a broad general issue. The two or three hundred guests of the evening surely demonstrated it and testified to the popularity of Miss Ashton personally, as well.

She had planned to hold the meeting in the big drawing-room of the Ashton mansion, but the audience overflowed into the library and other rooms. As the people assembled, it was interesting to see how for the moment at least they threw off the bitterness of the political campaign and met each other on what might be called neutral ground. Dorgan himself had been invited, but, in accordance with his custom of never appearing in public if he could help it, did not come. Langhorne was present, however, and I saw him once talking to a group of labour union leaders and later to Justice Pomeroy, an evidence of how successful the meeting was in hiding, if not burying, the hatchet.

Carton, naturally, was the lion of the evening, though he tried hard to keep in the background. I was amused to see his efforts. In fleeing from the congratulations of some of his own and Miss Ashton's society friends, he would run into a group of newspaper men and women who were lying in wait for him. Shaking himself loose from them would result in finding himself the centre of an enthusiastic crowd of Reform Leaguers.

Mrs. Ogleby was there, also, and both Kennedy and I watched her curiously. I wondered whether she might not feel just a little relieved to think that

Murtha was seemingly out of the way for the present. Her knowledge of the Black Book which had first given the tip to Carton had always been a mystery to Kennedy and was one of the problems which I knew he would like to solve to-night. She was keenly observant of Carton, which led us to suppose that she had not yet got out of her mind the idea that somehow it was he who had been responsible for the detectaphone record which so many of those present were struggling to obtain. Though Langhorne studiously avoided her, I noticed that each kept an eye on the other, and I felt that there was something common to both of them.

It was with an unexpressed air of relief to several members of the party that Miss Ashton at last rapped for order and after a short, pithy, pointed speech of introduction presented the several speakers of the evening. It was, like the audience, a well-balanced programme, which showed the tactfulness and political acumen of Miss Ashton. I shall pass over the speeches, however, as they had no direct bearing on the mystery which Kennedy and I found so engrossing.

The meeting had been cleverly planned so that in spite of its accomplishing much for the propaganda work of the " cause," it did not become tiresome and the speaking was followed by the entrance of one of the best little orchestras for dance music in the city.

Instantly, the scene transformed itself from a suffrage meeting to a social function that was unique.

Leaders of the smart set rubbed elbows, and seemed to enjoy it, with working girls and agitators. Conservative and radical, millionaire and muckraker succumbed to the spell of the Ashton hospitality and the lure of the new dances. It was a novel experience for all, a levelling-up of society, as contrasted to some of the levelling-down that we had recently seen.

Kennedy and I, having no mood as things stood for the festivities, drew aside and watched the kaleidoscopic whirl of the dancers. Across from us was a wide doorway that opened into a spacious conservatory, a nook of tropical and temperate beauty. Several couples had wandered in there to rest and, as the orchestra struck up something new that seemed to have the " punch " to its timeful measures, they gradually rejoined the dancers.

It had evidently suggested an idea to Kennedy, for a moment later he led me toward the coat room and uncovered the package which he had brought consisting of the two oaken boxes I had seen him adjusting in the laboratory.

We managed to reach the conservatory and found in a corner a veritable bower with a wide rustic seat under some palms. Quickly Kennedy deposited in the shadow of one of them an oaken box, sticking into it the plugs on the ends of the wires that I had brought. It was an easy matter here in the dim half light to conceal the wire behind the plants and a moment later he tossed the end through a swinging window in the glass and closed the window.

Casually we edged our way out among the dancers and around to the room into which he had thrown the wire. It was a breakfast room, I think, but at any rate we could not remain there for it was quite easy to see into it through the crystal walls of the conservatory. There was, however, what seemed to be a little pantry at the other end, and to this Kennedy deftly led the wires and then plugged them in on the other oaken box.

He turned a lever. Instantly from the wizard-like little box issued forth the strains of the dance music of the orchestra and the rhythmic shuffle of feet. Now and then a merry laugh or a snatch of gay conversation floated in to us. Though we were effectually cut off from both sight and hearing in the pantry, it was as though we had been sitting on the rustic bench in the conservatory.

"What is it?" I asked in amazement, gazing at the wonderful little instrument before us.

"A vocaphone," he explained, moving the switch and cutting off the sound instantly, "an improved detectaphone—something that can be used both in practical business, professional, and home affairs as a loud speaking telephone, and, as I expect to use it here, for special cases of detective work. You remember the detectaphone instruments which we have used?"

Indeed I did. It had helped us out of several very tight situations—and seemed now to have been used to get the organization into a very tight political place.

"Well, the vocaphone," went on Kennedy, "does even more than the detectaphone. You see, it talks right out. Those little apertures in the face act like megaphone horns increasing the volume of sound." He indicated the switch with his finger and then another point to which it could be moved. "Besides," he went on enthusiastically, "this machine talks both ways. I have only to turn the switch to that point and a voice will speak out in the conservatory just as if we were there instead of talking here."

He turned the switch so that it carried the sounds only in our direction. The last strains of the dance music were being followed by the hearty applause of the dancers.

As the encore struck up again, a voice, almost as if it were in the little room alongside us, said, "Why, hello, Mary, why aren't you dancing?"

There was an unmistakable air of familiarity about it and about the reply, "Why aren't you, Hartley?"

"Because I've been looking for a chance to have a quiet word with you," the man rejoined.

"Langhorne and Mrs. Ogleby," cried Craig excitedly.

"Sh!" I cautioned, "they might hear us."

He laughed. "Not unless I turn the switch further."

"I saw you down at the Criminal Courts Building this morning," went on the man, "but you didn't see me. What did you think of Carton?"

I fancied there was a trace of sarcasm or jealousy in his tone. At any rate, woman-like, she did not answer that question, but went on to the one which it implied.

"I didn't go to see Carton. He is nothing to me, has not been for months. I was only amusing myself when I knew him—leading him on, playing with him, then." She paused, then turned the attack on him. "What did you think of Miss Ashton? You thought I didn't see you, but you hardly took your eyes off her while I was in the hallway waiting to hear the verdict."

It was Langhorne's turn to defend himself. "It wasn't so much Margaret Ashton as that fellow Carton I was watching," he answered hastily.

"Then you—you haven't forgotten poor little me?" she inquired with a sincere plaintiveness in her voice.

"Mary," he said, lowering his voice, "I have tried to forget you—tried, because I had no right to remember you in the old way—not while you and Martin remained together. Margaret and I had always been friends—but I think Carton and this sort of thing,"—he waved his hand I imagined at the suffrage dancers—"have brought us to the parting of the ways. Perhaps it is better. I'm not so sure that it isn't best."

"And yet," she said slowly, "you are piqued—piqued that another should have won where you failed—even if the prize isn't just what you might wish."

Langhorne assented by silence. "Hartley," she went on at length, "you said a moment ago you had tried to forget me——"

"But can't," he cut in with almost passionate fierceness. "That was what hurt me when I—er—heard that you had gone with Murtha to that dinner of Dorgan's. I couldn't help trying to warn you of it. I know Martin neglects you. But I was mad —mad clean through when I saw you playing with Carton a few months ago. I don't know anything about it—don't want to. Maybe he was innocent and you were tempting him. I don't care. It angered me—angered me worse than ever when I saw later that he was winning with Margaret Ashton. Everywhere, he seemed to be crossing my trail, to be my nemesis. I—I wish I was Dorgan—I wish I could fight."

Langhorne checked himself before he said too much. As it was I saw that it had been he who had told Mrs. Ogleby that the Black Book existed. He had not told her that he had made it, if in fact he had, and she had let the thing out, never thinking Langhorne had been the eavesdropper, but supposing it must be Carton.

"Why—why did you go to that dinner with Murtha?" he asked finally, with a trace of reproach in his tone.

"Why? Why not?" she answered defiantly. "What do I care about Martin? Why should I not have my—my freedom, too? I went because it was wild, unconventional, perhaps wrong. I felt that way. If—if I had felt that you cared—perhaps—I could have been—more discreet."

" I do care," he blurted out. " I—I only wish I had known you as well as I do now—before you married—that's all."

" Is there no way to correct the mistake? " she asked softly. " Must marriage end all—all happiness? "

Langhorne said nothing, but I could almost hear his breathing over the vocaphone, which picked up and magnified even whispers.

" Mary," he said in a deep, passionate voice, " I— I will defend you—from this Murtha thing—if it ever gets out. I know it is always on your mind— that you couldn't keep away from that trial for fear that Carton, or Murtha, or *somebody* might say something by chance or drop some hint about it. Trust me."

" Then we can be—friends? "

" Lovers! " he cried fiercely.

There was a half-smothered exclamation over the faithful little vocaphone, a little flurried rustle of silk and a long, passionate sigh.

" Hartley," she whispered.

" What is it, Mary? " he asked tensely.

" We must be careful. Carton *must* be defeated. He must not have the power—to use that—record."

" No," ground out Langhorne. " Wait—he shall not. By the way, aren't those orchids gorgeous? "

The encore had ceased and over the vocaphone

we could hear gaily chatting couples wandering into the conservatory. The two conspirators rose and parted silently, without exciting suspicion.

For several minutes we listened to snatches of the usual vapid chatter that dancing seems to induce. Then the orchestra blared forth with another of the seductive popular pieces.

Kennedy and I looked at each other, amazed. From the underworld up to the smart set, the trail of graft was the same, debauching and blunting all that it touched. Here we saw the making of a full-fledged scandal in one of the highest circles.

We had scarcely recovered from our surprise at the startling disclosures of the vocaphone, when we heard two voices again above the music, two men this time.

" What—you here? " inquired a voice which we recognized immediately as that of Langhorne.

" Yes," replied the other voice, evidently of a young man. " I came in with the swells to keep my eye peeled on what was going on."

The voice itself was unfamiliar, yet it had a tough accent which denoted infallibly the section of the city where it was acquired. It was one of the gangsters.

" What's up, Ike? " demanded Langhorne suspiciously.

Craig looked at me significantly. It was Ike the Dropper!

The other lowered his voice. " I don't mind telling you, Mr. Langhorne. You're in the organization and we ain't got no grudge against you. It's Carton."

" Carton? " repeated Langhorne, and one could feel the expectant catch in his breath, as he added quickly: " You mean you fellows are going to try to get him right? "

" Bet your life," swaggered Ike, believing himself safe.

" How? "

The gangster hesitated, then reassured by Langhorne, said: " He's ordered a taxicab. We got it for him—a driver who is a right guy and'll drive him down where there's a bunch of the fellows. They ain't goner do nothing serious—but—well, he won't campaign much from a hospital cot," he added sagely. " Say—here he comes now with that girl. I better beat it."

Langhorne also managed to get away apparently, or else Carton and Miss Ashton were too engrossed in one another to notice him, for we heard no word of greeting.

A moment later Carton's and Miss Ashton's voices were audible.

" Must you go? " she was saying.

" I'm afraid so," he apologized. " I've a speech to prepare for to-morrow and I've had several hard days. It's been a splendid evening, Miss Ashton— splendid. I've enjoyed it ever so much and I think it has accomplished more than a hundred meetings —besides the publicity it will get for the cause. Shall I see you to-morrow at headquarters? "

"I shall make it a point to drop in," she answered in a tone as unmistakable.

"Mr. Carton—your cab is waiting, sir," announced a servant with an apology for intruding. "At the side entrance, sir, so that you can get away quietly, sir."

Carton thanked him.

I looked at Kennedy anxiously. If Carton slipped away in this fashion before we could warn him, what might not happen? We could hardly expect to get around and through the press of the dancers in time.

"I hate to go, Miss Ashton," he was adding. "I'd stay—if I saw any prospect of the others going. But—you see—this is the first time to-night —that I've had a word with you—alone."

It was not only an emergency, but there were limits to Kennedy's eavesdropping propensities, and spying on Carton's love affairs was quite another thing from Langhorne's.

Quickly Craig turned the lever all the way over.

"Carton—Miss Ashton—this is Kennedy," he called. "Back of the big palm you'll find a vocaphone. Don't take that cab! They are going to stick you up. Wait—I'll explain all in a moment!"

XVIII

THE WALL STREET WOLF

IT was a startled couple that we found when we reached the conservatory. As we made our hasty explanation, Carton overwhelmed us with thanks for the prompt and effective manner in which Kennedy had saved him from the machinations of the defeated gangsters.

Miss Ashton, who would have kept her nerves under control throughout any emergency, actually turned pale as she learned of the danger that had been so narrowly averted. I am sure that her feelings, which she made no effort to conceal, must have been such as to reassure Carton if he had still any doubt on that score.

The delay in his coming out, however, had been just enough to arouse suspicion, and by the time that we reached the side entrance to the house both Ike and the night-hawk taxicab which had evidently been drafted into service had disappeared, leaving no clue.

The result of the discovery over the vocaphone was that none of us left Miss Ashton's until much later than we had expected.

Langhorne, apparently, had gone shortly after he left the conservatory the last time, and Mrs. Ogleby had preceded him. When at last we managed to convince Miss Ashton that it was perfectly safe for Carton to go, nothing would suffice except that we should accompany him as a sort of body-guard to his home. We did so, without en-countering any adventure more thrilling than seeing an argument between a policeman and a late reveller.

"I can't thank you fellows too much," compli-mented Carton as we left him. "I was hunting around for you, but I thought you had found a suf-frage meeting too slow and had gone."

"On the contrary," returned Kennedy, equivo-cally, "we found it far from slow."

Carton did not appreciate the tenor of the re-mark and Craig was not disposed to enlighten him.

"What do you suppose Mrs. Ogleby meant in her references to Carton?" mused Kennedy when we reached our own apartment.

"I can't say," I replied, "unless before he came to really know Miss Ashton, they were intimate."

Kennedy shook his head. "Why will men in a public capacity get mixed up with women of the ad-venturess type like that, even innocently?" he rumi-nated. "Mark my words, she or someone else will make trouble for him before we get through."

It was a thought that had lately been in my own mind, for we had had several hints of that nature.

Kennedy said no more, but he had started my mind on a train of speculative thought. I could not imagine that a woman of Mrs. Ogleby's type could ever have really appealed to Carton, but that did not preclude the possibility that some unscrupulous

16

person might make use of the intimacy for base purposes. Then, too, there was the threat that I had
heard agreed on by both Langhorne and herself
over the vocaphone.

What would be the next step of the organization
now in its sworn warfare on Carton, I could not
imagine. But we did not have long to wait. Early
the following forenoon an urgent message came to
Kennedy from Carton to meet him at his office.

"Kennedy," he said, "I don't know how to thank
you for the many times you have pulled me through,
and I'm almost ashamed to keep on calling on you."

"It's a big fight," hastened Craig. "You have
opponents who know the game in its every crooked
turn. If I can be only a small cog on a wheel that
crushes them, I shall be only too glad. Your face
tells me that something particularly unpleasant has
happened."

"It has," admitted Carton, smoothing out some
of the wrinkles at the mere sight of Craig.

He paused a moment, as if he were himself in
doubt as to just what the trouble was.

"Someone has been impersonating me over the
telephone," he began. "All day long there have
been reports coming into my office asking me whether
it was true that I had agreed to accept the offer of
Dorgan that Murtha made, you know,—that is,
practically to let up on the organization if they
would let up on me."

"Yes," prompted Kennedy, "but, impersonation
—what do you mean by that?"

"Why, early to-day someone called me up, said he was Dorgan, and asked if I would have any objection to meeting him. I said I would meet him— only it would do no good. Then, apparently, the same person called up Dorgan and said he was myself, asking if he had any objection to meeting me. Dorgan said he'd see. Whoever it was, he almost succeeded in bringing about the fool thing—would have done it, if I hadn't got wise to the fact that there was something funny about it. I called up Dorgan. He said he'd meet me, as long as I had approached him first. I said I hadn't. We swore a little and called the fake meeting off. But it was too late. It got into the papers. Now, you'd think it wouldn't make any difference to either of us. It doesn't to him. People will think he tried to slip one over on *me*. But it does make a difference to me. People will think I'm trying to sell out."

Carton showed plainly his vexation at the affair.

"The old scheme!" exclaimed Kennedy. "That's the plan that has been used by a man down in Wall Street that they call, 'the Wolf.' He is a star impersonator—will call up two sworn enemies and put over something on them that double-crosses both."

"Wall Street," mused Carton. "That reminds me of another batch of rumours that have been flying around. They were that I had made a deal with Langhorne by which I agreed to support him in his fight to get something in the contracts of the new city planning scheme in return for his support of the part of the organization he could swing to me in the election,—another lie."

"It might have been Langhorne himself, playing the wolf," I suggested.

Kennedy had reached for the telephone book. "Also, it might have been Kahn," he added. "I see he has an office in Wall Street, too. He has been the legal beneficiary of several shady transactions down there."

"Oh," put in Carton, "it might have been any of them—they're all capable of it from Dorgan down. If Murtha was only out, I'd be inclined to suspect him."

He tossed over a typewritten sheet of paper. "That's the statement I gave out to the press," he explained.

It read: "My attention has been called to the alleged activities of some person or persons who through telephone calls and underground methods are seeking to undermine confidence in my integrity. A more despicable method of attempting to arouse distrust I cannot imagine. It is criminal and if any-one can assist me in placing the responsibility where it belongs I shall be glad to prosecute to the limit."

"That's all right," assented Kennedy, "but I don't think it will have any effect. You see, this sort of thing is too easy for anyone to be scared off from. All he has to do is to go to a pay station and call up there. You couldn't very well trace that."

He stopped abruptly and his face puckered with thought.

" There ought to be some way, though," I murmured, without knowing just what the way might
be, " to tell whether it is Dorgan and the organization crowd, or Langhorne and his pool, or Kahn and
the other shysters."

There *is* a way," cried Kennedy at last. " You
fellows wait here while I make a flying trip up to
the laboratory. If anyone calls us, just put him
off—tell him to call up later."

Carton continued to direct the work of his office,
of which there had been no interruptions even during the stress of the campaign. Now and then the
telephone rang and each time Carton would motion
to me, and say, " You take it, Jameson. If it seems
perfectly regular then pass it over to me."

Several routine calls came in, this way, followed
by one from Miss Ashton, which Carton prolonged
much beyond the mere time needed to discuss a phase
of the Reform League campaign.

He had scarcely hung up the receiver, when the
bell tinkled insistently, as though central had had
an urgent call which the last conversation had held
up.

I took down the receiver, and almost before I
could answer the inquiry, a voice began, " This is
the editor of the *Wall Street Record,* Mr. Carton.
Have you heard anything of the rumours about
Hartley Langhorne and his pool being insolvent?
The Street has been flooded with stories——"

" One moment," I managed to interrupt. " This
is not Mr. Carton, although this is his office. No—

he's out. Yes, he'll certainly be back in half an hour. Ring up then."

I repeated the scrap of gossip that had filtered through to me, which Carton received in quite as much perplexity as I had.

" Seems as if everybody was getting knocked," he commented.

" That may be a blind, though," I suggested.

He nodded. I think we both realized how helpless we were when Kennedy was away. In fact we made even our guesses with a sort of lack of confidence.

It was therefore with a sense of relief that we welcomed him a few minutes later as he hurried into the office, almost breathless from his trip uptown and back.

" Has anyone called up? " he inquired unceremoniously, unwrapping a small parcel which he carried.

I told him as briefly as I could what had happened. He nodded, without making any audible comment, but in a manner that seemed to show no surprise.

" I want to get this thing installed before anyone else calls," he explained, setting to work immediately.

" What is it? " I asked, regarding the affair, which included something that looked like a phonograph cylinder.

" An invention that has just been perfected," he replied without delaying his preparations, " by which it is possible for messages to be sent over the tele-

phone and automatically registered, even in the absence of anyone at the receiving end. Up to the
present it has been practicable to take phonograph
records only by the direct action of the human voice
upon the diaphragm of the instrument. Not long
ago there was submitted to the French Academy of
Sciences an apparatus by which the receiver of the
telephone can be put into communication with a
phonograph and a perfect record obtained of the
voice of the speaker at the other end of the wire,
his message being reproduced at will by merely
pressing a button."

"Wouldn't the telegraphone do?" I asked, remembering our use of that instrument in other cases.

"It would record," he replied, "but I want a
phonograph record. Nothing else will do in this
case. You'll see why, before I get through. Besides,
this apparatus isn't complicated. Between the
diaphragm of the telephone receiver and that of the
phonographic microphone is fitted an air chamber
of adjustable size, open to the outer atmosphere by
a small hole to prevent compression. I think," he
added with a smile, "it will afford a pretty good
means of collecting souvenirs of friends by preserv-
ing the sound of their voices through the telephone."

For several minutes we waited.

"I don't think I ever heard of such effrontery,
such open, bare-faced chicanery," fumed Carton impatiently.

"We'll catch the fellow yet," replied Kennedy
confidently. "And I think we'll find him a bad lot."

XIX

THE ESCAPE

AT last the telephone rang and Carton answered it eagerly. As he did so, he quickly motioned to us to go to the outside office where we, too, could listen on extensions.

"Yes, this is Mr. Carton," we heard him say.

"This is the editor of the *Wall Street Record*," came back the reply in a tone that showed no hesitation or compunction if it was lying. "I suppose you have heard the rumours that are current downtown that Hartley Langhorne and the people associated with him have gone broke in the pool they formed to get control of the public utilities that would put them in a position to capture the city betterment contracts?"

"No—I hadn't heard it," answered Carton, with difficulty restraining himself from quizzing the informant about himself. Kennedy was motioning to him that that was enough. "I'm sure I can't express any opinion at all for publication on the subject," he concluded brusquely, jamming down the receiver on the hook before his interlocutor had a chance to ask another question.

The bell continued to ring, but Craig seized the receiver off its hook again and called back, "Mr.

Carton has gone for the day," hanging it up again with a bang.

"Call up the *Record* now," advised Craig, disconnecting the recording instrument he had brought. "See what the editor has to say."

"This is the District Attorney's office," said Carton a moment later when he got the number. "You just called me."

"I called you?" asked the editor, non-plussed.

"About a rumour current in Wall Street."

"Rumour? No, sir. It must be some mistake."

"I guess so. Sorry to have troubled you. Goodbye."

Carton looked from one to the other of us. "You see," he said in disgust, "there it is again. That's the sort of thing that has been going on all day. How do I know what that fellow is doing now— perhaps using my name?"

I had no answer to his implied query as to who was the "wolf" and what he might be up to. As for Kennedy, while he showed plainly that he had his suspicions which he expected to confirm absolutely, he did not care to say anything about them yet.

"Two can play at 'wolf,'" he said quietly, calling up the headquarters of Dorgan's organization.

I wondered what he would say, but was disappointed to find that it was a merely trivial conversation about some inconsequential thing, as though Kennedy had merely wished to get in touch with the "Silent Boss." Next he called up the sanitarium to which Murtha had been committed, and after posing as Murtha's personal physician managed to have the rules relaxed to the extent of exchanging a few sentences with him.

"How did he seem—irrational?" asked Carton with interest, for I don't think the District Attorney had complete confidence in the commonly announced cause of Murtha's enforced retirement.

Kennedy shook his head doubtfully. "Sounded pretty far gone," was all he said, turning over the pages of the telephone book as he looked for another number.

This time it was Kahn whom he called up, and he had some difficulty locating him, for Kahn had two offices and was busily engaged in preparing a defence to the charges preferred against him for the jury fixing episode.

Among others whom he called up was Langhorne, and the conversation with him was as perfunctory as possible, consisting merely in repeating his name, followed by an apology from Kennedy for "calling the wrong number."

In each case, Craig was careful to have his little recording instrument working, taking down every word that was uttered and when he had finished he detached it, looking at the cylinder with unconcealed satisfaction.

"I'm going up to the laboratory again," he announced, as Carton looked at him inquiringly. "The investigation that I have in mind will take time, but I shall hurry it along as fast as I possibly can. I don't want any question about the accuracy of my conclusions."

We left Carton, who promised to meet us late in the afternoon at the laboratory, and started up-town. Instead, however, of going up directly, Craig telephoned first to Clare Kendall to shadow Mrs. Ogleby.

The rest of the day he spent in making micro-photographs of the phonograph cylinder and study-ing them very attentively under his high-powered lens.

Toward the close of the afternoon the first report of Miss Kendall, who had been "trailing" Mrs. Ogleby, came in. We were not surprised to learn that she had met Langhorne in the Futurist Tea Room in the middle of the afternoon and that they had talked long and earnestly. What did surprise us, though, was her suspicion that she had crossed the trail of someone else who was shadowing Mrs. Ogleby.

Kennedy made no comment, though I could see that he was vitally interested. What was the signifi-cance of the added mystery? Someone else had an interest in watching her movements. At once I thought of Dorgan. Could he have known of the intimacy of his guest at the Gastron dinner with Langhorne, rather than with Murtha, with whom she had gone? Suddenly another explanation occurred to me. What was more likely than that Martin Ogleby should have heard of his wife's escapade? He would certainly learn now to his surprise of her

meeting with Langhorne.   What would happen
then?

Kennedy had about finished with his microphoto-
graphic work and was checking it over to satisfy himself of the results, when Carton, as he had promised,
dropped in on us.

" What are you doing now? " he asked curiously,
looking at the prints and paraphernalia scattered
about.   " By the way, I've been inquiring into the
commitment of Murtha to that sanitarium for the
insane.   On the surface it all seems perfectly regular.   It appears that, unknown even to many of his
most intimate friends, he has been suffering from a
complication of diseases, the result of his high life,
and they have at last affected his brain, as they were
bound to do in time.   Still, I don't like his ' next
friends ' in the case.   One is his personal physician
—I don't know much about him.   But Dorgan is
one of the others."

" We'll have to look into it," agreed Kennedy.
" Meanwhile, would you like to know who your
' wolf ' is that has been spreading rumours about
broadcast? "

" I would indeed," exclaimed Carton eagerly.
" You were right about the statement I issued.   It
had no more effect than so many unspoken words.
The fellow has kept right on.   He even had the
nerve to call up Miss Ashton in my name and try
to find out whether she had any trace of the missing
Betty Blackwell.   How do you suppose they found
out that she was interested? "

" Not a very difficult thing," replied Kennedy.
" Miss Ashton must have told several organizations,
and the grafters always watch such societies pretty
closely. What did she say? "

" Nothing," answered Carton. " I had thought
that they might try something of the sort and fortunately I warned her to disregard any telephone
messages unless they came certainly from me. We
agreed on a little secret formula, a sort of password,
to be used, and I flatter myself that the ' wolf '
won't be able to accomplish much in that direction.
You say you have discovered a clue? How did you
get it? "

Kennedy picked up one of the microphotographs
which showed an enlargement of the marks on the
phonograph cylinder. He showed it to us and we
gazed curiously at the enigmatic markings, greatly
magnified. To me, it looked like a collection of
series of lines. By close scrutiny I was able to make
out that the lines were wavy and more or less continuous, being made up of collections of finer lines,
—lines within lines, as it were.

An analysis of their composition showed that the
centre of larger lines was composed of three continuous series of markings which looked, under the
lens, for all the world like the impressions of an end-
less straight series of molar teeth. Flanking these
three tooth-like impressions were other lines—varying in width and in number—I should say, about
four, both above and below the tooth-like impressions. When highly magnified one could distinguish

roughly parallel parts of what at even a low magnification looked like a single line.

"I have been studying voice analysis lately," explained Kennedy, "particularly with reference to the singing voice. Mr. Edison has made thousands and thousands of studies of voices to determine which are scientifically perfect for singing. That side of it did not interest me particularly. I have been seeking to use the discovery rather for detective purposes."

He paused and with a fine needle traced out some of the lines on the photographs before us.

"That," he went on, "is a highly magnified photograph of a minute section of the phonographic record of the voice that called you up, Carton, as editor of the *Wall Street Record*. The upper and lower lines, with long regular waves, are formed by a voice with no overtones. Those three broader lines in the middle, with rhythmic ripples, show the overtones."

Carton and I followed, fascinated by the minuteness of his investigation and knowledge.

"You see," he explained, "when a voice or a passage of music sounds or is sung before a phonograph, its modulations received upon the diaphragm are written by the needle point upon the surface of the cylinder or disc in a series of fine waving or zig-zag lines of infinitely varying depth and breadth.

"Close familiarity with such records for about forty years has taught Mr. Edison the precise meaning of each slightest variation in the lines. I have taken up and elaborated his idea. By examining them under the microscope one can analyze each tone with mathematical accuracy and can almost hear it—just as a musician reading the score of a song can almost hear the notes."

"Wonderful," ejaculated Carton. "And you mean to say that in that way you can actually iden-tify a voice?"

Kennedy nodded. "By examining the records in the laboratory, looking them over under a micro-scope—yes. I can count the overtones, say, in a singing voice, and it is on the overtones that the richness depends. I can recognize a voice—mathe-matically. In short," Craig concluded enthusiasti-cally, "it is what you might call the Bertillon meas-urement, the finger-print, the *portrait parlé* of the human voice!"

Incredible as it seemed, we were forced to be-lieve, for there on the table lay the graphic evidence which he had just so painstakingly interpreted.

"Who was it?" asked Carton breathlessly.

Kennedy picked up another microphotograph. "That is the record I took of one of the calls I made—merely for the purpose of obtaining samples of voices to compare with this of the impersonator. The two agree in every essential detail and none of the others could be confounded by an expert who studied them. Your 'wolf' was your old friend Kahn!"

"Fighting back at me by his usual underhand methods." exclaimed Carton in profound disguist.

"Or else trying himself to get control of the
Black Book," added Kennedy. "If you will stop
to think a moment, his shafts have been levelled
quite as much at discrediting Langhorne as yourself.
He might hope to kill two birds with one stone—
and incidentally save himself."

"You mean that he wants to lay a foundation
now for questioning the accuracy of the Black Book
if it ever comes to light?"

"Perhaps," assented Kennedy carefully.

"Surely we should take some steps to protect ourselves from his impostures," hastened Carton.

"I have no objections to your calling him up and
telling him that we know what he is up to and can
trace it to him—provided you don't tell him how we
did it—yet."

Carton had seized the telephone and was hastily
calling every place in which Kahn was likely to be.
He was not at either of his offices, nor at Farrell's,
but at each place successively Carton left a message
which told the story and which he could hardly fail
to receive soon.

As Carton finished, Kennedy seemed to be emerg-
ing from a brown study. He rose slowly and put
on his hat.

"Your story about Murtha's commitment interests me," he remarked, "particularly since you mentioned Dorgan's name in connection with it. I've
been thinking about Murtha myself a good deal
since I heard about his condition. I want to see him
myself."

Carton hesitated a minute. " I can break an engagement I had to speak to-night," he said. " Yes, I'll go with you. It's more important to look to the foundations than to the building just now."

A few minutes later we were all on our way in a touring car to the private sanitarium up in Westchester, where it had been announced that Murtha had been taken.

I had apprehended that we would have a great deal of difficulty either in getting admitted at all or in seeing Murtha himself. We arrived at the sanitarium, a large building enclosed by a high brick wall, and evidently once a fine country estate, at just about dusk. To my surprise, as we stopped at the entrance, we had no difficulty in being admitted.

For a moment, as we waited in the richly furnished reception room, I listened to the sounds that issued from other parts of the building. Something was clearly afoot, for things were in a state of disorder. I had not an extensive acquaintance with asylums for the care and treatment of the insane, but the atmosphere of excitement which palpably pervaded the air was not what one would have expected. I began to think of Poe's Dr. Tarr and Professor Fether, and wonder whether there might not have been a revolution in the place and the patients have taken charge of their keepers.

At last one of the attendants passed the door. No one had paid any attention to us since our admission and this man, too, was going to pass us without notice.

17

" I beg your pardon," interrupted Kennedy, who had heard his footsteps approaching and had placed himself in the hallway so that the attendant could not pass, " but we have called to see Mr. Murtha."

The attendant eyed us curiously. I expected him to say that it was against the rules, or to question our right to see the patient.

" I'm afraid you're too late," he said briefly, instead.

" Too late? " queried Kennedy sharply. " What do you mean? "

The man answered promptly as if that were the quickest way to get back to his own errand.

" Mr. Murtha escaped from his keepers this evening, just after dinner, and there is no trace of him."

XX

THE METRIC PHOTOGRAPH

MURTHA'S escape from the sanitarium had again thrown our calculations into chaos. We rode back to the city in silence, and even Kennedy had no explanation to offer.

Even at a late hour that night, although a widespread alarm had been sent out for him, no trace of the missing man could be found. The next morning's papers, of course, were full of the strange disappearance, but gave no hint of his discovery. In fact, all day the search was continued by the authorities, but without result.

On the face of it, it seemed incredible that a man who was so well known, especially to the thousands of police and others in the official and political life of the city, could remain at large unrecognized. Still, I recalled other cases where prominent men had disappeared. The facts in Murtha's case spoke for themselves.

Comparatively little occurred during the day, although the political campaign which had begun with the primaries many weeks before was now drawing nearer its close and the campaigners were getting ready for the final spurt to the finish.

With Kennedy's unmasking of the unprincipled

activities of Kahn, that worthy changed his tactics, or at least dropped out of our sight. Mrs. Ogleby lunched with Langhorne and I began to suspect that the shadow that had been placed on her could not have been engaged by Martin Ogleby, for he was not the kind who would take reports of the sort complaisantly. Someone else must be interested.

As for the Black Book itself, I wondered more as time went on that no one made use of it. Even though we gained no hint from Langhorne after the peculiar robbery of his safe, it was impossible to tell whether or not he still retained the detectaphone record. On the other hand, if Dorgan had obtained it by using the services of someone in the criminal hierarchy that Murtha had built up, it would not have been likely that we would have heard anything about it. We were in the position of men fighting several adversaries in the dark without knowing exactly whom we fought.

We had just finished dinner, that night, Kennedy and I, and, as had been the case in most of the waking hours of the previous twenty-four, had been speculating on the possible solution of the mysterious dropping out of sight of Murtha. The evening papers had contained nothing that the morning papers had not already published and Kennedy had tossed the last of an armful into the scrap basket when the buzzer on the door of our apartment sounded.

A young man stood there as I opened the door, and handed me a note, as he touched his hat. " A message for Professor Kennedy from Mr. Carton, sir," he announced.

I recognized him as Carton's valet as he stood impatiently waiting for Craig to read the letter.

"It's all right—there's no answer—I'll see him immediately," nodded Kennedy, tossing the hasty scrawl over to me as the valet disappeared.

"My study at home has been robbed, probably by sneak thieves," read the note. "Would you like to look it over? I can't find anything missing except a bundle of old and valueless photographs. Carton."

"Looks as if someone thought Carton might have got that Black Book from Langhorne," I commented, following the line on which I had been thinking at the time.

"And the taking of the photographs was merely a blind, after not finding it?" Kennedy queried, I cannot say much impressed by my theory.

"Perhaps," I acquiesced weakly, as we went out.

Instead of turning in the direction of Carton's immediately, Kennedy walked across the campus toward the Chemistry Building. At the laboratory we loaded ourselves with a large and heavy oblong case containing a camera and a tripod.

The Cartons lived in an old section of the city which still retained something of its aristocratic air, having been passed by, as it were, like an eddy in the stream of business that swirled uptown, engulfing everything.

It was an old four-story brownstone house which

had been occupied by his father and grandfather before him, and now was the home of Carton, his mother, and his sister.

"I'm glad to see you," Carton met us at the door. "This isn't quite as classy a robbery as Langhorne's —but it's just as mysterious. Must have happened while the family were at dinner. That's why I said it was a robbery by a sneak thief."

He was leading the way to his study, which was in an extension of the house, in the rear.

"I hope you've left things as they were," ventured Craig.

"I did," assured Carton. "I know your penchant for such things and almost the first thought I had was that you'd prefer it that way. So I shut the door and sent William after you. By the way, what have you done with him?"

"Nothing," returned Craig. "Isn't he back yet?"

"No—oh, well I don't need him right away."

"And nothing was taken except some old photographs?" asked Craig, looking intently at Carton's face.

"That is all I can find missing," he returned frankly.

Kennedy's examination of the looted study was minute, taking in the window through which the thief had apparently entered, the cabinet he had forced, and the situation in general. Finally he set up his camera with most particular care and took several flashlight pictures of the window, the cabinet, the doors—including the study—from every angle. Outside he examined the extension and back of the house carefully, noting possible ways of getting from the side street across the fences into the Carton yard.

With Carton we returned to Craig's splendidly equipped photographic studio and while Carton and I made the best of our time by discussing various phases of the case, Kennedy employed the interval in developing his plates.

He had ten or a dozen prints, all of exactly the same size, mounted on stiff cardboard in a space with scales and figures on all four margins. Carton and I puzzled over them.

" Those are metric photographs, such as Bertillon of Paris used to take," Craig explained. " By means of the scales and tables and other methods that have been worked out, we can determine from those pictures distances and many other things almost as well as if we were on the spot ourselves. Bertillon cleared up many crimes with this help, such as the mystery of the shooting in the Hotel Quai d'Orsay and other cases. The metric photograph, I believe, will in time rank with other devices in the study of crime."

He was going over the photographs carefully.

" For instance," he continued, " in order to solve the riddle of a crime, the detective's first task is to study the scene topographically. Plans and elevations of a room or house are made. The position of each object is painstakingly noted. In addition, the all-seeing eye of the camera is called into requisition. The plundered room is photographed, as in this case. I might have done it by placing a foot rule on a table and taking that in the picture. But a more scientific and accurate method has been devised by Bertillon. His camera lens is always used at a fixed height from the ground and forms its image on the plate at an exact focus. The print made from the negative is mounted on a card in a space of definite size, along the edges of which a metric scale is printed. In the way he has worked it out, the distance between any two points in the picture can be determined. With a topographical plan and a metric photograph one can study a crime, as a general studies the map of a strange country. There were several peculiar things that I observed at your house, Carton, and I have here an indelible record of the scene of the crime. Preserved in this way, it cannot be questioned. You are sure that the only thing missing is the photographs?"

Carton nodded, "I never keep anything valuable lying around."

"Well," resumed Kennedy, "the photographs were in this cabinet. There are other cabinets, but none of them seems to have been disturbed. Therefore the thief must have known just what he was after. The marks made in breaking the lock were not those of a jimmy, but of a screwdriver. No amazing command of the resources of science is needed so far. All that is necessary is a little scientific common sense."

Carton glanced at me, and I smiled, for it always did seem so easy, when Craig did it, and so impossible when we tried to go it alone.

"Now, how did the robber get in?" he continued, thoroughly engrossed in his study. "All the windows were supposedly locked. I saw that a pane had been partly cut from this window at the side— and the pieces were there to show it. But consider the outside, a moment. To reach that window even a tall man must have stood on a ladder or something. There were no marks of a ladder or even of any person in the soft soil of the garden under the window. What is more, that window was cut from the inside. The marks of the diamond which cut it plainly show that. Scientific common sense again."

"Then it must have been someone in the house or at least familiar with it?" I exclaimed.

Kennedy shook his head affirmatively.

I had been wondering who it could be. Certainly this was not the work of Dopey Jack, even if the far cleverer attempt on Langhorne's safe had been. But it might have been one of his gang. I had not got as far as trying to reason out the why of the crime.

"Call up your house, Carton," asked Craig. "See if William, your valet, has returned."

Carton did so, and a moment later turned to us with a look of perplexity on his face. "No," he reported, "he hasn't come back yet. I can't imagine where he is."

"He won't come back," asserted Kennedy positively. "It was an inside job—and he did it."

Carton gasped astonishment.

"At any rate," pursued Kennedy, "one thing we have which the police greatly neglect—a record. We have made some progress in reconstructing the crime, as Bertillon used to call it."

"Strange that he should take only photographs," I mused.

"What were they?" asked Kennedy, and again I saw that he was looking intently at Carton's face.

"Nothing much," returned Carton unhesitatingly, "just some personal photographs—of no real value except to me. Most of them were amateur photographs, too, pictures of myself in various groups at different times and places that I kept for the associations."

"Nothing that might be used by an enemy for any purpose?" suggested Kennedy.

Carton laughed. "More likely to be used by friends," he replied frankly.

Still, I felt that there must have been some sinister purpose back of the robbery. In that respect it was like the scientific cracking of Langhorne's safe. Langhorne, too, though he had been robbed, had been careful to disclaim the loss of anything of value. I frankly had not believed Langhorne, yet Carton was not of the same type and I felt that his open face would surely have disclosed to us any real loss that he suffered or apprehension that he felt over the robbery.

I was forced to give it up, and I think Kennedy, too, had decided not to worry over the crossing of any bridges until at least we knew that there were bridges to be crossed.

Carton was worried more by the discovery that one he had trusted even as a valet had proved unfaithful. He knew, however, as well as we did that one of the commonest methods of the underworld when they wished to pull off a robbery was to corrupt one of the servants of a house. Still, it looked strange, for the laying of such an elaborate plan usually preceded only big robberies, such as jewelery or silver. For myself, I was forced back on my first theory that someone had concluded that Carton had the Black Book, had concocted this elaborate scheme to get what was really of more value than much jewelry, and had found out that Carton did not have the precious detectaphone record, after all. I knew that there were those who would have gone to any length to get it.

A general alarm was given, through the police, for the apprehension of William, but we had small hope that anything would result from it, for at that time Carton's enemies controlled the police and I am not sure but that they would have been just a little more dilatory in apprehending one who had done Carton an injury than if it had been someone else. It was too soon, that night, of course, to expect to learn anything, anyhow.

It was quite late, but it had been a confining day for Kennedy who had spent the hours while not working on Carton's case in some of the ceaseless and recondite investigations of his own to which he was always turning his restless mind.

"Suppose we walk a little way downtown with Carton?" he suggested.

I was not averse, and by the time we arrived in the white light belt of Broadway the theatres were letting out.

Above the gaiety of the crowds one could hear the shrill cry of some belated newsboys, calling an "Extra Special"—the only superlative left to one of the more enterprising papers whose every issue was an "Extra."

Kennedy bought one, with the laughing remark, "Perhaps it's about your robbery, Carton."

It was only a second before the smile on his face changed to a look of extreme gravity. We crowded about him. In red ink across the head of the paper were the words:

"BODY OF MURTHA, MISSING, FOUND IN MORGUE"

Down in a lower corner, in a little box into which late news could be dropped, also in red ink, was the brief account:

This morning the body of an unknown man was found in The Bronx near the Westchester Railroad tracks. He had been run over and badly mutilated. After lying all day in the local morgue, it was transferred, still unidentified, to the city Morgue downtown.

Early this evening one of the night attendants recognized the unidentified body as that of Murtha, " the Smiling Boss," whose escape day before yesterday from an asylum in Westchester has remained a mystery until now.

" Well—what do you—think of that ! " ejaculated Carton. " Murtha—dead—and I thought the whole thing was a job they were putting up on me ! "

Kennedy crooked his finger at a cabby who was alertly violating the new ordinance and soliciting fares away from a public cab stand.

" The Morgue—quick ! " he ordered, not even noticing the flabbergasted look on the jehu's face, who was not accustomed to carrying people thither from the primrose path of Broadway quite so rapidly.

XXI

THE MORGUE

THERE had come a lull in the activities which never entirely cease, night or day, in the dingy building at the foot of East Twenty-sixth Street. Across the street in the municipal lodging-house the city's homeless were housed for the night. Even ever wakeful Bellevue Hospital nearby was comparatively quiet.

The last " dead boat " which carries the city's unclaimed corpses away for burial had long ago left, when we arrived. The anxious callers who pass all day through the portals of the mortuary chamber seeking lost friends and relatives had disappeared. Except for the night keeper and one or two assistants, the Morgue was empty save of the overcrowded dead.

Years before, as a cub reporter on the *Star*, I had had the gruesome assignment once of the Morgue. It was the same old place after all these years and it gave me the same creepy sensations now as it did then. Even the taxicab driver seemed glad to set down his fares and speed away.

It was ghoulish. I felt then and I did still that instead of contributing to the amelioration of conditions that could not be otherwise than harrowing, everything about the old Morgue lent itself to the increase of the horror of the surroundings.

As Kennedy, Carton, and I entered, we found that the principal chamber in the place was circular. Its walls were lined with the ends of caskets, which, fitting close into drawer-like apertures were constantly enveloped in the refrigerated air.

It seemed, even at that hour, that if these receptacles were even adequate to contain all of the daily tenants of the Morgue, much of the anguish and distress inseparable from such a place might be spared those who of necessity must visit the place seeking their dead. As it was, even for those bound by no blood ties to the unfortunates who found their way to the city Morgue, the room was a veritable chamber of horror.

We stood in horrified amazement at what we saw. On the floor, which should be kept clear, lay the overflow of the day's intake. Bodies for which there was no room in the cooling boxes, others which were yet awaiting claimants, and still more awaiting transfer to the public burying ground, lay about in their rough coffins, many of them brutally exposed.

It seemed, too, that if ever there was a time when conditions might have been expected to have halfway adjusted themselves to the pressure which by day brought out all too clearly the hopeless inadequacy of the facilities provided by the city to perform one of its most important and inevitable functions, it was at that early morning hour of our visit. Presumably preparation had been completed for the busy day about to open by setting all into some semblance of respectful order. But such was not the case. It was impossible.

In one group, I recall, which an attendant said had been awaiting his removal for a couple of days, the rough board coffins, painted the uniform brown of the city's institutions, lay open, without so much as face coverings over the dead.

They lay as they had been sent in from various hospitals. Most of them were bereft of all the decencies usual with the dead, in striking contrast, however, with the bodies from Bellevue, which were all closely swathed in bandages and shrouds.

One body, that of a negro, which had been sent in to the Morgue from a Harlem hospital, lay just as it came, utterly bare, exposing to public view all the gruesome marks of the autopsy. I wondered whether anything like that might be found to be the fate of the once jovial and popular Murtha, when we found him.

I almost forgot our mission in the horror of the place, for, nearby was an even more heartrending sight. Piled in several heaps much higher than a man's head and as carelessly as cordwood were the tiny coffins holding the babies which the authorities are called on by the poor of the city to bury in large numbers—far too poor to meet the cost of the cheapest decent burial. Atop the stack of regulation coffins were the nondescript receptacles made use of by the very poor—the most pathetic a tiny box from the corner grocery. The bodies, some dozens of them, lay like so much merchandise, awaiting shipment.

"What a barbarity!" I heard Craig mutter, for even he, though now and then forced to visit the place when one of his cases took him there, especially when it was concerned with an autopsy, had never become hardened to it.

Often I had heard him denounce the primitive appointments, especially in the autopsy rooms. The archaic attempts to utilize the Morgue for scientific investigation were the occasion for practices that shocked even the initiated. For the lack of suitable depositories for the products of autopsies, these objects were plainly visible in rude profusion when a door was opened to draw out a body for inspection. About and around the slabs whereon the human bodies lay, in bottles and in plates, this material which had no place except in the cabinets of a laboratory was inhumanly displayed in profusion, close to corpses for which a morgue is expected to provide some degree of reverential care.

"You see," apologized the keeper, not averse to throwing the blame on someone else, for it indeed was not his but the city's fault, "one reason why so many bodies have to remain uncared for is that I could show you cooling box after cooling box with some subject which figured during the past few months in the police records. Why victims of murders committed long ago should be held indefinitely, and their growing numbers make it impossible to give proper places to each day's temporary bodies,

18

I can't say. Sometimes," he added with a sly dig at Carton, " the only explanation seems to be that the District Attorney's office has requested the pres-ervation of the grisly relics."

I could see that Carton was making a mental note that the practice would be ended as far as his office was concerned.

" So—you saw the story in the newspapers about Mr. Murtha," repeated the keeper, not displeased to see us and at the publicity it gave him. " It was I that discovered him—and yet ma-any's the times some of the boys that must have handled the body since it was picked up beside the tracks must have seen him. It was too late to get anyone to take the body away to-night, but the arrangements have all been made, and it will be done early in the morning before anyone else sees Pat Murtha here, as he shouldn't be. We've done what we could for him ourselves—he was a fine gentleman and many's the boy that owes a boost up in life to him."

Reverentially even the hardened keeper drew out one of the best of the drawer-like boxes. On the slab before us lay the body. Carton drew back, ex-citedly, shocked.

" It *is* Murtha ! " he exclaimed.

I, too, looked at it quickly. The name as Carton pronounced it, in such a place, had, to me at least, an unpleasant likeness to " murder."

Kennedy had bent down and was examining the mutilated body minutely.

" How do you suppose such a thing is possible—

that he could lie about the city, even here until the
night keeper came on,—unknown? " asked Carton,
aghast.

" I don't know," I said, " but I imagine that in
connection with the actual inadequacy of the equip-
ment one would find reflected the same makeshift
character in the attitude and actions of those who
handle the city's dead. It used to be the case, at
least, that the facilities for keeping records were
often almost totally neglected, and not through the
fault of the Morgue keepers, entirely. But, I understand it is better now."

" This is terrible," repeated Carton, averting his
face. " Really, Jameson, it makes me feel like a
hound, for ever thinking that Murtha might have
been putting up a game on me. Poor old Murtha—
I should have preferred to remember him as the
' Smiling Boss ' as everyone always called him ! "

I called to mind the last time we had seen Murtha,
in Carton's office as the bearer of an offer which
had made Carton almost beside himself with anger
at the thought of the insult that he would compromise with the organization. What a contrast, this,
with the Murtha who, in turn, had been trembling
with passion at Carton's refusal !

And yet I could not but reflect on the strangeness
of it all—the fact that the organization, of which
Murtha was a part, had by its neglect and failure
to care for the human side of government when
there was graft to be collected, brought about the
very conditions which had made possible such neg-

lect of the district leader's body, as it had been bandied back and forth, unwittingly by many who owed their very positions to the organization.

I could not help but think that if he had served humanity with one-half the zeal which he had served graft, this could not have happened.

The more I contemplated the case, the more tragic did it seem to me. I longed for the assignment of writing the story for the *Star*—the chance I would have had in the old days to bring in a story that would have got me a nod of approval from my superior. I determined, as soon as possible, to get the *Star* on the wire and try to express some of the thoughts that were surging through my brain in the face of this awful and unexpected occurrence.

There he lay, alone, uncared for except by such rude hands as those of the Morgue attendants. I could not help reflecting on the strange vicissitudes of human life, and death, which levelled all distinctions between men of high and low degree. Murtha had almost literally sprung from the streets. His career had been one possible only in the social and political conditions of his times. And now he had only by the narrowest chance escaped a burial in a pauper's grave at the hands of the city which he had helped Dorgan to debauch.

Carton, too, I could see was overwhelmed. For the moment he did not even think of how this blow to the System might affect his own chances. It was only the pitiful wreck of a human being before us that he saw.

I was not an expert on study of wounds, such as was Kennedy, who was examining Murtha's body with minute care, now and then muttering under his breath at the rough and careless handling it had received in its various transfers about the city. But there were some terrible wounds and disfigurements on the body, which added even more to the horror of the case.

One thing, I felt, was fortunate. Murtha had had no family. There had been plenty of scandal about him, but as far as I knew there was no one except his old cronies in the organization to be shocked by his loss, no living tragedy left in the wake of this.

" How do you suppose it happened? " I asked the night keeper.

He shook his head doubtfully. " No one knows, of course," he replied slowly. " But I think the big fellow got worse up there in that asylum. He wasn't used to anything but having his own way, you know. They say he must have waited his chance, after the dinner hour, when things were quiet, and then slipped out while no one was looking. He may have been crazy, but you can bet your life Pat Murtha was the smartest crazy man they ever had up there. *They* couldn't hold him."

" I see," I said, struck by the faith which the man had inspired even in those who held the lowest of city positions. " But I meant how do you suppose he was killed? "

The attendant looked at me thoughtfully a while. " Young man," he answered, " I ain't saying nothing and it may have been an accident after all. Have you ever been up in that part of town?"

I had not and said so.

"Well," he continued, "those electric trains do sneak up on a fellow fast. It may have been an accident, all right. The coroner up there said so, and I guess he ought to know. It must have been late at night—perhaps he was wandering away from the ordinary roads for fear of being recaptured. No one knows—I guess no one will know, ever. But it's a sad day for many of the boys. He helped a lot of 'em. And Mr. Dorgan—he knows what a loss it is, too. I hear that it's hit the Chief hard."

The attendant, rough though he was and hardened by the daily succession of tragedies, could not restrain an honest catch in his voice over the passing of the "big fellow," as some of them called the "Smiling Boss." It was a pretty good object lesson on the power of the system which the organization had built up, how Murtha, and even the more distant Dorgan himself, had endeared himself to his followers and henchmen. Perhaps it was corrupt, but it was at least human, and that was a great deal in a world full of inhumanities. In the face of what had happened, one felt that much might be forgiven Murtha for his shortcomings, especially as the era of the Murthas and Dorgans was plainly passing.

"Here at least," whispered Carton, as we withdrew to a corner to escape the palling atmosphere, "is one who won't worry about what happens to that Black Book any more. I wonder what he really knew about it—what secrets he carried away with him? "

" I can't say," I returned. " But, one thing it does. It must relieve Mrs. Ogleby's fears a bit. With Murtha out of the way there is one less to gossip about what went on at Gastron's that night of the dinner."

He said nothing and just then Kennedy straightened up, as though he had finished his examination. We hurried over to him. I thought the look on Craig's face was peculiar.

" What is it—what did you find? " both Carton and I asked.

Kennedy did not answer immediately.

" I—I can't say," he answered slowly at length, as we thanked the Morgue keeper for his courtesy and left the place. " In fact I'd rather not say—until I know."

I knew from previous experiences that it was of no use to try to quiz Kennedy. He was a veritable Gradgrind for facts, facts, facts. As for myself, I could not help wondering whether, after all, Murtha might not have been the victim of foul play—and, if so, by whom?

XXII

THE CANARD

WE did not have to wait long for the secret of the robbery of Carton to come out. It was not in any " extras," or in the morning papers the next day, but it came through a secret source of information to the Reform League.

" A clerk in the employ of the organization who is really a detective employed by the Reform League," groaned Carton, as he told us the story himself the next morning at his office, " has just given us the information that they have prepared a long and circumstantial story about me—about my intimacy with Mrs. Ogleby and Murtha and some others. The story of the robbery of my study is in the papers this morning. To-morrow they plan to publish some photographs—alleged to have been stolen."

" Photographs—Mrs. Ogleby," repeated Kennedy. " Real ones ? "

" No," exclaimed Carton quickly, " of course not —fakes. Don't you see the scheme ? First they lay a foundation in the robbery, knowing that the public is satisfied with sensations, and that they will be sure to believe that the robbery was put up by some muckrakers to obtain material for an exposé. I wasn't worried last night. I knew I had nothing to conceal."

" Then what of it? " I asked naïvely.

" A good deal of it," returned Carton excitedly, " The story is to be, as I understand it, that the fake pictures were among those stolen from me and that in a roundabout way they came into the possession of someone in the organization, without their knowing who the thief was. Of course they don't know who took them and the original plates or films are destroyed, but they've concocted some means of putting a date on them early in the spring."

" What are they that they should take such pains with them? " persisted Kennedy, looking fixedly at Carton.

Carton met his look without flinching. " They are supposed to be photographs of myself," he repeated. " One purports to represent me in a group composed of Mrs. Ogleby, Murtha, another woman whom I do not even know, and myself. I am standing between Murtha and Mrs. Ogleby and we look very familiar. Another is a picture of the same four riding in a car, owned by Murtha. Oh, there are several of them, of that sort."

He paused as a dozen unspoken questions framed themselves in my mind. " I don't hesitate to admit," he added, " that a few months ago I knew Mrs. Ogleby—socially. But there was nothing to it. I never knew Murtha well, and the other woman I never saw. At various times I have been present at affairs where she was, but I know that no pictures were ever taken, and even if there had been, I would not care, provided they told the truth about them. What I do care about is the sworn allegation that, I understand, is to accompany these—these fakes."

His voice broke. "It's a lie from start to finish, but just think of it, Kennedy," he went on. "Here is the story, and here, too, are the pictures—at least they will be, in print, to-morrow. Now, you know nothing could hurt the reform ticket worse than to have a scandal like this raised at this time. There may be just enough people to believe that there is some basis for the suspicion to turn the tide against me. If it were earlier in the campaign, I might accept the issue, fight it out to a finish, and in the turn of events I should have really the best sort of campaign material. But it is too late now to expose such a knavish trick on the Saturday before election."

"Can't we buy them off?" I ventured, perplexed beyond measure at this new and unexpected turn of events.

"No, I won't," persisted Carton, shutting his square jaw doggedly. "I won't be held up—even if that is possible."

"Miss Ashton on the wire," announced a boy from the outer office.

The look on Carton's face was a study. I saw directly what was the trouble—far more important to him than a mere election.

"Tell her—I'm out—will be back soon," he muttered, for the first time hesitating to speak to her.

"You see," he continued blackly, "I'll fight if

it takes my last dollar, but I won't allow myself to be blackmailed out of a cent—no, not a cent," he thundered, a heightened look of determination fixing the lines on his face as he brought his fist down with a rattling bang on the desk.

Kennedy was saying nothing. He was letting Carton ease his mind of the load which had been suddenly thrust upon it. Carton was now excitedly pacing the floor.

"They believe plainly," he continued, growing more excited as he paced up and down, "that the pictures will of course be accepted by the public as among those stolen from me, and in that, I suppose, they are right. The public will swallow it. If I say I'll prosecute, they'll laugh and tell me to go ahead, that they didn't steal the pictures. Our informant tells us that a hundred copies have been made of each and that they have them ready to drop into the mail to the leading hundred papers, not only of this city but of the state, in time for them to appear Sunday. They think that no amount of denying on our part can destroy the effect."

"That's it," I persisted. "The only way is to buy them off."

"But, Jameson," argued Carton, "I repeat— they are false. It is a plot of Dorgan's, the last fight of a boss, driven into a corner, for his life. And it is meaner than if he had attempted to forge a letter. Pictures appeal to the eye much more than letters. That's what makes the thing so dangerous. Dorgan knows how to make the best use of such a roorback

on the eve of an election and even if I not only deny
but prove that they are a fake, I'm afraid the harm
will be done.   I can't reach all the voters in time.
Ten see such a charge to one who sees the denial."

He looked from one to the other of us helplessly.
" If we had a week or two, it might be all right.   But
I can't make any move to-day without making a fool
of myself, nothing until they are published, as the
last big thing of the campaign.   Monday and Tuesday morning do *not* give me time to reply in the
papers and hammer it in.   Even if they were out
now, it would not give me time to make of it an
asset instead of a liability.   And then, too, it means
that I am diverted by this thing, that I let up in the
final efforts that we have so carefully planned to cap
the campaign.   That in itself is as much as Dorgan
wants, anyway."

Kennedy had been, so far, little more than an interested listener, but now he asked pointedly, " You
have copies of the pictures? "

" No—but I've been promised them this morning."

" H'm," mused Craig, turning the crisis over in
his mind.   " We've had alleged stolen and forged
letters before, but alleged stolen and forged photographs are new.   I'm not surprised that you are
alarmed, Carton,—nor that Walter suggests buying
them off.   But I agree with you, Carton—it's best to
fight, to admit nothing, as you would imply by any
other method."

" Then you think you can trace down the forger

of those pictures before it is too late?" urged Carton, leaning forward almost like a prisoner in the dock to catch the words of the foreman of the jury.

"I haven't said I can do that—yet," measured Craig with provoking slowness.

"Say, Kennedy, you're not going to desert me?" reproached Carton.

Kennedy laughed as he put his hand on Carton's shoulder.

"I've been afraid of something like this," he said, "ever since I began to realize that you had once been —er—foolish enough to become even slightly acquainted with that adventuress, Mrs. Ogleby. My advice is to fight, not to get in wrong by trying to dicker, for that might amount to confession, and suit Dorgan's purpose just as well. Photographs," he added sententiously, "are like statistics. They don't lie unless the people who make them do. But it's hard to tell what a liar can accomplish with either, in an election. I—I don't know that I'd desert you —if the pictures were true. I'd be sure there was some other explanation."

"I knew it," responded Carton heartily. "Your hand on that, Kennedy. Say, I think I've shaken hands with half the male population of this city since I was nominated, but this means more than any of them. Spare no reasonable expense and—get the goods, no matter whom it hits higher up—Langhorne—anybody. And, for God's sake get it in time —there's more than an election that hangs on it!"

Carton looked Kennedy squarely in the eye again,

and we all understood what it was he meant that
was at stake. It might be possible after all to gloss
over almost anything and win the election, but none
of us dared to think what it might mean if Miss
Ashton not only suspected that Carton had been
fraternizing with the bosses but also that there had
been or by some possibility could be anything really
in common between him and Mrs. Ogleby.

That, after all, I saw was the real question. How
would Miss Ashton take it? Could she ever forgive him if it were possible for Langhorne to turn
the tables and point with scorn at the man who had
once been his rival for her hand? What might be
the effect on her of any disillusionment, of any ridi-
cule that Langhorne might artfully heap up? As we
left Carton, I shared with Kennedy his eagerness to
get at the truth, now, and win the fight—the two
fights.

"I want to see Miss Ashton, first," remarked
Kennedy when we were outside.

Personally I thought that it was a risky business,
but felt that Kennedy must know best.

When we arrived at the Reform League headquarters, the clerks and girls had already set to work,
and the office was a hive of industry in the rush of
winding up the campaign. Typewriters were click-
ing, clippings were being snipped out of a huge stack
of newspapers and pasted into large scrapbooks,
circulars were being folded and made ready to mail
for the final appeal.

Carton's office there had been in the centre of the

suite. On one side were the cashier and bookkeeper, the clerical force and the speakers' bureau, where spellbinders of all degrees were getting instructions, final tours were being laid out, and reports received of meetings already held.

On the other side was the press bureau, with its large and active force, in charge of Miss Ashton.

As we entered we saw Miss Ashton very busy over something. Her back was toward us, but the moment she turned at hearing us we could see that something was the matter.

Kennedy wasted no time in coming to the point of his visit. We had scarcely seated ourselves beside her desk when he leaned over and said in a low voice, " Miss Ashton, I think I can trust you. I have called to see you about a matter of vital importance to Mr. Carton."

She did not betray even by a fleeting look on her proud face what the true state of her feelings was.

" I don't know whether you know, but an attempt is being made to slander Mr. Carton," went on Kennedy.

Still she said nothing, though it was evident that she was thinking much.

" I suppose in a large force like this that it is not impossible that your political enemies may have a spy or two," observed Kennedy, glancing about at the score or more clerks busily engaged in getting out the " literature."

" I have sometimes thought that myself," she murmured, " but of course I don't know. There isn't anything for them to discover in *this* office, though."

Kennedy looked up quickly at the significant stress on the word "this." She saw that Kennedy was watching. Margaret Ashton might have made a good actress, that is, in something in which her personal feelings were not involved, as they were in this case. She was now pale and agitated.

"I—I can't believe it," she managed to say. "Oh, Mr. Kennedy—I would almost rather not have known it at all,—only I suppose I must have known it sooner or later."

"Believe me, Miss Ashton," soothed Kennedy, "you ought to know. It is on you that I depend for many things. But, tell me, how do you know already? I didn't think—it was known."

She was still pale, and replied nervously, "Our detective in the organization brought the pictures up here—one of the girls opened them by mistake—it got about the office—I couldn't help but know."

"Miss Ashton," remonstrated Kennedy soothingly, "I beg you to be calm. I had no idea you would take it like this, no idea. Please, please. Remember pictures can lie—just like words."

"I—I hope you're right," she managed to reply slowly. "I'm all broken up by it. I'm ready to resign. My faith in human nature is shaken. No, I won't say anything about Mr. Carton to anyone. But it cuts me to have to think that Hartley Langhorne may have been right. He always used to say that every man had his price. I am afraid this will do great harm to the cause of reform and through it to the woman suffrage cause which made me cast myself in with the League. I—I can hardly believe——"

Kennedy was still looking earnestly at her. " Miss Ashton," he implored, " believe nothing. Remember one of the first rules of politics in the organization you are fighting is loyalty. Wait until——"

" Wait? " she echoed. " How can I? I hate Mr. Carton for—for even knowing——" she paused just in time to substitute Mr. Murtha for Mrs. Ogleby—" such men as Mr. Murtha—secretly."

She bit her lip at thus betraying her feelings, but what she had seen had evidently affected her deeply. It was as though the feet of her idol had turned to clay.

" Just think it over," urged Kennedy. " Don't be too harsh. Don't do anything rash. Suspend judgment. You won't regret it."

Kennedy was apparently doing some rapid thinking. " Let me have the photographs," he asked at length.

" They are in Mr. Carton's office," she answered, as if she would not soil her hands by touching the filthy things.

We excused ourselves and went into Carton's office.

There they were wrapped up, and across the package was written by one of the clerks, " Opened by mistake."

Kennedy opened the package again. Sure enough,

19

there were the photographs—as plain as they could be, the group including Carton, Mrs. Ogleby, Murtha, and another woman, standing on the porch of a gabled building in the sunshine, again the four speeding in a touring car, of which the number could be read faintly, and other less interesting snapshots.

As I looked at them I said nothing, but I must admit that the whole thing began to assume a suspicious look in my mind in connection with various hints I had heard dropped by organization men about probing into the past, and other insinuations. I felt that far from aiding Carton, things were now getting darker. There was nothing but his unsupported word that he had not been in such groups to counterbalance the existence of the actual pictures themselves, on the surface a graphic clincher to Dorgan's story. Kennedy, however, after an examination of the photographs clung no less tenaciously to a purpose he already had in mind, and instead of leaving them for Carton, took them himself, leaving a note instead.

He stopped again to speak to Margaret Ashton. I did not hear all of the conversation, but one phrase struck me, "And the worst of it is that he called me up a little while ago and tried to act toward me in the same old way—and that after I know what I know. I—I could detect it in his voice. He knew he was concealing something from me."

What Kennedy said to her, I do not know, but I don't think it had much effect.

"That's the most difficult and unfortunate part of the whole affair," he sighed as we left. "She believes it."

I had no comment that was worth while. What was to be done? If people believed it generally, Carton was ruined.

XXIII

THE CONFESSION

DORGAN was putting up a bold fight, at any rate. Everyone, and most of all his opponents who had once thought they had him on the run, was forced to admit that. Moreover, one could not help wondering at his audacity, whatever might be the opinion of his dishonesty.

But I was quite as much struck by the nerve of Carton. In the face of gathering misfortunes many a man of less stern mettle might have gone to pieces. Not so with the fighting District Attorney. It seemed to spur him on to greater efforts.

It was a titanic struggle, this between Carton and Dorgan, and had reached the point where quarter was given or asked by neither.

Kennedy had retired to his laboratory with the photographs and was studying them with an increasing interest.

It was toward the close of the afternoon when the telephone rang and Kennedy motioned to me to answer it.

"If it's Carton," he said quickly, "tell him I'm not here. I'm not ready for him yet and I can't be interrupted."

I took down the receiver, prepared to perjure my

immortal soul. It was indeed Carton, bursting with news and demanding to see Kennedy immediately.

Almost before I had finished with the carefully framed, glib excuse that I was to make, he shouted to me over the wire, "What do you think, Jameson? Tell him to come down right away. The impossible has happened. I have got under Dopey Jack's guard—he has confessed. It's big. Tell Kennedy I'll wait here at my office until he comes."

He had hung up the receiver before I could question him further. I think it cured Kennedy, temporarily of asking me to fib for him over the telephone. He was as anxious as I to see Carton, now, and plunged into the remaining work on the photographs eagerly.

He finished much sooner than he would, otherwise, and only to preserve the decency of the excuse that I had made did not hasten down to the Criminal Courts Building before a reasonable time had elapsed.

As we entered Carton's office we could tell from the very atmosphere of the halls that something was happening. The reporters in their little room outside were on the *qui vive* and I heard a whisper and a busy scratching of pencils as we passed in and the presence of someone else in the District Attorney's office was noted.

Carton met us in a little ante-room. He was all excitement himself, but I could see that it was a clouded triumph. His mind was really elsewhere than on the confession that he was getting. Although he did not ask us, I knew that he was thinking only of Margaret Ashton and how to regain the ground that he had apparently lost with her. Still, he said nothing about the photographs. I wondered whether it was because of his confidence that Kennedy would pull him through.

"You know," he whispered, "I have been working with my assistants on Dopey Jack ever since the conviction, hoping to get a confession from him, holding out all sorts of promises if he would turn state's evidence and threats if he didn't. It all had no effect. But Murtha's death seems to have changed all that. I don't know why—whether he thinks it was due to foul play or not, for he won't say anything about that and evidently doesn't know —but it seems to have changed him."

Carton said it as though at last a ray of light had struck in on an otherwise black situation, and that was indeed the case.

"I suppose," suggested Craig, "that as long as Murtha was alive he would rather have died than say anything that would incriminate him. That's the law of the gang world. But with Murtha no longer to be shielded, perhaps he feels released. Besides, it must begin to look to him as though the organization had abandoned him and was letting him shift pretty much for himself."

"That's it," agreed Carton. "He has never got it out of his head that Kahn swung the case against him and I've been careful not to dwell on the truth of that Kahn episode."

Carton led us into his main office, where Rubano was seated with two of Carton's assistants who were quizzing him industriously and obtaining an amazing amount of information about gang life and political corruption. In fact, like most criminals when they do confess, Dopey Jack was in danger of confessing too much, in sheer pride at his own prowess as a bad man.

Outside, I knew that it was being well noised abroad, in fact I had nodded to an old friend on the *Star* who had whispered to me that the editor had already called him up and offered to give Rubano any sum for a series of articles for the Sunday supplement on life in the underworld. I knew, then, that the organization had heard of it, by this time— too late.

Most of the confession was completed by the time we arrived, but as it had all been carefully taken down we knew we had missed nothing.

"You see, Mr. Carton," Rubano was saying as we three entered and he turned from the assistant who was quizzing him, "it's like this. I can't tell you all about the System. No one can. You understand that. All any of us know is the men next to us—above and below. We may have opinions, hear gossip, but that's no good as evidence."

"I understand," reassured Carton. "I don't expect that. You must tell me the gossip and rumours, but all I am bartering a pardon for is what you really know, and you've got to make good, or the deal is off, see?"

He said it in a tone that Dopey Jack could understand and the gangster protested. "Well, Mr. Carton, haven't I made good?"

"You have so far," grudgingly admitted Carton who was greedy for everything down to the uttermost scrap that might lead to other things. "Now, who was the man above you, to whom you reported?"

"Mr. Murtha, of course," replied Jack, surprised that anyone should ask so simple a question.

"That's all right," explained Carton. "I knew it, but I wanted you on record as saying it. And above Murtha?"

"Why, you know it is Dorgan," replied Dopey, "only, as I say, I can't prove that for you any better than you can."

"He has already told about his associates and those he had working under him," explained Carton, turning to us. "Now Langhorne—what do you know about him?"

"Know about Langhorne—the fellow that was— that I robbed?" repeated Jack.

"You robbed?" cut in Kennedy. "So you knew about thermit, then?"

Dopey smiled with a sort of pride in his work, much as if he had received a splendid recommendation.

"Yes," he replied. "I knew about it—got it from a peterman who has studied safes and all that sort of thing. I heard he had some secret, so one night I takes him up to Farrell's and gets him stewed and he tells me. Then when I wants to use it, bingo! there I am with the goods."

"And the girl—Betty Blackwell—what did she have to do with it?" pursued Craig. "Did you get into the office, learn Langhorne's habits, and so on, from her?"

Dopey Jack looked at us in disgust. "Say," he replied, "if I wanted a skirt to help me in such a job, believe me I know plenty that could put it all over that girl. Naw, I did it all myself. I picked the lock, burnt the safe with that powder the guy give me, and took out something in soft leather, a lot of typewriting."

We were all on our feet in unrestrained excitement. It was the Black Book at last!"

"Yes," prompted Carton, "and what then—what did you do with it?"

"Gave it to Mr. Murtha, of course," came back the matter-of-fact answer of the young tough.

"What did he do with it?" demanded Carton.

Dopey Jack shook his head dubiously. "It ain't no use trying to kid you, Mr. Carton. If I told you a fake you'd find it out. I'd tell you what he did, if I knew, but I don't—on the level. He just took it. Maybe he burnt it—I don't know. I did my work."

Unprincipled as the young man was, I could not help the feeling that in this case he was telling only the truth as he knew it.

We looked at each other aghast. What if Murtha had got it and had destroyed it before his death? That was an end of the dreams we had built on its

capture. On the other hand, if he had hidden it
there was small likelihood now of finding it. The
only chance, as far as I could see, was that he had
passed it along to someone else. And of that Dopey
Jack obviously knew nothing.

Still, his information was quite valuable enough.
He had given us the first definite information we
had received of it.

Carton, his assistants, and Kennedy now vigorously proceeded in a sort of kid glove third degree,
without getting any further than convincing themselves that Rubano genuinely did not know.

" But the stenographer," reiterated Carton, returning to the line of attack which he had temporarily abandoned. " Something became of her. She
disappeared and even her family haven't a trace of
her, nor any other institutions in the city. We've got
something on you, there, Rubano."

Jack laughed. " Mr. Carton," he answered easily,
" the police put me through the mill on that without
finding anything, and I don't believe you have anything. But just to show you that I'm on the square
with you, I don't mind telling you that I got her
away."

It was dramatic, the off-hand way in which the
gangster told of this mystery that had perplexed us.

" Got her away—how—where? " demanded Carton fiercely.

" Mr Murtha gave me some money—a wad. I
don't know who gave it to him, but it wasn't his
money. It was to pay her to stay away till this all

blew over. Oh, they made it worth her while. So I dolled up and saw her—and she fell for it—a pretty good sized wad," he repeated, as though he wished some of it had stuck to his own hands.

We fairly gasped at the ease and simplicity with which the fellow bandied facts that had been beyond our discovery for days. Here was another link in our chain. We could not prove it, but in all probability it was Dorgan who furnished the money. Even if the Black Book were lost, it was possible that in the retentive memory of this girl there might be much that would take its place. She had seen a chance for providing for the future of herself and her family. All she had to do was to take it and keep quiet.

"You know where she is, then?" shot out Kennedy suddenly.

"No—not now," returned Dopey. "She was told to meet me at the Little Montmartre. She did. I don't think she knew what kind of place it was, or she wouldn't have come."

He paused, as though he had something on his mind.

"Go on," urged Kennedy. "Tell all. You must tell all."

"I was just thinking," he hesitated. "I remember I saw Ike the Dropper and Marie Margot there that day, too, with Martin Ogleby——"

"Martin Ogleby!" interrupted Carton in surprise.

"Yes, Martin Ogleby. He hangs about the Montmartre and the Futurist, all those joints. Say—I've been thinking a heap since this case of mine came up. I wonder whether it was all on the level—with me. I gave the money. But was that a stall? Perhaps they tried to get back. Perhaps she played into their hands—I saw her watching the sports, there, and believe me, there are some swell lookers. Oh well, *I* don't know. All I know is my part. I don't know anything that happened after that. I can't tell what I don't know, can I, Mr. Carton?"

"Not very well," smiled the prosecutor. "But you can tell us anything you suspect."

"I don't know what I suspect. I was only a part of the machine. Only after I read that she disappeared, I began to think there might have been some funny business—I don't know."

Eager as we were, we could only accept this unsatisfactory explanation of the whereabouts of Betty.

"After all, I was only a part," reiterated Jack. "You better ask Ike—that's all."

Just then the telephone buzzed. Carton was busy and Kennedy, who happened to be nearest, answered it. I fancied that there was a puzzled expression on his face, as he placed his hand over the transmitter and said to Carton, "Here—it's for you. Take it. By the way, where's that thing I left down here for recording voices?"

"Here in my desk. But you took the cylinder with you."

"Haven't you got another? Don't you ever use them for dictating letters?"

Carton nodded and sent his stenographer to get a new one.

"Just a minute, please," cut in Kennedy. "Mr. Carton will be here in a few moments, now."

Carton took the telephone and placed his hand over it, until, with a nod from Kennedy as he affixed the machine, he answered.

"Yes—this is the District Attorney," we heard him answer. "What? Rubano? Why you can't talk to him. He's a convicted man. Here? How do you know he's here? No—I wouldn't let you talk to him if he was. Who are you, anyway? What's that—you threaten him—you threaten me? You'll get us both, will you? Well, I want to tell you, you can go plumb—the deuce! The fellow's cut himself off!"

As Carton finished, a peculiar smile played about Rubano's features. "I expected that, but not so soon," he said quietly. "New York'll be no place for me, Mr. Carton, after this. You've got to keep your word and smuggle me out. South Africa, you know—you promised."

"I'll keep my word, Rubano, too," assured Carton. "The nerve of that fellow. Where's Kennedy?"

We looked about. Craig had slipped out quietly during the telephone conversation. Before we could start a search for him, he returned.

"I thought there was something peculiar about the voice," he explained. "That was why I wanted a record of it. While you were talking I got your switchboard operator to connect me with central on another wire. The call was from a pay station on the west side. There wasn't a chance to get the fellow, of course—but I have the voice record, anyhow."

Dopey Jack's confession occupied most of the evening and it was late when we got away. Carton was overjoyed at the result of his pressure, and eager to know, on the other hand, whether Kennedy had made any progress yet with his study of the photographs.

I could have told him beforehand, however, that Craig would say nothing and he did not. Besides, he had the added mystery of the new phonograph cylinder to engross him, with the result that we parted from Carton, a little piqued at being left out of Craig's confidence, but helpless.

As for me, I knew it was useless to trail after Kennedy and when he announced that he was going back to the laboratory, I balked and, in spite of my interest in the case, went home to our apartment to bed, while Kennedy made a night of it.

What he discovered I knew no better in the morning than when I left him, except that he seemed highly elated.

Leisurely he dressed, none the worse for his late work and after devouring the papers as if there were nothing else in the world so important, he waited until the middle of the morning before doing anything further.

"I merely wanted to give Dorgan a chance to

get to his office," he surprised me with, finally. " Come, Walter, I think he must be there now."

Amazed at his temerity in bearding Dorgan in his very den, I could do nothing but accompany him, though I much feared it was almost like inviting homicide.

The Boss's office was full of politicians, for it was now approaching " dough day," when the purse strings of the organization were loosed and a flood of potent argument poured forth to turn the tide of election by the force of the only thing that talks loud enough for some men to hear. Somehow, Kennedy managed to see the Boss.

" Mr. Dorgan," began Kennedy quietly, when we were seated alone in the little Sanctum of the Boss, " you will pardon me if I seem to be a little slow in coming to the business that has brought me here this morning. First of all I may say that you probably share the idea that ever since the days of Daguerre photography has been regarded as the one infallible means of portraying faithfully any object, scene, or action. Indeed, a photograph is admitted in court as irrefutable evidence. For, when everything else fails, a picture made through the photographic lens almost invariably turns the tide. However, such a picture upon which the fate of an important case may rest should be subjected to critical examination, for it is an established fact that a photograph may be made as untruthful as it may be reliable."

He paused. Dorgan was regarding him keenly,

but saying nothing. Kennedy did not mind, as he resumed.

"Combination photographs change entirely the character of the initial negative and have been made for the past fifty years. The earliest, simplest, and most harmless photographic deception is the printing of clouds in a bare sky. But the retoucher with his pencil and etching tool to-day is very skilful. A workman of ordinary ability can introduce a person taken in a studio into an open-air scene well blended and in complete harmony without a visible trace of falsity."

Dorgan was growing interested.

"I need say nothing of how one head can be put on another body in a picture," pursued Craig, "nor need I say what a double exposure will do. There is almost no limit to the changes that may be wrought in form and feature. It is possible to represent a person crossing Broadway or walking on Riverside Drive, places he may never have visited. Thus a person charged with an offence may be able to prove an alibi by the aid of a skilfully prepared combination photograph.

"Where, then," asked Kennedy, "can photography be considered as irrefutable evidence? The realism may convince all, except the expert and the initiated after careful study. A shrewd judge will be careful to insist that in every case the negative be submitted and examined for possible alterations by a clever manipulator."

Kennedy bent his gaze on Dorgan. "Now, I

do not accuse you, sir, of anything. But a photograph has come into my possession in which Mr. Carton is represented as standing in a group on a porch, with Mr. Murtha, Mrs. Ogleby, and an unknown woman. The first three are in poses that show the utmost friendliness. I do not hesitate to say that was originally a photograph of yourself, Mr. Murtha, Mrs. Ogleby, and a woman whom you know well. It is a pretty raw deal, a fake in which Carton has been substituted by very excellent photographic forgery."

"A fake—huh!" repeated Dorgan, contemptuously. "How about the story of them? There's no negative. You've got to show me that the original print stolen from Carton, we'll say, is a fake. You can't do it. No, sir, those pictures were taken this summer."

Kennedy quietly laid down the bundle of photographs copied from those alleged to have been stolen from Carton. He was pointing to a shadow of a gable on the house.

"You see that shadow of the gable, Dorgan?" he asked. "Perhaps you never heard of it, but it is possible to tell the exact time at which a photograph was taken from a study of the shadows. It is possible in theory and practice, and it can be trusted absolutely. Almost any scientist, Dorgan, may be called in to bear testimony in court nowadays, but you probably think the astronomer is one of the least likely.

"Well, the shadow in this picture can be made to

20

prove an alibi for someone. Notice. It is seen prominently to the right, and its exact location on the house is an easy matter. The identification of the gable casting the shadow ought to be easy. To be exact, I have figured it out as 19.62 feet high. The shadow is 14.23 feet down, 13.10 feet east, and 3.43 feet north. You see, I am exact. I have to be. In one minute it moves 0.080 feet upward, 0.053 feet to the right, and 0.096 feet in its apparent path. It passes the width of a weatherboard, 0.37 foot, in four minutes and thirty-seven seconds."

Kennedy was talking rapidly of data which he had derived from the study of the photograph as from plumb line, level, compass, and tape, astronomical triangle, vertices, zenith, pole, and sun, declination, azimuth, solar time, parallactic angles, refraction, and a dozen other bewildering terms.

"In spherical trigonometry," he concluded, "to solve the problem three elements must be known. I know four. Therefore, I can take each of the known, treat it as unknown, and have four ways to check my result. I find that the time might have been either three o'clock, twenty-one minutes and twelve seconds in the afternoon, or 3 : 21 : 31 or 3 : 21 : 29, or 3 : 21 : 33. The average is 3 : 21 : 26 and there can be no appreciable error except for a few seconds. I tell you that to show you how close I can come. The important thing, however, is that the date must have been one of two days, either May 22 or July 22. Between these two dates we must decide on evidence other than the shadow. It

must have been in May, as the immature condition
of the foliage shows. But even if it had been in
July, that would be far from the date you allege.
Why, I could even tell you the year. Then, too, I
could look up the weather records and tell something
from them. I can really answer, with an assurance
and accuracy superior to the photographer himself,
if you could produce him and he were honest, as to
the real date. The original picture, aside from being doctored, was actually taken last May. Science
is not fallible, but exact in this matter."

Kennedy felt that he had scored a palpable hit.
Dorgan was speechless. Still, Craig hurried on.

" But, you may ask, how about the automobile picture? That also is an unblushing fake. Of course
I must prove that. In the first place you know that
the general public has come to recognize the distortion of a photograph as denoting speed. A picture
of a car in a race that doesn't lean is rejected. People demand to see speed, speed, more speed, even in
pictures. Distortion does indeed show speed, but
that, too, can be faked.

" Almost everyone knows that the image is projected upside down by the lens on the plate, and that
the bottom of the picture is taken before the top.
The camera mechanism admits light, which makes
the picture, in the manner of a roller blind curtain.
The slit travels from the top to the bottom and, the
image on the plate being projected upside down, the
bottom of the object appears on the top of the plate.
For instance, the wheels are taken before the head

of the driver. If the car is moving quickly, the image moves on the plate and each successive part is taken a little in advance of the last. The whole leans forward. By widening the slit and slowing the speed of the shutter, there is more distortion.

"Now, that is just what has been done. A picture has been taken of a car owned once by Murtha, probably at rest, with perhaps yourself, Murtha, Mrs. Ogleby, and your friend in it. The matter of faking Carton or anyone else is simple. If, with an enlarging lantern, the image of this faked picture is thrown on the printing paper like a lantern slide, and if the right-hand side is moved a little further away than the left, the top further away than the bottom, you can in that way print a fraudulent high-speed picture ahead.

"True, everything else in the picture, even if motionless, is distorted, and the difference between this faking and the distortion of the shutter can be seen by an expert. But it will pass with most people. In this case, however," added Kennedy suddenly, "the faker was so sure of it that he was careless. Instead of getting the plate further from the paper on the right, he did so on the left. It was further away on the bottom than on the top. He got the distortion, all right, enough to satisfy anyone. But it is distortion in the wrong direction! The top of the wheel, which goes fastest and ought to be most indistinct, is, in the fake, as sharp as any other part. It is a small mistake that was made, but fatal. Your picture is not of a joy ride at all. It is really high speed—backwards! It is too raw, too raw."

" You don't think people are going to swallow all that stuff, do you? " asked Dorgan coolly, in spite of the exposures. " What of it all? " he asked surlily. " I have nothing to do with it, anyhow. Why do you come to me? Take it to the proper authorities."

" Shall I? " asked Kennedy quietly, leaning over and whispering a few words in Dorgan's ear. I could not hear what he said, but Dorgan appeared to be fairly staggered.

When Kennedy passed out of the Boss's office there was a look of quiet satisfaction on his face which I could not fathom. Not a word could I extract from him on the subject, either. I was still in the dark as to the result of his visit.

XXIV

THE DÉBACLE OF DORGAN

SUNDAY morning came and with it the huge batch of papers which we always took. I looked at them eagerly, though Kennedy did not seem to evince much interest, to see whether the Carton photographs had been used. There were none.

Kennedy employed the time in directing some work of his own and had disappeared, I knew not where, though I surmised it was on one of his periodic excursions into the underworld in which he often knocked about, collecting all sorts of valuable and interesting bits of information to fit together in the mosaic of a case.

Monday came, also, the last day before the election, with its lull in the heart-breaking activities of the campaign. There were still no pictures published, but Kennedy was working in the laboratory over a peculiar piece of apparatus.

"I've been helping out my own shadows," was all the explanation he vouchsafed of his disappearances, as he continued to work.

"Watching Mrs. Ogleby?" I hinted.

"No, I didn't interfere any more with Miss Kendall. This was someone else—in another part of the city."

He said it with an air that seemed to imply that I would learn all about it shortly and I did not pursue the subject.

Meanwhile, he was arranging something on the top of a large, flat table. It seemed to be an instrument in two parts, composed of many levers and discs and magnets, each part with a roll of paper about five inches wide.

On one was a sort of stylus with two silk cords attached at right angles to each other near the point. On the other was a capillary glass tube at the junction of two aluminum arms, also at right angles to each other.

It was quite like old times to see Kennedy at work in his laboratory again, and I watched him curiously. Two sets of wires were attached to each of the instruments, and they lead out of the window to some other wires which had been strung by telephone linemen only a few hours before.

Craig had scarcely completed his preparations when Carton arrived. Things were going all right in the campaign again, I knew, at least as far as appeared on the surface. But his face showed that Carton was clearly dissatisfied with what Craig had apparently accomplished, for, as yet, he had not told Carton about his discovery after studying the photographs, and matters between Carton and Margaret Ashton stood in the same strained condition that they had when last we saw her.

I must say that I, too, was keenly disappointed by the lack of developments in this phase of the case.

Aside from the fact that the photographs had not actually been published, the whole thing seemed to me to be a mess. What had Craig said to Dorgan? Above all, what was his game? Was he playing to spare the girl's feelings merely by allowing the election to go on without a scandal to Carton? I knew the result of the election was now the least of Carton's worries.

Carton did not say much, but he showed that he thought it high time for Kennedy to do something.

We were seated about the flat table, wondering when Kennedy would break his silence, when suddenly, as if by a spirit hand, the stylus before us began to move across one of the rolls of paper.

We watched it uncomprehendingly.

At last I saw that it was actually writing the words. " How is it working? "

Quickly Craig seized the stylus on the lower part of the instrument and wrote in his characteristic scrawl, " All right, go ahead."

" What is the thing? " asked Carton, momentarily forgetting his own worries at the new marvel before us.

" An instrument that was invented many years ago, but has only recently been perfected for practical, every-day use, the telautograph, the long-distance writer," replied Kennedy, as we waited. " You see, with what amounts to an ordinary pencil I have written on the paper of the transmitter. The silk cord attached to the pencil regulates the current which controls another capillary glass tube-pen at the

other end of the line.   The receiving pen moves
simultaneously with my stylus.   It is the same prin-
ciple as the pantagraph, cut in half as it were, one
half here, the other half at the other end of the line,
two elephone wires in this case connecting the halves.
Ah,—that's it.   The pencil of the receiving instrument is writing again.   Just a moment.   Let us see
what it is."

I almost gasped in astonishment at the words that
I saw.   I looked again, for I could not believe my
eyes.   Still, there it was.   My first glance had been
correct, impossible as it was.

" I, Patrick Murtha," wrote the pen.

" What is it? " asked Carton, awestruck.   " A
dead hand? "

" Stop a minute," wrote Kennedy hastily.

We bent over him closely.   Craig had drawn from
a packet several letters, which he had evidently secured in some way from the effects of Murtha.   Carefully, minutely, he compared the words before us
with the signatures at the bottom of the letters.

" It is genuine ! " he cried excitedly.

" Genuine ! " Carton and I echoed.

What did he mean?   Was this some kind of spirit-
ism?   Had Kennedy turned medium and sought a
message from the other world to solve the inexplicable problems of this?   It was weird, uncanny,
unthinkable.   We turned to him blankly for an explanation of the mystery.

" That wasn't Murtha at all whose body we saw
at the Morgue," he hurried to explain.   " That was

all a frame-up. I thought as soon as I saw it that there was something queer."

I recalled now the peculiar look on his face which I had interpreted as indicating that he thought Murtha had been the victim of foul play.

" And the other night, when we were in Carton's office and someone called up threatening you, Carton, and Dopey Jack, I saw at once that the voice was concealed. Yet there was something about it that was familiar, though I couldn't quite place it. I had heard that voice before, perhaps while we were getting the records to discover the ' wolf.' It occurred to me that if I had a record of it I might identify it by comparing it with those we had already taken. I got the record. I studied it. I compared it with what I already had, line, and wave, and overtone. You can imagine how I felt when I found there was only one voice with which it corresponded, and that man was supposed to be dead. Something more than intuition as I looked at the body that night had roused my suspicions. Now they were confirmed. Fancy how that information must have burned in my mind, during these days while I knew that Murtha was alive, but could say nothing ! "

Neither Carton nor I could say a word as we thought of this voice from the dead, as it almost seemed.

" I hadn't found him," continued Craig, " but I knew he had used a pay station on the West Side. I began shadowing everyone who might have helped

him, Dorgan, Kahn, Langhorne, all. I didn't find
him. They were too clever. He was hiding somewhere in the city, a changed personality, waiting for
the thing to blow over. He knew that of all places
a city is the best to hide in, and of all cities New
York is safest.

"But, though I didn't actually find his hiding
place, I had enough on some of his friends so that
I could get word to him that his secret was known
to me, at least. I made him an offer of safety. He
need not come out of his hiding place and I would
agree to let him go where and when he pleased
without further pursuit from me, if he would let
me install a telautograph in a neutral place which
he could select and the other end in this laboratory.
I myself do not know where the other place is. Only
a mechanic sworn to secrecy knows and neither Murtha nor myself know him. If Murtha comes across,
I have given my word of honour that before the
world he shall remain a dead man, free to go where
he pleases and enjoy such of his fortune as he was
able to fix so that he could carry it with him into his
new life."

Carton and I were entranced by the romance of
the thing.

Murtha was alive!

The commitment to the asylum, the escape, the
search, the finding of a substitute body, mutilated beyond ordinary recognition, the mysterious transfers,
and finally the identification in the Morgue—all had
been part of an elaborately staged play!

We saw it all, now. Carton had got too close to
him in the conviction of Dopey Jack and the proceedings against Kahn. He had seen the handwrit-
ing on the wall for himself. In Carton's gradual
climbing, step by step, for the man higher up, he
would have been the next to go.

Murtha had decided that it was time to get out,
to save himself.

Suddenly, I saw another aspect of it. By dropping out as though dead, he destroyed a link in the
chain that would reach Dorgan. There was no way
of repairing that link if he were dead. It was missing and missing for good.

Dorgan had known it. Had it been a hint as to
that which had finally clinched whatever it was that
Kennedy had whispered to the Silent Boss that morning when we had seen him in his office?

All these thoughts and more flashed through my
head with lightning-like rapidity.

The telautograph was writing again, obedient to
Kennedy's signal that he was satisfied with the sig-
nature.

" . . . . in consideration of Craig Kennedy's
agreement to destroy even this record, agree to give
him such information as he has asked for, after
which no further demands are to be made and the
facts as already publicly recorded are to stand."

" Just witness it," asked Kennedy of us. " It is
a gentleman's agreement among us all."

Nervously we set our names to the thing, only
too eager to keep the secret if we could further the

case on which we had been almost literally sweating blood so long.

Prepared though we were for some startling disclosures, it was, nevertheless, with a feeling almost of faintness that we saw the stylus above moving again.

"The Black Book, as you call it," it wrote, "has been sent by messenger to be deposited in escrow with the Gotham Trust Company to be delivered, Tuesday, the third of November, on the written order of Craig Kennedy and John Carton. An officer of the trust company will notify you of its receipt immediately, which will close the entire transaction as far as I am concerned."

Kennedy could not wait. He had already seized his own telephone and was calling a number.

"They have it," he announced a moment later, scrawling the information on the transmitter of the telautograph.

A moment it was still, then it wrote again.

"Good-bye and good luck," it traced. "Murtha!"

The Smiling Boss could not resist his little joke at the end, even now.

"Can—we—get it?" asked Carton, almost stunned at the unexpected turn of events.

"No," cautioned Kennedy, "not yet. To-morrow. I made the same promise to Murtha that I made to Dorgan, when I went to him with Walter, although Walter did not hear it. This is to be a fair fight, for the election, now."

"Then," said Carton earnestly, "I may as well tell you that I shall not sleep to-night. I can't, even if I can use the book only after election in the clean-up of the city!"

Kennedy laughed.

"Perhaps I can entertain you with some other things," he said gleefully, adding, "About those photographs."

Carton was as good as his word. He did not sleep, and the greater part of the night we spent in telling him about what Craig had discovered by his scientific analysis of the faked pictures.

At last morning came. Though Kennedy and I had slept soundly in our apartment, Carton had in reality only dozed in a chair, after we closed the laboratory.

Slowly the hours slipped away until the trust company opened.

We were the first to be admitted, with our order ready signed and personally delivered.

As the officer handed over the package, Craig tore the wrapper off eagerly.

There, at last, was the Black Book!

Carton almost seized it from Kennedy, turning the pages, skimming over it, gloating like a veritable miser.

It was the débacle of Dorgan—the end of the man highest up!

XXV

THE BLOOD CRYSTALS

MUCH as we had accomplished, we had not found Betty Blackwell. Except for her shadowing of Mrs. Ogleby, Clare Kendall had devoted her time to winning the confidence of the poor girl, Sybil Seymour, whom we had rescued from Margot's. Meanwhile, the estrangement of Carton and Margaret Ashton threw a cloud over even our success.

During the rest of the morning Craig was at work again in the laboratory. He was busily engaged in testing something through his powerful microscopes and had a large number of curious microphotographs spread out on the table. As I watched him, apparently there was nothing but the blood-stained gauze bandage which had been fastened to the face of the strange, light-haired woman, and on the stains on this bandage he was concentrating his attention. I could not imagine what he expected to discover from it.

I waited for Kennedy to speak, but he was too busy more than to notice that I had come in. I fell to thinking of that woman. And the more I thought of the fair face, the more I was puzzled by it. I felt somehow or other that I had seen it somewhere before, yet could not place it.

A second time I examined the unpublished photograph of Betty Blackwell as well as the pictures that had been published. The only conclusion that I could come to was that it could not be she, for although she was light-haired and of fair complexion, the face as I remembered it was that of a mature woman who was much larger than the slight Betty. I was sure of that.

Every time I reasoned it out I came to the same contradictory conclusion that I had seen her, and I hadn't. I gave it up, and as Kennedy seemed indisposed to enlighten me, I went for a stroll about the campus, returning as if drawn back to him by a lodestone.

About him was still the litter of test tubes, the photographs, the microscopes; and he was more absorbed in his delicate work than ever.

He looked up from his examination of a little glass slide and I could see by the crow's feet in the corners of his eyes that he was not looking so much at me as through me at a very puzzling problem.

"Walter," he remarked at length, "did you notice anything in particular about that blonde woman who dashed down the steps into the taxicab and escaped from the dope joint?"

"I should say that I did," I returned, glad to ease my mind of what had been perplexing me ever since. "I don't want to appear to be foolish, but, frankly, I thought I had seen her before, and then when I tried to place her I found that I could not recognize her at all. She seemed to be familiar, and yet when I tried to place her I could think of no one with just those features. It was a foolish impression, I suppose."

" That's exactly it," he exclaimed. " I thought at first it was just a foolish impression, too, an intuition which my later judgment rejected. But often those first impressions put you on the track of the truth. I reconsidered. You remember sne had dropped that bandage from her face with the blood-stain on it. I picked it up and it occurred to me to try a little experiment with these blood-stains which might show something."

He paused a moment and fingered some of the microphotographs.

" What would you say," he went on, " if I should tell you that a pronounced blonde, with a fair complexion and thin, almost hooked, nose, was in reality a negress? "

" If it were anyone but you, Craig," I replied frankly, " I'd be tempted to call him something. But you—well, what's the answer? How do you know? "

" I wonder if you have ever heard of the Reichert blood test? Well, the Carnegie Instituion has recently published an account of it. Professor Edward Reichert of the University of Pennsylvania has discovered that the blood crystals of all animals and men show characteristic differences.

" It has even been suggested that before the

21

studies are over photographs of blood corpuscles
may be used to identify criminals, almost like finger-
prints. There is much that can be discovered already by the use of these hemoglobin clues. That
hemoglobin, or red colouring matter of the blood,
forms crystals has been known for a long time.
These crystals vary in different animals, as they are
studied under the polarizing microscope, both in
form and molecular structure. That is of immense
importance for the scientific criminologist.

" A man's blood is not like the blood of any other
living creature, either fish, flesh, or fowl. Further,
it is said that the blood of a woman or a man and of
different individuals shows differences that will re-
veal themselves under certain tests. You can take
blood from any number of animals and the scientists
to-day can tell that it is not human blood, but the
blood, say, of an animal.

" The scientists now can go further. They even
hope soon to be able to tell the difference between
individuals so closely that they can trace parentage
by these tests. Already they can actually distinguish
among the races of men, whether a certain sample
of blood, by its crystals, is from a Chinaman, a Caucasian, or a negro. Each gives its own characteristic crystal. The Caucasian shows that he is more
closely related to one group of primates; the negro
to another. It is scientific proof of evolution.

" It is all the more wonderful, Walter, when you
consider that these crystals are only 1-2250th of an
inch in length and 1-9000th of an inch in width."

" How do you study them?" I asked.

" The method I employed was to take a little of the blood and add some oxalate of ammonium to it, then shake it up thoroughly with ether to free the hemoglobin from the corpuscles. I then separated the ether carefully from the rest of the blood mixture and put a few drops of it on a slide, covered them with a cover slip and sealed the edges with balsam. Gradually the crystals appear and they can be studied and photographed in the usual way—not only the shapes of the crystals, but also the relation that their angles bear to each other. So it is impossible to mistake the blood of one animal for another or of one race, like the white race, for that of another, like the black. In fact the physical characteristics by which some physicians profess to detect the presence of negro blood are held by other authorities to be valueless. But not so with this test."

" And you have discovered in this case?" I asked.

" That the blood on the bandage from the face of that woman who escaped was not the blood of a pure Caucasian. She shows traces of negro blood, in fact exactly what would have been expected of a mulatto."

It dawned on me that the woman must have been Marie, after all; at least that that was what he meant.

" But," I objected, " one look at her face was enough to show that she was not the dark-skinned Marie with her straight nose, her dark hair and

other features. This woman was fair, had a nose
that was almost hooked and hair that was almost
flaxen. Remember the *portrait parlé.*"

"Just so—the *portrait parlé.* That is what I am
remembering. You recall Carton discovered that
in some way these people found out that we were
using it? What would they do? Why, they have
thought out the only possible way in which to beat
it, don't you see?

"Marie, Madame Margot, whatever you call her,
had a beauty parlour. Oh, they are clever, these
people. They reasoned it all out. What was a
beauty parlour, a cosmetic surgery, for, if it could
not be used to save them? They knew we had her
scientific description. What was the thing to do,
then? Why, change it, of course, change *her!*"

Kennedy was quite excited now.

"You know what Miss Kendall said of decora-
tive surgery, there? They change noses, ears, fore-
heads, chins, even eyes. They put the thing up to
Dr. Harris with his knives and bandages and lotions.
He must work quickly. It would take all his time.
So he disappeared into Margot's and stayed
there. Marie also stayed there until such time as
she might be able to walk out, another person entirely. Harris must have had charge of her features.
The attendants in Margot's had charge of her complexion and hair—those were the things in which
they specialized.

"Don't you see it all now? She could retire a
few days into the dope joint next door and she would

emerge literally a new woman ready to face us, even with Bertillon's *portrait parlé* against her."

It was amazing how quickly Kennedy pieced the facts together into an explanation.

"Yes," he concluded triumphantly, "that blonde woman was our dark-skinned mulatto made over— Marie. But they can't escape the power of science, even by using science themselves. She might change her identity to our eyes, but she could not before the Reichert test and the microscope. No, the Ethiopian could not change her skin before the eye of science."

It was late in the afternoon that Kennedy received a hurried telephone call from Miss Kendall. I could tell by the scraps of conversation which I overheard that it was most important.

"That girl, Sybil Seymour, has broken down," was all he said as he turned from the instrument. "She will he here to-day with Miss Kendall. You must see Carton immediately. Tell him not to fail to be here, at the laboratory, this afternoon at three, sharp."

He was gone before I could question him further and there was nothing for me to do but to execute the commission he had laid on me.

I met Carton at his club, relating to him all that I could about the progress of the case. He seemed interested but I could see that his mind was really not on it. The estrangement between him and Margaret Ashton outweighed success in this case and even in the election.

Half an hour before the appointed time, however, we arrived at the laboratory in Carton's car, to find Kennedy already there, putting the finishing touches on the preparations he was making to receive his " guests."

" Dorgan will be here," he answered, evading Carton's question as to what he had discovered.

" Dorgan? " we repeated in surprise.

" Yes. I have made arrangements to have Martin Ogleby, too. They won't dare stay away. Ike the Dropper, Dr. Harris, and Marie Margot have not been found yet, but Miss Kendall will bring Sybil Seymour. Then we shall see."

The door opened. It was Ogleby. He bowed stiffly, but before he could say anything, a noise outside heralded the arrival of someone else.

It proved to be Dorgan, who had come from an opposite direction. Dorgan seemed to treat the whole affair with contempt, which he took pleasure in showing. He was cool and calm, master of himself, in any situation no matter how hostile.

As we waited, the strained silence, broken only by an occasional whisper between Carton and Kennedy, was relieved even by the arrival of Miss Kendall and Sybil Seymour in a cab. As they entered I fancied that a friendship had sprung up between the two, that Miss Kendall had won her fight for the girl. Indeed, I suspect that it was the first time in years that the girl had had a really disinterested friend of either sex.

I thought Ogleby visibly winced as he caught sight

of Miss Seymour. He evidently had not expected her, and I thought that perhaps he had no relish for the recollection of the Montmartre which her presence suggested.

Miss Seymour, now like herself as she had appeared first behind the desk at the hotel, only subdued and serious, seemed ill at ease. Dorgan, on the other hand, bowed to her brazenly and mockingly. He was evidently preparing against any surprises which Craig might have in store, and maintained his usual surly silence.

" Perhaps," hemmed Ogleby, clearing his throat and looking at his watch ostentatiously, " Professor Kennedy can inform us regarding the purpose of this extra-legal proceeding? Some of us, I know, have other engagements. I would suggest that you begin, Professor."

He placed a sarcastic emphasis on the word " professor," as the two men faced each other—Craig tall, clean-cut, earnest; Ogleby polished, smooth, keen.

" Very well," replied Craig with that steel-trap snap of his jaws which I knew boded ill for someone.

" It is not necessary for me to repeat what has happened at the Montmartre and the beauty parlour adjoining it," began Kennedy deliberately. " One thing, however, I want to say. Twice, now, I have seen Dr. Harris handing out packets of drugs— once to Ike the Dropper, agent for the police and a corrupt politician, and once to a mulatto woman, almost white, who conducted the beauty parlour and dope joint which I have mentioned, a friend and associate of Ike the Dropper, a constant go-between from Ike to the corrupt person higher up.

" This woman, whom I have just mentioned, we have been seeking by use of Bertillon's new system of the *portrait parlé*. She has escaped, for the time, by a very clever ruse, by changing her very face in the beauty parlour. She is Madame Margot herself ! "

Not a word was breathed by any of the little audience as they hung on Kennedy's words.

" Why was it necessary to get Betty Blackwell out of the way ? " he asked suddenly, then without waiting for an answer, " You know and District Attorney Carton knows. Someone was afraid of Carton and his crusade. Someone wanted to destroy the value of that Black Book, which I now have. The only safety lay in removing the person whose evidence would be required in court to establish it— Betty Blackwell. And the manner ? What more natural than to use the dope fiends and the degenerates of the Montmartre gang ? "

" That's silly," interrupted Ogleby contemptuously.

" Silly ? You can say that—you, the tool of that —that monster ? "

It was a woman's voice that interrupted. I turned. Sybil Seymour, her face blazing with resentment, had risen and was facing Ogleby squarely.

" You lie ! " exclaimed the Silent Boss, forgetting both his silence and his superciliousness.

The situation was tense as the girl faced him.

" Go on, Sybil," urged Clare.

" Be careful, woman," cried Dorgan roughly.

Sybil Seymour turned quickly to her new assailant. " You are the man for whom we were all coined into dollars," she scorned, " Dorgan—politician, man higher up! You reaped the profits through your dirty agent, Ike the Dropper, and those over him, even the police you controlled. Dr. Harris, Marie Margot, all are your tools—and the worst of them all is this man Martin Ogleby! "

Dorgan's face was livid. For once in his life he was speechless rather than silent, as the girl poured out the inside gossip of the Montmartre which Kennedy had now stamped with the earmarks of legal proof.

She had turned from Dorgan, as if from an unclean animal and was now facing Ogleby.

" As for you, Martin Ogleby, they call you a club-man and society leader. Do you want to know what club I think you really belong to—you who have involved one girl after another in the meshes of this devilish System? You belong to the Abduction Club—that is what I would call it—you—you libertine! "

XXVI

THE WHITE SLAVE

CARTON had sprung to his feet at the direct charge and was facing Ogleby.

"Is that true—about the Montmartre?" he demanded.

Ogleby fairly sputtered. "She lies," he almost hissed.

"Just a moment," interrupted Dorgan. "What has that to do with Miss Blackwell, anyhow?"

Sybil Seymour did not pause.

"It is true," she reiterated. "This is what it has to do with Betty Blackwell. Listen. He is the man who led me on, who would have done the same to Betty Blackwell. I yielded, but she fought. They could not conquer her—neither by drugs nor drink, nor by clothes, nor a good time, nor force. I saw it all in the Montmartre and the beauty parlour—all."

"Lies—all lies," hissed Ogleby, beside himself with anger.

"No, no," cried Sybil. "I do not lie. Mr. Carton and this good woman, Miss Kendall, who is working for him, are the first people I have seen since you, Martin Ogleby, brought me to the Montmartre, who have ever given me a chance to become again what I was before you and your friends got me."

"Have a care, young woman," interrupted Dorgan, recovering himself as she proceeded. "There are laws and——"

"I don't care a rap about laws such as yours. As for gangs—that was what you were going to say—I'd snap my fingers in the face of Ike the Dropper himself if he were here. You could kill me, but I would tell the truth.

"Let me tell you my case," she continued, turning in appeal to the rest of us, "the case of a poor girl in a small city near New York, who liked a good time, liked pretty clothes, a ride in an automobile, theatres, excitement, bright lights, night life. I liked them. He knew that. He led me on, made me like him. And when I began to show the strain of the pace—we all show it more than the men— he cast me aside, like a squeezed-out lemon."

Sybil Seymour was talking rapidly, but she was not hysterical.

"Already you know Betty Blackwell's story— part of it," she hurried on. "Miss Kendall has told me—how she was bribed to disappear. But beyond that—what?"

For a moment she paused. No one said a word. Here at last was the one person who held the key to the mystery.

"She did disappear. She kept her word. At last she had money, the one thing she had longed for. At last she was able to gratify those desires to play the fashionable lady which her family had always felt. What more natural, then, than while she must keep in hiding to make one visit to the beauty parlour to which so many society women went—Margot's? It was there that she went on the day that she disappeared."

We were hanging breathlessly now on the words of the girl as she untangled the sordid story.

" And then? " prompted Kennedy.

" Then came into play another arm of the System," she replied. " They tried to make sure that she would disappear. They tried the same arts on her that they had on me—this man and the gang about him. He played on her love of beauty and Madame Margot helped him. He used the Montmartre and the Futurist to fascinate her, but still she was not his. She let herself drift along, perhaps because she knew that her family was every bit the equal socially of his own. Madame Margot tried drugs; first the doped cigarette, then drugs that had to be forced on her. She kept her in that joint for days by force; and there where I went for relief day after day from my own bitter thoughts I saw her, in that hell which Miss Kendall now by her evidence will close forever. Still she would not yield.

" I saw it all. Maybe you will say I was jealous because I had lost him. I was not. I hated him. You do not know how close hate can be to love in the heart of a woman. I could not help it. I had to write a letter that might save her.

" Miss Kendall has told me about the typewritten

letters; how you, Professor Kennedy, traced them
to the Montmartre. I wrote them, I admit, for
these people. I wrote that stuff about drugs for
Dr. Harris. And I wrote the first letter of all to
the District Attorney. I wrote it for myself and
signed it as I am—God forgive me—'An Outcast.' "

The poor girl, overwrought by the strain of the
confession that laid bare her very soul, sank back
in her chair and cried, as Miss Kendall gently tried
to soothe her.

Dorgan and Ogleby listened sullenly. Never in
their lives had they dreamed of such a situation as
this.

There was no air of triumph about Kennedy now
over the confession, which with the aid of Miss Kendall, he had staged so effectively. Rather it was a
spirit of earnestness, of retribution, justice.

"You know all this?" he inquired gently of the
girl.

"I saw it," she said simply, raising her bowed
head.

Dorgan had been doing some quick thinking. He
leaned over and whispered quickly to Ogleby.

"Why was she not discovered then when these
detectives broke into the private house—an act which
they themselves will have to answer for when the
time comes?" demanded Ogleby.

It seemed as if the mere sound of his voice roused
the girl.

"Because it was dangerous to keep her there any

longer," she replied. " I heard the talk about the
hotel, the rumour that someone was using this new
French detective scheme. I heard them blame the
District Attorney—who was clever enough to have
others working on the case whom you did not know.
While you were watching his officers, Mr. Kennedy
and Miss Kendall were gathering evidence almost
under your very eyes.

" But you were panic-stricken. You and your
agents wanted to remove the danger of discovery.
Dr. Harris and Marie Margot had a plan which
you grasped at eagerly. There was Ike the Dropper, that scoundrel who lives on women. Between
them you would spirit her away. You were glad to
have them do it, little realizing that, with every step,
they had you involved deeper and worse. You forgot everything, all honour and manhood in your
panic; you were ready to consent, to urge any course
that would relieve you—and you have taken the
course that involves you worse than any other."

" Who will believe a story like that? " demanded
Ogleby. " What are you—according to your own
confession? Am I to be charged with everything
this gang, as you call it, does? You are their agent,
perhaps working for this blackmailing crew. But
I tell you, I will fight, I will not be blackened
by——"

Sybil laughed, half hysterically.

" Blackened? " she repeated. " You who would
put this thing all off on others who worked for you,
who played on your vices and passions, not because

you were weak, but because you thought you were above the law!

"You did not care what became of that girl, so long as she was where she could not accuse you. You left her to that gang, to Ike, to Marie, to Harris." She paused a moment, and flashed a quick glance of scorn at him. "Do you want to know what has become of her, what you are responsible for?

"I will tell you. They had other ideas than just getting her out of the way of your selfish career. They are in this life for money. Betty Blackwell to them was a marketable article, a piece of merchandise in the terrible traffic which they carry on. If she had been yielding, like the rest of us, she might now be apparently free, yet held by a bondage as powerful and unescapable as if it were of iron, a life from which she could not escape. But she was not yielding. They would break her. Perhaps you have tried to ease your conscience, if you have any, by the thought that it is they, not you, who have her hidden away somewhere now. You cannot escape that way; it was you who made her, who made others of us, what we are."

"Let her rave, Ogleby," sneered Dorgan.

"Yes—raving, that's it," echoed Ogleby. But his expression belied him.

"There it is," she continued. "You have not even an opinion of your own. You repeat even the remarks of others. They have you in their power. You have put yourself there."

"All very pretty," remarked Dorgan with biting sarcasm. "All very cleverly thought out. So nice here! Wait until you have to tell that story in court. You know the first rule of equity? Do you go into court with clean hands? There is a day of reckoning coming to you, young woman, and to these other meddlers here—whether they are playing politics or meddling just because they are old-maidish busybodies."

She was facing the politician with burning cheeks.

"You," she scorned, "belong to an age that is passing away. You cannot understand these people like Miss Kendall, like Mr. Carton, who cannot be bought and controlled like your other creatures. You do not know how the underworld can turn on the upperworld. You would not pull us up—you shoved us down deeper, in your greed. But if we go down, we shall drag you, too. What have we to lose? You and your creatures, like Martin Ogleby, have taken everything from us. We——"

"Come, Ogleby," interposed Dorgan, deliberately turning his back on her and slowly placing his hat on his half-bald head. "We are indebted to Professor Kennedy for a pleasant entertainment. When he has another show equally original we trust he will not forget the first-nighters who have enjoyed this farce."

Dorgan had reached the door and had his hand on the knob. I had expected Kennedy to reply. But he said nothing. Instead his hand stole along the edge of the table beside which he was standing,

"Good-night," bowed Dorgan with mock sol-
emnity. "Thank you for laying the cards on the
table. We shall know how to play——"

Dorgan cut the words short.

Kennedy had touched the button of an electric
attachment which was under the table by which he
could lock every door and window of the laboratory
instantly and silently.

"Well?" demanded Dorgan fiercely, though
there was a tremble in his voice that had never been
heard before.

"Where is Betty Blackwell?" demanded Craig,
turning to Sybil Seymour. "Where did they take
her?"

We hung breathlessly on the answer. Was she
being held as a white slave in some obscure den?
I knew that that did not mean that she was necessarily imprisoned behind locked doors and barred
windows, although even that might be the case. I
knew that the restraint might be just as effective,
even though it was not actually or wholly physical.

An ordinary girl, I reasoned, with little knowledge of her rights or of the powers which she might
call to her aid if she knew how to summon them,
might she not be so hemmed in by the forces into
whose hands she had fallen as to be practically held
in bonds which she could not break?

Here was Sybil herself! Once she had been like
Betty Blackwell. Indeed, when she seemed to have
every chance to escape she did not. She knew how
she could be pursued, hounded at every turn, forced

back, and her only course was to sink deeper into the life. The thought of what might be accomplished by drugs startled me.

Clare bent over the poor girl reassuringly. What was it that seemed to freeze her tongue now? Was it still some vestige of the old fear under which she had been held so long? Clare strove, although we could not hear what she was saying, to calm her.

At last Sybil raised her head, with a wild cry, as if she were sealing her own doom.

" It was Ike. He kept us all in terror. Oh, if he hears he will kill me," she blurted out.

" Where did he take her? " asked Clare.

She had broken down the girl's last fear.

" To that place on the West Side—that black and tan joint, where Marie Margot came from before the gang took her in."

" Carton," called Kennedy. " You and Walter will take Miss Kendall and Miss Seymour. Let me see. Dorgan, Ogleby, and myself will ride in the taxicab."

Carton was toying ostentatiously with a police whistle as Dorgan hesitated, then entered the cab.

I think at the joint, as we pulled up with a rush after our wild ride downtown, they must have thought that a party of revellers had dropped in to see the sights. It was perhaps just as well that they did, for there was no alarm at first.

As we entered the black and tan joint, I took another long look at its forbidding exterior. Below, it was a saloon and dance hall; above, it was a "hotel." It was weatherbeaten, dirty, and unsightly, without, except for the entrance; unsanitary, ramshackle, within, except for the tawdry decorations. At every window were awnings and all were down, although it was on the shady side of the street in the daytime and it was now getting late. That was the mute sign post to the initiated of the character of the place.

Instead of turning downstairs where we had gone on our other visit, Kennedy led the way up through a door that read, "Hotel Entrance—Office."

A clerk at a desk in a little alcove on the second floor mechanically pushed out a register at us, then seeming to sense trouble, pulled it back quickly and with his foot gave a sharp kick at the door of a little safe, locking the combination.

"I'm looking for someone," was all Kennedy said. "This is the District Attorney. We'll go through——"

"Yes, you will!"

It was Ike the Dropper. He had heard the commotion, and, seeing ladies, came to the conclusion that it was not a police plainclothes raid, but some new game of the reformers.

He stopped short in amazement at the sight of Dorgan and Ogleby.

"Well—I'll be——"

"Carton! Walter!" shouted Kennedy. "Take care of him. Watch out for a knife or gun. He's soft, though. Carton—the whistle!"

Our struggle with the redoubtable Ike was short

and quickly over. Sullen, and with torn clothes and bleeding face, we held him until the policeman arrived, and turned him over to the law.

At a room on the same floor Craig knocked.

"Come in," answered a woman's voice.

He pushed open the door. There was the woman who had fled so precipitately from the dope joint.

Evidently she did not recognize us.

"You are under arrest," announced Kennedy.

The blonde woman laughed mockingly.

"Under arrest? For what?"

"You are Marie Margot. Never mind about your alias. All the arts of your employees and Dr. Harris himself cannot change you so that I cannot recognize you. You may feel safe from the *portrait parlé*, but there are other means of detection that you never dreamed of. Where is Betty Blackwell? Marie, it's all off!"

All the brazen assurance with which she had met us was gone. She looked from one to the other and read that it was the end. With a shriek, she suddenly darted past us, out of the door. Down the hall was Ike the Dropper with the policeman and Carton. Beside her was a stairway leading to the upper floors. She chose the stairs.

Following Kennedy we hurried through the hotel, from one dirty room to another, with their loose and creaking floors, rotten and filthy, sagging as we walked, covered with matting that was rotting away. Damp and unventilated, the air was heavy and filled with foul odours of tobacco, perfumery, and cheap disinfectants. There seemed to have been no attempt to keep the place clean.

The rooms were small and separated by thin partitions through which conversations in even low tones could be heard. The furniture was cheap and worn with constant use.

Downstairs we could hear the uproar as the news spread that the District Attorney was raiding the place. As fast as they could the sordid crowd in the dance hall and cabaret was disappearing. Now and then we could hear a door bang, a hasty conference, and then silence as some of the inmates realized that upstairs all escape was cut off.

On the top floor we came to a door, locked and bolted. With all the force that he could gather in the narrow hall, Kennedy catapulted himself against it. It yielded in its rottenness with a crash.

A woman, in all her finery, lay across the foot of a bed, a formless heap. Kennedy turned her over. It was Marie, motionless, but still breathing faintly. In an armchair, with his hands hanging limply down almost to the floor, his head sagging forward on his chest, sprawled Harris.

Kennedy picked up a little silver receptacle on the floor where it lay near his right hand. It was nearly empty, but as he looked from it quickly to the two insensible figures before us he muttered: " Morphine. They have robbed the law of its punishment."

He bent over the suicides, but it was too late to do anything for them. They had paid the price.

"My heavens!" he exclaimed suddenly, as a thought flashed over his mind. "I hope they have not carried the secret of Betty Blackwell with them to the grave. Where is Miss Kendall?"

Down the hall, cut off from the rest of the hotel into a sort of private suite, Clare had entered one of the rooms and was bending over a pale, wan shadow of a girl, tossing restlessly on a bed. The room was scantily furnished with a dilapidated bureau in one corner and a rickety washstand equipped with a dirty washbowl and pitcher. A few cheap chromos on the walls were the only decorations, and a small badly soiled rug covered a floor innocent for many years of soap.

I looked sharply at the girl lying before us. Somehow it did not occur to me who she was. She was so worn that anyone might safely have transported her through the streets and never have been questioned, in spite of the fact that every paper in the country which prints pictures had published her photograph, not once but many times.

It was Betty Blackwell at last, struggling against the drugs that had been forced on her, half conscious, but with one firm and acute feeling left—resistance to the end.

Kennedy had dropped on his knees before her and was examining her closely.

"Open the windows—more air," he ordered. "Walter, see if you can find some ice water and a little stimulant."

While Craig was taking such restorative measures

as were possible on the spur of the moment, Miss Kendall gently massaged her head and hands.

She seemed to understand that she was in the hands of friends, and though she did not know us her mute look of thanks was touching.

Don't get excited, my dear," breathed Miss Kendall into her ear. " You will be all right soon."

As the wronged girl relaxed from her constant tension of watching, it seemed as if she fell into a stupor. Now and then she moaned feebly, and words, half-formed, seemed to come to her lips only to die away.

Suddenly she seemed to have a vision more vivid than the rest.

" No—no—— Mr. Ogleby—leave me. Where —my mother—oh, where is mother? " she cried hysterically, sitting bolt upright and staring at us without seeing us.

Kennedy passed the broad palm of his hand over her forehead and murmured, " There, there, you are all right now." Then he added to us: " I did not send for her mother because I wasn't sure that we might find her even as well as this. Will someone find Carton? Get the address and send a messenger for Mrs. Blackwell."

Sybil was on her knees by the bedside of the girl, holding Betty's hand in both of her own.

" You poor, poor girl," she cried softly. It is— dreadful."

She had sunk her head into the worn and dirty covers of the bed. Kennedy reached over and took

hold of her arm. " She will be all right, soon," he
said reassuringly. " Miss Kendall will take good
care of her."

As we descended the stairs, we could see Carton
at the foot. A patrol wagon had been backed up
to the curb in front and the inmates of the place
were being taken out, protesting violently at being
detained.

Further down the hall, by the " office," Dorgan
and Ogleby were storming, protesting that " influence " would " break " everyone concerned, from
Carton down to the innocent patrolmen.

Kennedy listened a moment, then turned to Clare
Kendall.

" I will leave Miss Blackwell in your care," he
said quietly. " It is on her we must rely to prove
the contents of the Black Book."

Clare nodded, as, with a clang, Carton drove off
with his prisoners to see them safely entered on the
" blotter."

" Our work is over," remarked Kennedy, turning
again to Miss Kendall, in a tone as if he might have
said more, but refrained.

Looking Craig frankly in the eye, she extended
her hand in that same cordial straight-arm shake
with which she had first greeted us, and added,
" But not the memory of this fight we have won."

XXVII

THE ELECTION NIGHT

IT was election night. Kennedy and Carton had arranged between them that we were all to receive the returns at the headquarters of the Reform League, where one of the papers which was particularly interested, had installed several special wires.

The polls had scarcely closed when Kennedy and I, who had voted early, if not often, in spite of our strenuous day, hastened up to the headquarters. Already it was a scene of activity.

The first election district had come in, one on the lower East Side, which was a stronghold of Dorgan, where the count could be made quickly, for there were no split tickets there. Dorgan had drawn first blood.

"I hope it isn't an omen," smiled Carton, like a good sport.

Kennedy smiled quietly.

We looked about, but Miss Ashton was not there. I wondered why not and where she was.

The first returns had scarcely begun to filter in, though, when Craig leaned over and whispered to me to go out and find her, either at her home, or if not there, at a woman's club of which she was one of the leading members.

I found her at home and sent up my card. She had apparently lost interest in the election and it was with difficulty that I could persuade her to accompany me to the League headquarters. However, I argued the case with what ability I had and finally she consented.

The other members of the Ashton family had monopolized the cars and we were obliged to take a taxicab. As our driver threaded his way slowly and carefully through the thronged streets it gave us a splendid chance to see some of the enthusiasm. I think it did Margaret Ashton good, too, to get out, instead of brooding over the events of the past few days, as she had seen them. Her heightened colour made her more attractive than ever.

The excitement of any other night in the year paled to insignificance before this.

Distracted crowds everywhere were cheering and blowing horns. Now a series of wild shouts broke forth from the dense mass of people before a newspaper bulletin board. Now came sullen groans, hisses, and catcalls, or all together, with cheers, as the returns swung in another direction. Not even baseball could call out such a crowd as this.

Enterprising newspapers had established places at which they flashed out the returns on huge sheets on every prominent corner. Some of them had bands, and moving pictures, and elaborate forms of entertainment for the crowds.

Now and then, where the crowd was more than usually dense, we had to make a wide détour. Even the quieter streets seemed alive. On some boys had built huge bonfires from barrels and boxes that had been saved religiously for weeks or surreptitiously purloined from the grocer or the patient house-holder. About the fires, they kept an ever watchful eye for the descent of their two sworn enemies—the policeman and the rival gang privateering in the name of a hostile candidate.

Boys with armfuls of newspapers were every-where, selling news that in the rapid-fire change of the statistics seemed almost archeologically old.

Lights blazed on every side. Automobiles honked and ground their gears. The lobster palaces, where for weeks, François, Carl, and William had been taking small treasury notes for tables reserved against the occasion, were thronged. In theatres people squirmed uneasily until the ends of acts, in order to listen to returns read from the stage before the curtain. Police were everywhere. People with horns, and bells, and all manner of noise-making de-vices, with confetti and " ticklers " pushed up on one side of Broadway and down on the other.

At every square they congested foot and vehicle traffic, as they paused ravenously to feed on the meagre bulletins of news.

Yet back of all the noise and human energy, as a newspaperman, I could think only of the silent, sys-tematic gathering and editing of the news, of the busy scenes that each journal's office presented, the haste, the excitement, the thrill in the very smell of the printer's ink.

Miss Ashton, I was glad to note, as we proceeded downtown, fell more and more into the spirit of the adventure.

High up in the League headquarters in the tower, when we arrived, it was almost like a newspaper office, to me. A corps of clerks was tabulating returns, comparing official and semi-official reports. As first the city swung one way, then another, our hopes rose and fell.

I could not help noticing, however, after a while that Miss Ashton seemed cold and ill at ease. There was such a crowd there of Leaguers and their friends that it was easily possible for her not to meet Carton. But as I circulated about in the throng, I came upon him. Carton looked worried and was paying less attention to the returns than seemed natural. It was evident that, in spite of the crowd, she had avoided him and he hesitated to seek her out.

There were so many things to think of thrusting themselves into one's attention that I could follow none consistently. First I found myself wondering about Carton and Miss Ashton. Before I knew it I was delivering a snap judgment on whether the uptown residence district returns would be large enough to overcome the hostile downtown vote. I was frankly amazed, now, to see how strongly the city as a whole was turning to the Reform League.

A boy, pushing through the crowd, came upon

Kennedy and myself, talking to Miss Ashton. He
shoved a message quickly into Craig's hand and
disappeared.

"For heaven's sake!" he exclaimed as he tore
open the envelope and read. "What do you think of
that? My shadows report that Martin Ogleby has
been arrested and his confession will be enough, with
the Black Book and Betty Blackwell, to indict Dorgan. Kahn has committed suicide! Hartley Langhorne has sailed for Paris on the French line, with
Mrs. Ogleby!"

"Mary Ogleby—eloped?" repeated Miss Ashton, aghast.

The very name seemed to call up unpleasant associations and her face plainly showed it. Kennedy
had said nothing to her since the day when he had
pleaded with her to suspend judgment.

"By the way," he said in a low voice, leaning over
toward her, "have you heard that those pictures
of her were faked? It was really Dorgan, and some
crook photographer cut out his face and substituted
Carton's. We got the Black Book, this morning,
too, and it tells the story of Mrs. Ogleby's misad-
ventures—as well as a lot of much more important
things. We got it from Mr. Murtha and——"

"Mr. Murtha?" she inquired, in surprise.

"It is a secret, but I think I can violate it to
a certain extent for Mr. Carton is a party to it
and——"

Kennedy paused. He was speaking with the assurance of one who assumed that John Carton and

Margaret Ashton had no secrets. She saw it, and coloured deeply.

Then he lowered his voice further to a whisper and when he finished, her face was even a deeper scarlet. But her eyes had a brightness they had lacked for days. And I could see the emotion she felt as her slight form quivered with excitement.

Kennedy excused himself and we worked our way through the press toward Carton.

" Dorgan has lost his nerve!" ejaculated Craig as we came up with him, watching district after district which showed that the Boss's usual pluralities were being seriously reduced.

" Lost his nerve?" repeated Carton.

" Yes. I told him I would publish the whole affair of the photographs just as I knew it, not caring whom it hit. I advised him to read his revised statutes again about money in elections and I added the threat, ' There will be no " dough day " or it will be carried to the limit, Dorgan, and I will resurrect Murtha in an hour!' You should have seen his face! There was no dough day. That's what I meant when I said it was to be a fair fight. You see the effect on the returns."

Carton was absolutely speechless. The tears stood in his eyes as he grasped Kennedy's hand, then swung around to me.

A terrific cheer broke out among the clerks in the outer office. One of them rushed in with a still unblotted report.

Kennedy seized it and read:

" Dorgan concedes the city by a safe plurality to Carton, fifty-two election districts estimated. This clinches the Reform League victory."

I turned to Carton.

Behind us, through the crowd, had followed a young lady and now Carton had no ears for anything except the pretty apology of Margaret Ashton.

Kennedy pulled me toward the door.

" We might as well concede Miss Ashton to Carton," he beamed. " Let's go out and watch the crowd."

THE END